PURE HUMANS

THE END OF THE BEGINNING

By

DeLawrence Thomas

ISBN-13: 978-1495470301

ISBN-10: 149547030X

DEDICATED TO THE LOVING MEMORY
OF
NICOLE ANGELIQUE THOMAS

TABLE OF CONTENTS

CHAPTER 1
THE OPPOSITE SEX

About half an hour passed and Lori hadn't said a word. Michael began to wonder if she was lost. He then noticed it had become very quiet. There was only the rustling of their feet crunching the dead leaves and twigs beneath them.

Listening even closer, he couldn't hear a single bird chirping in the trees. He looked up, distinctively remembering hearing a symphony of cheery tweeting when they first entered the forest. But now they alone were breaking the silence of the woodland.

"Where have all the birds gone?" Michael asked.

"What?" Lori answered, as if she were pulled from a deep thought.

"I asked where all the birds are. There's not one chirping. I've never heard a forest this quiet before."

"You're right," she said and slowed her steps until she came to a complete stop. Carefully turning her head from left to right, Lori then circled around and looked behind them without saying a single word. Finally, she looked up as if she were expecting a storm.

"What's wrong?" Michael asked, searching her face for any sign of worry.

"Shhh," Lori replied before he could even fully finish his last word. She had a disturbed look on her face he hadn't seen before. The fact that she was uncomfortable on her own turf made him instantly alert. Michael could actually feel his fluids pulsing through him. He wondered if the flow was blood or adrenalin. Either way, he was more concerned with not looking frightened in Lori's presence than whatever it was that had her attention.

"Michael, before we take another step on this journey, you must realize something very important. And you may already know it, but right now you need to believe it. Just as clear as I can see your face right now, I can see you have a pure heart. With that, you must understand you were chosen by Him before you were born. Michael, I've said this only as a reminder that you are in this world, but you are not of it. Do you understand?"

"Not really. Why are you telling me this now?"

"Because right now you need to abandon all the influences this world has over you. Right now you need to open your mind to the fact that man has not solved or even seen all the mysteries of creation."

"Lori, what are you saying?" he asked, feeling even more confused.

"I'm saying you may see things here which defy the laws of man's nature. Just remember that man didn't make this world. So don't consider everything you've ever heard or read as fact." She looked up into the trees once again. "Don't move," she whispered. "And don't speak."

Michael began to reflect on all the events which had led up to this moment, back to the very first day he met Lori, when his life and the entire world began to change forever.

The absolute silence of the still room was shattered by a violent rustling of sheets and heavy breathing as Michael suddenly wakened. He sat up to feel a brilliant blade of sunlight on his face that sliced its way between the almost-closed drapes. With cold beads of sweat skiing down his skin, he became conscious of his morning reality.

The college dorm was like any other. Two twin-size beds and a wooden desk on one wall of the room. The parallel wall held a matching desk with two closets. The tan wood of the furniture almost matched the color of the curtains that the Arizona morning sun was trying its hardest to penetrate.

"Not again," Michael whispered to himself, mourning the broken bed beneath him. He swung his feet over the side of the defeated mattress onto the floor and held his head in his hands.

Suddenly, before Michael could even hear the key enter the door, it swung open.

"Well, look at what we have here. Hmmm." Michael's roommate, Eric, snickered as he looked Michael over. "Let's see. We have a college freshman on a broken bed who seems to have sweated up a serious workout with…himself," Eric continued through obnoxious laughter. "Man, that had to be some intense self-handling session."

"How about I was doing push-ups until I collapsed on the bed and broke it?" Michael suggested, trying to ease the awkwardness of the scene. "Why is sophisticated, high-powered masturbation your first guess anyway?"

"Well, we came by earlier and tried to wake you to eat with us, but you were sound asleep," Eric said, still chuckling. "The door must've woken you when we left you here alone to just go all out on yourself."

"We, us?" Michael burst out. "Who is this us and we?"

"Oh, I almost forgot, this is Stacey," Eric said as if someone were behind him. "Stacey?"

"Yeah," a small voice whimpered, followed by an eruption of thundering laughter. "I'm sorry," she cried as the door slowly opened, revealing Eric's latest conquest. A different, yet more attractive, female than the one he had introduced to Michael last week. He couldn't help but notice the short skirt and revealing blouse, which seemed to be the uniform for all his girls.

"Nice to meet you," Michael said in a cordial voice, trying to present himself as more decent than his roommate. Although he felt the effort was in vain, since he was still sitting dripping with sweat on his busted bed.

"I wouldn't shake his hand if I were you." Eric chuckled.

"You know, I really appreciate your support with this little circumstance I'm waking up to. I couldn't ask for a better friend or roommate. I mean, really, thank you," Michael joked.

"C'mon, man, don't get all sensitive on me," Eric said, switching his tone. "Stacey, you see how nice his body looks, all glistening and muscular? Can't you get one of your friends to go out with him?"

"Thank you, but no thank you, Stacey," Michael interrupted. "Now I may not be the best-looking guy around, I know that but just because you think your friend is attractive, it doesn't mean I will. Then I'm stuck trying to be nice, but not so nice that she likes me. And I don't enjoy hurting the feelings of anyone unattractive," Michael said smiling, trying to simplify his blind dating philosophy. "I hope that doesn't sound arrogant, I've just had some bad experiences."

"You see what I have to work with?" Eric asked Stacey, loud enough for Michael to hear. "This is why he's single." He turned back to Michael with a grin. "Don't you have class in an hour?"

"An hour and a half," Michael replied with a deep yawn.

"Well, you'll probably need that long to wash yourself...off of yourself," Eric joked with another short round of laughter.

"That was actually kind of funny for you. Not true, but funny."

"Well, Stacey, let's go and let loverboy get cleaned up," Eric said as he winked and escorted Stacey back into the hallway.

"Nice to meet you, Michael," she said with a couple of left-over giggles as her ponytail swung with her turn.

The door closed and Michael was once again left alone in silence. He looked down at himself and also gave a little chuckle.

Eric is a decent roommate, he thought. His side of the room was kept clean, and even though Eric was on the university track team, Michael never had to suffer the stench of the athlete's practice uniforms. He figured Eric probably needed the room to stay fresh and clean for all his female company. Michael enjoyed his sense of humor and respected his honesty. And although Eric was a little wild, Michael actually found his conversation intriguing.

He had seen Eric with several women in the four months he'd known him. Eric argued that there were one or two qualities he desired in each of the women he dated so only by dating them all could he experience the perfect female. Eric simply believed it was impossible to find everything he wanted in one woman. A part of Michael envied his shameless roommate but he knew such a lifestyle wasn't for him.

Looking at his folded mattress, Michael thought about the first time he woke up in a dripping-cold sweat as a child. No nightmare he could recall, just a panting and shaking body on a busted bed. After a few confusing episodes like that, he began dragging his mattress to the bedroom floor each night then back onto the box spring each morning. Problem solved. But now in a college dorm, he wasn't sure how to deal with the episodes.

Michael knew very little of his biological parents. He was told by his adoptive parents, Drake and Debra, of how his casework had been grossly mishandled. When he did try and look up his birthmother, he was told by adoption offices that she was "off the grid." There was no record of her after his birth. Drake told Michael that if his biological mother or father wanted to find him then they'd look him up.

Michael loved Drake but couldn't help feeling a little distant. He knew Drake loved him as well but they never played catch or did any other father-son activities in the limited time they had together. Employed by the federal government, Drake was constantly called away on assignments. Michael figured he held a very important position since Drake wouldn't discuss what he actually did at work with him or anyone else. Michael often wanted to ask if they could go to a ball game or something they might both enjoy, but he always shied away from the idea. Since Drake never initiated a bond, Michael eventually became afraid to. Deep down, Michael supposed there'd be no pain of rejection if he himself didn't try.

On the other hand, Michael was closer to Debra. She taught him to keep his word and treat women with respect. All of her other lessons branched off of these two concepts. When he had a problem, she wouldn't simply give him the answer. She'd give him the tools to find the answers on his own. She always told him that her intentions were only to make him more responsible.

Michael grabbed a towel and his keys to clear his mind with a relaxing shower. The public bathroom for the dorm floor was conveniently across from his room. Feeling the steamy streams of water on his face, Michael considered sliding a row of cinder blocks under his bed.

Thoughts of why he had to constantly endure such a bizarre circumstance only left him frustrated and insecure. His desperate movements during these intense dreams were held responsible for the broken beds. He imagined himself ten years into the future with a wife who would be afraid to sleep alongside him. With no other explanations, Michael and his parents had learned to live with this unusual condition.

The freedom of being a college freshman had been both exciting and intimidating for Michael. Living without a curfew or supervision was a teenager's dream, though it would soon prove who was responsible and who was not. His future was very important to him. He wanted to become a major success so one day his biological parents would regret ever giving him up.

Walking on campus, Michael felt engulfed by the sea of faces herding from building to building each day. At times he could relate to the students referred to as "weirdoes," the students who wanted to stand out amongst conformity and display their own individuality. He wasn't fond of being another face in the crowd yet he enjoyed this new adventure of finding himself.

Michael hadn't yet set his mind on a career. He actually thought it wasn't the best system or idea to have students deciding what they would do for the rest of their lives at such a young age. Since Debra was a high school teacher, Michael had always done well in all his classes. Anytime his grades slipped, she explained his mistakes in very simple words. He was never afraid to ask her a question. He could still hear her saying, "A good education ensures a good celebration."

Michael found no problem entertaining himself. It was never an issue for him to make friends either, but he had very few. The family had to move frequently because of Drake's job so Michael never had an opportunity to develop a lasting friendship with anyone. Instead, he spent a lot of time in random thought, lost in his own imagination. Most people liked him so he saw no reason to make any more effort in calling or keeping in touch. It was hard for him to find meaning in all of the minor updates of another person's life; just as it was equally difficult for him to volunteer his. Nevertheless, his sense of humor and quick wit made his personality addictive to others.

Just as Michael began to appreciate the autumn Arizona sun, he was swallowed by the cold brick building of the lecture hall. He had been encouraged to take easy electives for his first semester to ease the shock but he couldn't wait to take psychology. He had no interest in being a psychologist but embraced any subject that could help him learn more about himself.

Michael knew he struggled with identity issues. It wasn't surprising for someone who was adopted to have these feelings, but Michael wanted to understand them. He often wondered if meeting an actual blood relative would ease his concerns of not fully knowing himself.

As Michael approached an empty seat in the massive auditorium, his attention was totally captured by a painfully attractive young woman. She was four seats to his left in the row ahead of him. By the time he realized he was moving in slow motion while staring at this girl, the damage was done. He quickly resumed a more customary speed as he sat down in embarrassment. Michael just knew, out of all the people flocking into the lecture hall, someone had seen him. He strategically placed his left hand over his brow to shield his face of guilt from any spectators.

"She's cute. You shouldn't be ashamed," came a voice so small and intimate that it almost seemed as if he were talking to himself.

Realizing this was a real voice he'd heard, Michael slowly looked to his right to see the biggest and deepest brown eyes he'd ever seen. As his gaze fell from this set of magnificent eyes, a set of moist lips began to pull back and show the most stunning smile. Michael sat there, speechless. He could only respond with subtle squinting at the radiance he felt from her beauty.

"You should talk to her," the stranger advised as her smile slightly shortened to release her words.

"Who?" Michael responded in total sincerity.

"Her," she said, nodding to the attractive girl who'd first caught his attention.

The girl he'd embarrassed himself over just seconds ago had completely slipped his mind. Although startled, Michael was instantly intrigued by this new stranger. He'd just sat down and there was no one there. It was like she'd just appeared.

"Where did you come from?" he asked in a mystified tone.

"I think an introduction is appropriate before we start getting into where we're from. Hello, my name is Lori," she said, extending her soft hand.

"I'm sorry, my name is Michael. And when I asked where you came from, I meant that I just sat down and there was no one here. When did you sit down?"

"Well, it was probably while you were preoccupied in your super-slow motion clip. You know, where you heard some love song in your head with cartoon birds chirping around your face. I think you tuned the rest of the class out," she said smiling.

Michael wanted so much to tell this creature of perfection that she'd been the only person in the room since she first whispered to him but the words escaped him. Everything just happened too quickly for him to devise a smooth response. He just gazed at her with the smile of a child.

"Good morning and welcome to Psych 101," the professor began, saving Michael from the awkward moment.

While Michael was looking at the professor and pretending to pay attention, all he saw was Lori's face. Now he could easily think of twenty different things he should've said, but the moment had passed. Maybe he could get a couple of words in on the way out, he thought to himself. He tried not to think about her as the class proceeded, but she remained a distraction in his peripheral vision.

By the end of class, Michael had armed himself with premeditated flirting ammunition. As he picked up his book bag and turned around, he saw that she'd begun chatting with another girl. He walked past them slowly, and even thought about waiting for her to finish their conversation. But then he told himself he wouldn't display any stalker-like behavior. He'd learned from prior mistakes that everyone needs a challenge. Showing too much interest in a woman could be a turn-off. He tried to make eye contact as he walked past but she was absorbed in small talk.

As Michael left the class, he told himself she'd probably never go out with him. He felt she was way out of his league. Trying not to think about her anymore, Michael noticed the sun didn't have the same shine as it did before. It was still sunny outside but the warmth didn't feel the same across his face.

Later that evening, Michael and Eric met back at their dorm before dinner. Eric finished track practice around the same time Michael's last class was over. The timing made it routine for them to eat together.

"Is Stacey coming to dinner with us?" Michael asked, already knowing the answer.

"I haven't talked to her since earlier. Why, have you changed your mind about meeting one of her friends?" Eric asked, fixing his clothes in the mirror.

"What if I did? Let's just say I did want to talk to one of her friends and we really connected. What happens when she comes back here with me one day and finds you with another girl? She'd have to stay true to their 'girl code' and tell Stacey."

"That would never happen," Eric said with a calm confidence.

"Why not?"

"Because you'd give me a heads up beforehand," he said, smiling.

"True, but you're missing the point," Michael said, grinning through his frustration. "If I was to make one of Stacey's friends my girlfriend, then-"

"Hold it right there. See, that's your problem. Why are you trying to make each girl you meet your girlfriend? You haven't even met the girl yet and you're picturing yourself in a relationship with her. This is college, *man. Come on!*"

"Look, I'm not trying to tell you what to do. I'm just saying it isn't smart to play with people's feelings. We both know how crazy we can make women," Michael said.

"All right, so when you're married with kids and have that same woman for the rest of your life, you'll be curious about every short skirt that smiles at you. On the other hand, I'll be a better husband because I'll have already tried almost every girl out there," Eric said, chuckling. "I'll be confident that, of all the women I've tried out, my wife is the one. Not to mention with all the nights of experience I'll have accumulated, I'll be a much better lover than you."

"I don't even know why I try," Michael said, joking, throwing his hands up.

"Because you want to make yourself feel better about not having any girls. If you make me look bad then the reason for your loneliness is decency," Eric said with a straight face, still perfecting himself in the mirror.

"Actually, *Doctor Phil,* my problem is that girls don't know how to let me go. See, when you dump a woman, she feels better off anyway. They aren't as dumb as you think. But I dump a girl and she feels as if her whole world is crashing," Michael said, smiling. This was only meant to strengthen his point since he'd never dumped anyone in his life. "See, I'm the type of guy girls want to keep forever, so I can't just love and leave like you."

"Okay then, why don't you have at least one girl right now?"

"Actually I met one today."

"Really?" Eric said, finally turning from the mirror.

"Yeah, her name is Lori," Michael said nonchalantly.

"I can't wait to meet her," Eric replied with a sarcastic smirk.

"Why? You don't believe me?"

"Yeah, I just can't wait to meet her," he said, continuing his sarcasm while focused on neatly folding his track sweats.

"She puts all your girls to shame too," Michael insisted.

"Yeah, most fantasies do," Eric whispered to himself, turning into his closet.

"Are you ready to eat yet? And don't think I don't hear you over there whispering." Although Michael didn't agree with Eric, he enjoyed and respected their friendly sparring matches.

This particular topic touched a nerve within Michael because he still had feelings for his ex-girlfriend, Rachel. The loss of his high school sweetheart was still a fresh wound for him no one knew about. It had only been three months ago she decided that, since they were going to different schools in different states, they should "be adults" and end the relationship. Thinking back he saw the logic in breaking up, but what really hurt Michael was how easy it was for her. She was his first. If it was up to Michael, he would've married her right after college. As Eric's words echoed in his head, he considered that his first real heartbreak could be the reason he lacked the motivation to approach more women.

CHAPTER 2
I KNOW WOMEN

Michael couldn't wait for his next psychology class. He tried to tell himself that Lori may not even show up that day, or he may not even see her in the large and congested lecture hall. Still, he laughed to himself at how he'd paid special attention to what he wore and how his hair looked that day.

He tried to sit in his same seat as before but it was already occupied by a guy in a tattered baseball cap, bobbing his head to an MP3 player. Instead, Michael chose the empty row behind his original seat. Now, he thought, the ball would be in her court. It'd be up to her to decide to sit next to him or the bobble-head MP3 guy. What if she sits right next to me without leaving the empty middle seat? he thought.

The class started and Lori was nowhere to be seen. Michael reluctantly snapped out of his disappointment and began taking notes on the professor's lecture. He couldn't help but take random glances around the crowded room, growing frustrated with himself for even getting so excited over a partial conversation. I'm not in college for women anyway, he kept thinking.

As the professor's glasses reflected the ceiling lights, he spoke of how humans only use about ten percent of their brain. Michael wondered how much of his ten percent was being divided between his psychology class and Lori at that moment.

When class was over, Michael had given up. *Why did I even allow myself to get all worked up over someone I know is out of my league anyway?* he thought. He chuckled at the thought of Eric's reaction when there would be no Lori.

Stepping down the stairs of the building, Michael saw the sunlight hit Lori's face so perfectly that every premature feeling for her that he'd just denounced instantly resurfaced. He took three or four steps towards her before realizing she was talking to someone. And not only talking, but laughing, with a tall, handsome, muscular football player. He'd seen this giant before, laughing and joking with the other giants, all wearing the same athletic department-issued jerseys. Michael tried to redirect his path to avoid hearing any of the smiling words in their dialogue.

"Michael!" the vaguely familiar voice shouted. He looked over and calmly pretended to be surprised to see her when, in reality, his heart was racing in overdrive. "I'll talk to you later, I've gotta go," Lori told the athletic titan before turning back to Michael.

She was even more beautiful than he remembered. As Michael went to meet her, he noticed the football player scanning him before turning away.

"Hey, how've you been?" Lori asked.

"All right. You know, just staying busy." Michael pictured himself finishing his statement with, *thinking about you.* But he knew that was Eric's influence and she wouldn't buy it, not even if it was true.

"Too busy to go over what I missed today in class with me?" she asked.

"I think I can squeeze you in," he said, in his best effort not to sound excited.

"Great, what time is best for you?"

"Um, how about seven?"

"Sounds good, here's my number and my address," she said, scribbling on a folded piece of paper.

"Okay, I'll give you a call around six forty-five to let you know I'm on the way."

"Sounds good, I'll see you then," she said, walking away.

This conversation left Michael content. He had seen her long enough to imprint her flawless features into his memory. He couldn't wait to tell Eric about his date but, of course, this was the one day that Eric was late getting home from track practice. Michael hoped he would walk in any minute, but then decided it didn't matter. Lori was real and he was going to have some one-on-one time with her. He decided against changing clothes because that might insinuate he was trying too hard. He preferred a safer, more casual perception. Besides, he thought, she could be dating Mr. Football Man.

After calling, Michael headed towards Lori's all-girl dorm. It made Michael feel better knowing she wasn't surrounded by men all day and night. The co-ed dorm he lived in made Eric's choice almost limitless. He figured if Lori was a wild girl then she wouldn't be living in an all-girl facility. What if she's a lesbian, he thought, slowing his steps. That idea left him feeling disappointed, yet more excited at the same time. "I think too much," he said aloud to himself.

As he approached the entrance of the building, Michael saw Lori with an older man, under a tree. Leaning on one of the rusted steel bicycle racks, she was looking up to this stranger with a more serious face than Michael had seen her with in their short talks. The older students had always seemed professional but this man was in his early forties and didn't look like a student. Although his clothes were clean, they were wrinkled and worn. His arm was in a sling and encased in a fresh white cast, leaving only the tips of his fingers and thumb exposed.

When Lori noticed Michael, she waved him over.

"This is Richard." She introduced them with another display of her glorious smile. A part of Michael was grateful that her signature smile hadn't surfaced until she saw him.

"How do you do?" the stranger asked in a polite voice, extending a thin but strong hand. The tree shaded the details of his face from the light of the surrounding lampposts.

Michael gripped the man's good hand, wondering if this could be her father. "I'm doing fine, sir, how about yourself?"

"Every day is another chance to do better," he said with a rugged smile.

"I like that," Michael said, smiling back.

"I got it from a little angel," he said, looking over at Lori.

Lori's eyes smiled at Richard for a moment. "Okay, so I'll see you next Wednesday, around six?"

"Yes ma'am, I'll see you then. You kids have fun. Peace and love."

"Peace and love to you, Richard," Lori replied.

Michael felt like a third wheel. He wanted to join in with this "peace and love" but that seemed to be their personal expression. Richard disappeared into the dark distance, finally leaving him alone with Lori.

"Sorry about that." Lori said, turning her key into the door and escorting Michael into the sweet-smelling, all-girl community.

"It's fine, he seems like a real nice guy."

"He has a pure heart. He's just made some bad decisions."

"Is he your father?" Michael asked, but then instantly regretted the question when Lori looked at him with a confused yet sympathetic look. "I'm sorry, that was totally inappropriate. I don't even know you well enough to ask you about your family life or personal business."

"No, I don't mind. I guess that would be the best guess when someone sees me with Richard. And no, he's not my father. But your question did make me think of my own family and how much I miss them."

"Well, if you don't mind me asking, how do you know him?" he asked as they reached her room door.

Lori sighed and looked up at Michael. "He tried to assault me. But before you respond, please understand he's changed from that person. And it was only an attempt, so I obviously haven't been traumatized," Lori explained.

"When you say assault, do you mean he tried to rob, or rape you?" Michael asked, feeling a shot of heat bloom in his chest. Instantly he became more interested in the stranger he just shook hands with.

"Well, since it never got that far, I didn't know at first. But after talking to him, I learned that it was an attempted sexual assault."

"Do the police know that he comes to see you?"

"No, jail is not the place for Richard. I told you, he has a pure heart."

"So he tried to rape you and you didn't report it?" Michael asked in confusion. He couldn't believe what she was saying.

"Who would that have helped?" Lori argued. "Neither myself nor Richard."

"It may stop him from raping the next girl on a big college campus. Even if you don't want him punished for what he did to you, I still think it's important for other women to know this man is out there, walking around."

"In most cases you're right, but Richard is different," she countered in a calm and warm voice. "I've spent time a fair amount of time with him, talking about his decisions and intentions. I've heard his apologies and his story. I've heard the pain that he's endured and how he suppressed it. I've taken the time to see another side of him, and I've forgiven him. I see the potential in him that the courts would not see. I see a man who needs to be shown love, instead of the same dish this world keeps serving."

Michael stood there, speechless. He'd never heard of such forgiveness and goodwill. He felt as if she was on the verge of being naïve but her words had the conviction and strength of a wise and experienced humanitarian. He wondered if he'd become too excited in his disbelief and rudely pushed Lori into defending her actions. "I'm sorry; I don't think I've ever met anyone like you. I mean, when I picture him trying to hurt you after seeing you two casually shooting the breeze, I just can't understand it."

"That's because you have a very protective spirit," she answered with a smile. "And don't misunderstand me, that's good. But you've also lived in a society bent on revenge cloaked in justice."

"And what society are you from?"

"One much different than this. A lot simpler," Lori answered.

"That's vague. It can't be too different, your English is perfect."

"I've spent enough time here to learn the language but there's still so much that I don't understand about the people or the laws here."

"Don't even worry about that. If you don't understand the people or the laws here then you're no different from the average American," Michael joked, but found it peculiar that she was being so candid about where she was from.

"Well, what about you, Mr. Twenty Questions. I've told you enough about me for a while, what about you?"

"Fair enough. I was adopted by two loving parents here in Phoenix. No other sisters or brothers. That's about it."

"After everything I've told you, that's it?"

"I'm sorry my life isn't as exciting and I'm not from the *secret society*," Michael said with playful sarcasm.

Lori smiled back. "I know it may sound weird but I'm kind of self-conscious about my home. I feel there's no way that I could tell someone and they not automatically pass a sort of judgment on me. I'm sorry. Maybe if we get to know each other a little better, you'll crack the case."

"I don't care where you're from, as long as you're not a terrorist," he said chuckling. "It would be a shame to see such a pretty girl blow herself up." Michael immediately regretted what he said. It was corny and even somewhat disrespectful to terrorist victims. Still, he was relieved to see her give a charitable smile.

"Okay, let's get to business," she said. "What did I miss in class?"

Going over his notes with Lori, he saw that she was freakishly smart. He'd describe a concept and she would give about four or five examples to assure him that she understood. At times he wanted to take notes on what she was saying.

After all the material had been reviewed, Michael stretched his arms up as far as he could and gave out a sigh as if he had a long day. "You hungry?" he asked, looking down at his Seiko, which showed almost eight o'clock.

"I could eat a little bit," Lori answered.

A neglected television sat silently in the corner of the room flashing scenes of fish washing up dead on beaches.

"Have you been seeing all these crazy things going on lately?" she asked.

"You mean the dead fish because of all the oil spills?" Michael replied, looking to the television, but wondering what this had to do with his dinner proposal.

"No, not just that. There's also all been all these birds falling from the sky as well. It's been all over the news."

"I haven't been watching too much of the news lately. It's been kind of depressing. I think they should report on more positive stories."

"But you still have to wonder what's going on with all these bizarre incidents?" Lori asked.

"Yeah, I don't know. Maybe global warming?"

"Maybe...I just worry sometimes that we're in the last days. You know, Armageddon and all that," she said with a concerned look.

"Really?" Michael said, totally taken by surprise. "I guess I hadn't put it all together like that."

"Well, hopefully it's not. But it's a scary thought."

"It is," Michael said, still confused about where she was going with all this. "Do you want to eat before the world ends?"

She smiled. "There are so many restaurants in the cafeteria."

"Aren't there any restaurants where you're from?"

"No, but the food where I 'm from is incomparable to the food here."

"Good or bad incomparable?"

"The food where I'm from isn't as fast but it tastes fresher and is much better for you," she said with pride. "But my tongue does enjoy the sensations from these new tastes here."

Walking down the hall with her made him feel good. He was proud to be seen with such a gorgeous young woman. He decided that he should hold his feelings back until he found out if she even had a boyfriend. Michael thought about Mr. Football. He could've been a passing friend or the love of her life. It was smart to just play it cool for now.

Michael's dinner consisted of his favorite, sweet and sour Chinese chicken. Lori sat before a Lean Cuisine platter on what he considered their first date. "You seem pretty smart, but can you figure out riddles?" he asked. "Do they have riddles where you're from?"

"Yes, I know all about riddles. What do you have for me?"

"Ok, what's big, red, and eats rocks?"

"A type of red-colored rock erosion that's used in shaping stones?" Lori answered without any hesitation.

"Well, I guess I can't say no to that, can I?" he answered with a smile.

"If that's not it then what is?"

"What's big, red, and eats rocks? A big, red rockeater. The moral of the riddle is that sometimes the answers are simple. We search all around for solutions that maybe right in front of our faces."

She looked up at him. "You're really smooth."

"What do you mean?" he asked in innocence.

Lori giggled a little. "Well, since we're in front of each other's faces right now, I would have to say that was a cute and subtle little line. Are you suggesting that you're the solution that I've been searching for?"

Michael had no intention of giving her that underlying message, but it worked out perfectly. He was just telling a corny riddle but if she thought it was cute then that was fine with him. "I didn't think you had a problem that needed a solution but if you do, then I'm definitely your man."

"You're cute."

Michael felt a small chill from her words. "Not as cute as you though." He was going all the way now. "I mean it, I can't even look directly at you for too long. It's like looking at the sun. You're just too much."

"Just like the girl I saw you staring at in psychology class when we first met?" Lori asked.

"I admit that I was staring at whoever she was but since I turned and saw your face, I haven't been able to look at another girl on campus without realizing there's no competition. But enough of my rambling for one day. I'm going to call it a night and head home now. It was nice having dinner with you," he said quickly, retreating from the table and leaving half of his food uneaten.

"Nice talking with you too," she said, half smiling, with a look on her face somewhere between flattered and confused.

Michael walked away, not knowing if he had spoken too soon or said too much, but it felt like a heavy weight had been lifted off of his shoulders. He was proud of himself. Even if she never spoke to him again, he wouldn't have changed one bold word.

Michael no longer had to convince himself that he was over his high school sweetheart, Rachel. He'd moved on. She orchestrated the break-up with such ease that he knew she wasn't sitting around thinking of him. When he was around Lori, she eclipsed any thoughts of Rachel. He felt better now that he'd spent time with her and saw she was a beautiful person as well as a walking work of art.

His only fear now was that she was too good for him. Michael didn't consider himself a bad guy but Lori was so perfectly faultless that he felt as if he couldn't compare to her high standards. He'd never felt this kind of insecurity before. He still couldn't get over her total forgiveness of someone who'd tried to rape her. He doubted if he had those types of principles.

Eric was standing in his closet, still wearing his track practice sweats, when Michael returned to the room. "You've never missed dinner. What did you have, a date or something?" Eric said with a chuckle.

"Actually I did."

"You know, that's actually believable because you're back so early." Eric chuckled again, pulling a clean sweat suit out of his closet. "Who was it, this Laura girl?"

"Well I'm impressed you even remembered her name started with an L. Lori, her name is Lori, and I think I just blew it with her but I don't regret it."

"So you think you messed up your chances with this girl you really like, and you don't regret it?" Eric asked with sincerity in his voice.

"Not at all. We were sitting down eating dinner and I told her how beautiful she was and how she made me feel. Then I said goodnight and walked home."

"You did what?" Eric said in total disbelief. "Okay, first, you never tell women how you feel. You save that until you mess up. You have to keep your feelings in the bank, like money; only withdrawing when you're in trouble. If you give women flowers every day then what do you give them when you mess up? Now you have to buy her a car or a ring."

"How about you just don't mess up with your girl?" Michael asked, lying back on his bed.

"Look, we're men, it's inevitable. You've probably messed up with Lori already and don't even know it."

Michael thought of how she'd caught him looking at the other girl when they first met, but wouldn't give Eric the satisfaction of mentioning it. "I don't see anything wrong with being honest and telling someone how you feel."

"You see, attractive women all know that men want them. They know they can just walk out their door and grab almost any man they want. So, because of this, they're more attracted to the man that's harder to get. A man they may actually have to work to get. I'm trying to school you, youngster," Eric preached, getting more motivated with each point he drove home.

"First of all, you're like one year older than I am, so I don't know how you can call me youngster. Second, you're about as hard to get as wet in water. Since when is playing hard to get part of your agenda in a relationship?"

"Okay, first of all, you're not even in any relationship yet. You just met the girl and walked out on a study date. Second, you've never seen me in action. You see, first I pay the girl that I want the least amount of attention. Then, after she notices me, I come on strong. It's like letting them think they're choosing you. They need to think they're in control at first. And third, did you ever stop and think about what she would've had to say back?"

"I guess I wanted her to think it over before she got back to me," Michael said in reflection.

"Okay, even if this is true, you left her sitting at the table alone. You didn't even fulfill your gentlemanly duty of escorting her back to her door. Even I do that. It's where you get your first kiss."

He hadn't thought of that. Eric had finally found a loophole. Michael couldn't come up with a response, so he had to concede. "You're right. It doesn't happen a lot, but I can admit you got me on that one."

"So let me get this straight. After you told her, you just chickened out and ran for it, huh?" Eric asked as he stared Michael down.

After a brief silence, Michael looked over at Eric and they erupted in a boisterous round of laughter. They continued until Michael's abdomen became sore.

"You remind me of myself in tenth grade, back when I was still innocent. You'll be alright, son," Eric said, still laughing.

"It's just that I don't know if she has a boyfriend," Michael confessed.

"Well, she could've said to meet her at the library, but she invited you to her room. See now when I'm in that situation with a girl, we never study. Besides, does it matter if she has a boyfriend? May the best man win is how I look at it. I mean, don't get me wrong. If I see a guy and a girl together, I won't approach her out of respect for him. But if she approaches me, or if I don't know that she has a boyfriend, it's on…like hot buttered popcorn."

"See now that's the difference between you and a person like myself. Let's say I want a girl and she has someone. Then she leaves him for me. In whatever way, I must've been better than the man she left. But then, I'll always wonder what'll happen when someone comes along better than me. And I know there's someone better than me out there. It would just be a matter of time before she meets him and then leaves me to repeat the cycle. This just continues until she finds the best mate that she can get."

"I know what's wrong with you. Someone broke your heart and now your confidence is shot. Look, you don't have to admit it, but it happens to us all. And later on down the line, it makes us stronger. You should never feel like there's someone better than you out there. Whatever strengths you have are specific to you, which makes you perfect for someone. A guy could come around in an Ashton Martin coupe, with piles of money, a good sense of humor, and just be a great guy. But he doesn't have whatever it is that makes you, Michael. And if that's what Lori loves, then there's no guy better for her than you."

"That was pretty profound for you," Michael said with a smile.

"All jokes aside, you're a good dude. And I don't like hearing you say that there are 'better guys.' If I was like you, I wouldn't have to lie to women. I'd just use that innocent and corny charm of yours. Women love that more than my smooth lines. As a matter of fact, I want to meet this Lori and see if she's good enough for my boy."

"You have to really be on your best behavior, she's a good girl."

"Like a Ms. Goodie Two Shoes?" Eric asked.

"No, not like that, she's just good. I don't know how to describe it. She's the kind of girl that makes you want to better yourself because she's on top of her game. And she's cool too, but just super nice."

"So I can't mention how I came in from breakfast to find you on your broken bed, alone and dripping with sweat?" Eric asked as he chuckled.

"Sure, you can go into all kinds of detail about that. Just expect to have one eyebrow shaved off when you wake up the next day."

"You'd shave my eyebrow off for a girl?"

"Only if you were to use my embarrassment as entertainment in front of a girl I really like."

"Touché," Eric said, smiling.

Michael thought if he could adopt some of Eric's positive qualities, and vice versa, they'd both be better men. He liked Eric when they first met but never thought he'd be able to seriously respect anything Eric said, much less take something from their conversations and apply it to his life. He felt Eric had taken a big brother approach to their relationship. And since Michael had grown up without any siblings, he found himself slowly beginning to accept this side of their friendship.

CHAPTER 3
MYSTERIES &
MISUNDERSTANDINGS

All of Michael's other courses were dull compared to his psychology class although he did find it easier to focus in other classes because Lori wasn't in them. As Michael and a mob of other students were spewing from a pair of lecture hall doors, his cell phone rang. "Hello."

"Hello, may I speak to Michael?" the sweet familiar voice asked.

"This is Michael. Is this Lori?"

"Yes, you remembered my voice. What are you doing right now?"

"Just heading out of class, about to grab some lunch. How did you get my number?"

"You called to tell me you were on the way when you came over. Remember?"

"Oh yeah, caller ID," he said, slightly disappointed. For a split second, Michael thought she may have gone to the trouble of looking him up.

"Is it okay that I called you?" she asked.

"Yeah, that's fine. What's up?"

"I was just getting out of class too, so I thought I'd call to see if you wanted to grab some lunch with me?"

"Perfect timing. Where are you?"

"Look behind you."

He turned around in total surprise to see her stunning eyes smiling at him. "You stalker," he said grinning, trying to downplay his excitement.

"No, I think you've been stalking me since before class even started. You found some way to hack into the school database and found my schedule. Then you took a class in this building that would be over at the same time as mine."

"The fact that you could even come up with such an elaborate scheme like that off the top of your head makes you a stalker." He laughed and was happy to see her laughing. He didn't know what to expect after he'd just ran away the other night.

"Well, now that we've stalked each other down, let's go eat," she said, with that radiant smile that made him consider buying sunglasses.

As they began walking, Michael knew they couldn't take too many more steps before the other night would resurface so he decided to play it by the worst possible scenario. "I hope we can still be friends, even if you don't feel the same way about me. You seem like a very special person I'd like in my life. Even if only as a friend."

"So after everything you said, you're backing out on me? Okay," she said, purposely looking away into the distance.

"No, I'm not backing out," he said so sternly that he paused to lower his voice. "I was just saying there would be no pressure if you only wanted to be friends. You know, making it easier on you. I mean, you probably have to turn guys down every other day," he said, feeling proud of himself for how smoothly his words came together.

"That was sweet. Just like what you said to me the other night."

"Sorry I didn't walk you back to your door."

"That did cross my mind. Especially after I told you about Richard. But then I put myself in your shoes. If I was to spill my feelings out like that, I might try to find the nearest exit too," she said, smiling.

Michael took it as a good sign that she was sympathetic to his lack of nerve. "Our student cards work at all the dorms; you want to eat here?" he asked, trying to avoid his dorm cafeteria where they might see Eric. Their one-on-one conversation was going well, and he was afraid the addition of Eric might disrupt the flow.

"Sure. I've never eaten here and I love new scenery," Lori answered.

As they sat down to eat, Michael liked how all the new faces looked at them. He felt as if everyone's stares were their appreciation of a nice couple. Or maybe everyone was just looking at her, he thought.

"So why aren't you dating anyone?" she asked.

"I should probably explain this whole dating thing is new to me," he confessed.

"I figured that when I gave you my number and you didn't call back. Even after you told me you were interested."

"I had one serious relationship in high school and she broke up with me over the phone. But not just over the phone. In a text."

"Mmmm," Lori said with a lemon-juice face.

"Yeah. She said since we both were at different schools, that we should just go our separate ways."

"I've heard that happens a lot. It's a part of growing up."

"Enough about her, though. I'd rather talk about you," Michael said, looking back into her inviting eyes.

"What about?"

"How old are you?"

"Now one thing I do know is you should never ask a lady that question," she said, squinting with a smile. "I'm pretty sure that's universal for all cultures."

"Yeah, for older women who still look like they're twenty or thirty-something. I know you're not in your thirties…right?"

"This is only my second year of college."

"Okay, so you're either eighteen or nineteen like me. Or you're a twenty-something who was held back a couple of times while being homeschooled." They both laughed, but Michael still felt a little tension from Lori. "Anyway, what do you like to do besides volunteer for every charity in your zip code? I mean, for fun."

"Well," she said, trying to contain her laugh, "I like to read, I like to swim, and I like movies."

"What would you be doing if you were back in your hometown right now?" Michael didn't mean to ask about her home again, but it slipped out.

"We'll get to that very soon, I promise. Maybe I'll even get you to visit."

"Whoa, you're talking about meeting the parents. That's fast. I was just asking where you were from."

"You're so silly."

Michael had begun to feel more comfortable around Lori. Before talking with Eric, he really couldn't see himself with someone in her league. He always thought he was an attractive guy but he figured women who looked like her were reserved for guys on their way to becoming professional athletes. The more he talked and joked with her, the less intimidating she was to him, both physically and socially. The more time he spent with her, the more he could see himself being with her. Making her laugh and smile made him feel like he could relax and be himself.

After lunch, Michael wouldn't make the same mistake again. He walked her to her door, teaching her the words to one of his favorite songs.

"The sound of her voice just takes you to a different mood. I have almost all her albums downloaded if you'd like to listen sometime," he said, trying to slip in a subtle invitation to see her again.

"Music is an experience to you?"

"Exactly. Like being cradled in the arms of an angel."

Lori looked over at him as if he were about to continue with something else, but he was done.

"What?" he asked.

"I was just thinking of what you said. I know songs like that too."

"You want to sing one for me?"

"No!" she said quickly.

"Why? You can't sing? No need to be embarrassed around me."

"No, it's because I don't know the words. I just know the sound." She closed her eyes and smiled for a moment. "Well, I'm going to take a nap before my evening class. The food here makes me sleepy."

"Okay, well, it was really nice to see you. Maybe we can do it again sometime."

"We'll see," she said.

He smiled back and turned off into the crowded campus traffic of shuffling feet and backpacks. The sun was hitting his face the way he liked it again. It seemed as if the pieces of his puzzle were beginning to form a picture that he wanted. He was breezing through all his first semester courses, he was on good terms with his roommate, and he was building a relationship with the girl of his dreams. Everything seemed too good to be true. He couldn't help but feel something was bound to go wrong. All the more reason to enjoy this moment while it lasted, he thought.

Eric had invited Michael to his open track practice, but he'd never gone. He appreciated the confidence he'd gained from their last conversation, so today he figured he'd go. He passed by his dorm and continued down a long, wide, yet shallow, hill that led to the sports facilities. He could smell the determination and sweat in the air.

At first it was hard to find Eric in the population of uniformed team members. Sure enough, Michael spotted him entertaining two ladies with his wicked smile. The closer he came, the louder he could hear Eric's laughter.

"Michael. You finally came by!" Eric said, with excitement. "Katie, this is Michael, who doesn't like to be called Mike."

"That's fine because I hate to be called Kate," she said, smiling and reaching her hand out for Michael's. "So, you're Eric's roommate?"

"Yeah," he said, finally noticing that she was yet another beautiful girl.

"And this is Monica-" Eric continued.

"He was just inviting us over for dinner and a game of pool. Will you be home tonight?" Katie interrupted.

"Yeah," Michael answered, totally stunned.

"Cool. Let's go warm up, Monica. See you guys tonight, around eight thirty?" Katie said as they jogged off.

"That sounds perfect. We'll see you ladies later," Eric said, smiling, his eyes wide enough to pop out of his head. "Look at Michael. Did you see that? She cut me off when I was introducing Monica to make sure you'd be home tonight. I don't even think she was planning on coming until you walked up. Look at Michael, of all people, about to get Katie. Killer Katie!"

"First of all, what do you mean, *of all people*? Second, why are you calling her Killer

Katie? You're making me nervous."

"Did you not see her? You had to see how cute she is, that's why all you said the whole time was *yeah...yeah*. Everybody on the track team wants her."

"Everybody?"

"Everybody. Even the girls," Eric said.

"Your mom must not have taken her prenatal vitamins or something," Michael said, laughing. "You have mental issues."

"I'm serious. She's the one everyone talks about. A legend in the making. And don't take this personally, but I still can't believe she wants you over me."

"Oh, now why would anybody take that personally?"

"This is just hard for a man of my history to accept, although my confidence is strong enough to take a hit like that and still do all I can to assist my wingman. Besides, Monica is no slouch by any means."

"What if I'm not trying to have a double date with you and whoever?" Michael asked.

"Oh, that's right, I forgot about Lori. Well, she's not your girlfriend yet. It can't be cheating if there's no established relationship."

"Who said that? You're talking as if you're quoting this from somewhere. Where are you getting this from?" Michael asked playfully, but really wanted an answer.

"That's it," Eric said, as if he had had an epiphany.

"What's it?"

"Me. I'm saying all that. I should write a book."

"Did you not just hear me say that you have mental issues? People with mental issues don't write books."

"Anyway, I've got to warm up. Are you going to stay and see me smoke these guys?"

"Yeah, I'll stay for a little bit and check out your skills."

"Alright, I'll talk to you later. Oh yeah, if you get a chance, clean up a little when you get back."

"All my side is clean," Michael said. "And *I* never invited anyone over."

"Come on, man…I didn't ask you to clean up your side. I won't have time to clean up and take a shower. It's hard being a student athlete."

"Alright, crybaby."

"My man," Eric said as if he were proud.

Michael sat back and watched the display of pain versus will in amazement and respect. He wondered how much of these athletes' abilities were from pure talent, and how much was strict discipline.

Michael began to see where Eric's confidence came from. He was really being truthful about smoking the other guys. There were no other runners even close to him. Michael could see Eric easing up as he approached the finish line with no one around to push him. "Finish strong," the coach shouted. Eric would complete his repetition then turn around to cheer-in everyone else. This made the other runners look even worse since they were out of breath and wheezing as they crossed the line. Eric was only a sophomore. Michael knew there had to be juniors and seniors in the group that Eric was leaving half way down the track. About thirty minutes later, Michael decided to head home to prepare for their guests.

After cleaning and showering, Michael sat and reflected on what he'd let Eric get him into. I don't even know this girl, he kept thinking to himself. And although he had no plans, he began to feel guilty for saying he'd be home.

Eric suddenly swung in like a hurricane, tearing at his clothes in a frenzy to hurry into the shower. "I see you're all fresh and clean," Eric said, still in overdrive.

"I don't even know if I want to get to know this girl," Michael said with wrinkles in his forehead.

"I've got to see this Lori of yours. I mean, Katie is more than a pretty girl. She's an opportunity to plant a memory that you'll cherish for years to come."

"Look. I'll be friendly but I won't jeopardize what I could have with Lori. I haven't had time to tell you but we had lunch today. And I believe we're on our way to being a couple soon," Michael said in a sincere tone, so Eric would know he was serious.

"All I can ask is for you to be friendly. I mean, I can't make you date a potential future supermodel."

"You're right. I could possibly be doing that on my own."

"I seriously have to meet her. If you really made Lori up, just tell me now," Eric said with a sympathetic look.

"I'll see if I can get her to come over here for dinner tomorrow."

"Good, because if she's like you say, then I promise I'll back off."

"Why is who, or if, I date important to you, anyway?"

"Because I feel like when it comes to girls, I'm feasting. And you...well, you're starving. So being the man that I am, it's hard for me to watch someone I care about in a female famine."

"Eloquently put," Michael said, laughing.

"I'm going to take a shower while you just sit there and focus on being friendly," Eric said, rushing out.

"So this is what college is really like," Michael said, falling back on his bed. First there were no girls, and now they're coming in flurries. It was easy to see how students could get caught up in the party life and lose sight of what was important. It was just as easy to see how a man could live as promiscuously as Eric. Sometimes Michael wondered if he was missing out on life. Sometimes he wished he could indulge in some of the pleasures that his peers enjoyed, but he had his conscious to blame.

After Eric had showered and dressed, they made their way to the cafeteria and reserved a table. When the girls arrived, Michael was both surprised and impressed by how Katie looked. She wore black spandex pants that showed every attractive curve a man would want to see, and a pink tank-top that was working as hard as it could to hold back the goods. Monica also wore black spandex pants with a turquoise top. Her appeal also called for attention, but Katie was the main attraction.

"Long time no see," Eric joked, as the two striking young women approached the table. "You guys remember Michael, right?"

"Nice outfits," Michael said, unable to hide his admiration of the female body.

"We need to do laundry, to be honest," Monica said, smiling.

"Plus we do evening stretching before we go to bed," Katie added as they sat down. Michael instantly found himself fighting off the mental imagery of the two attractive girls contorting themselves in different stretching positions.

"Coach Lewis wore us out today. Was it a hard practice for the guys too?" Monica asked Eric.

"Mondays, Wednesdays, and Fridays are always our hard days in the off season," Eric replied with a business face that Michael rarely saw. He began to see how serious track and field was to him.

While looking at Eric as he spoke, Michael glanced over at Katie to find her staring directly at him with a mischievous smile. He also noticed her subtly moving around in her seat, as if her legs had a mind of their own. When he looked back at Eric to see if he'd noticed her behavior, he saw the same wicked look

34

on Eric's face as he stared at Monica. At first Michael thought some weird team joke was about to unfold, until he saw that Monica looked normal.

"Yeah...but today's practice was even challenging for a hard day," Eric continued.

Just when Michael thought all the staring and moving around was becoming too awkward, Katie broke the silence. "I need to go to the ladies room and freshen up; wanna come with me, Monica?"

"Sure," Monica said, with the innocence of not recognizing that anything was happening.

After the girls left the table Eric leaned over to Michael. "You know they just left to go talk about us. Females think they're so slick. Monica wants me. She's been playing footsies with me the last few minutes. Rubbing her foot all up my leg and looking all innocent about it. She's probably making plans with Katie about how to get me alone right now. What can I say? Some guys don't even have to try. Katie seems quiet; you getting any vibes off her?"

Michael chuckled a little as the scenario had finally begun to make sense to him. The chuckle became a laugh when he pictured Katie smiling at him, and Eric smiling at Monica.

"What's so funny?" Eric asked.

Just as Michael's laugh was slowing and he was able to speak, Katie and Monica came walking back to the table. Michael quickly nudged Eric and shook his head.

Eric looked back at Michael and nodded his head with an overconfident smile. "That was quick," Eric said, still smiling. "How about we go up to our room and order pizza?"

"That sounds perfect." Katie quickly replied, her eyes excited.

Things were spinning out of control so quickly that Michael couldn't find a pause to try and clarify the situation. He was the only one at the table who noticed the misunderstanding that decisions were being made from.

While they were all getting up from the table, Katie grabbed Michael's hand. "Why don't you two go ahead? I'd like to walk with Michael and get to know him a little better."

"Good idea, we'll meet you two upstairs in a little while," Eric said, looking at Monica.

Michael wanted to just stop everything right there and say what really happened, but he couldn't. He felt as if he would turn the evening into an awkward catastrophe.

Besides, what if Monica did like Eric? Michael didn't want to sabotage their night and put the friendship that he and Eric were building in jeopardy. So he went with the flow as the two couples went their separate ways.

"I must admit I'm really attracted to you," Katie said, looking up at Michael with seductive eyes.

Michael couldn't contain himself anymore. He rubbed his hands over his face and gave a loud exhale that ended with a chuckle. "I'm sorry. I let this whole night get out of hand."

"What do you mean?"

"It wasn't me that you were playing footsies with under the table."

"What?" Katie said, with bulging eyes and a wide open mouth.

"It was Eric. And he thinks it was Monica who was rubbing her foot up his leg."

Katie stopped walking and paused before releasing a bellowing laugh. "Wait a minute, how do you know Eric thinks it was Monica?"

"Well," he said, smiling as the situation became more humorous to him the more that Katie laughed. "I saw you staring and smiling at me, and then I saw Eric smiling at Monica all weird. So when you two went to the ladies room, he told me he thought it was Monica rubbing his leg. But then you two came back before I could tell him."

"Yeah, we didn't really have to freshen up. I just wanted to ask Monica if she could keep Eric company so we could get to know each other. But he helped out with the pizza idea before we could even get our plan out," she said with another shrieking bolt of laughter.

"Is it really that funny?" Michael asked, looking around at the attention she was attracting with her gaudy laughing.

"You don't understand," she said, wiping traces of tears from her eyes. "Monica likes Eric but she wouldn't even kiss Eric until he totally committed to her. And sex would probably be out of the question until she was engaged or married," Katie said, laughing again.

Now seeing the entire picture, Michael indulged in a new round of laughter himself. "Shouldn't we go back and tell them?" he asked.

"Well, let's just see how they play out first. Does he have a girlfriend?"

"It's the Bro Code; no comment," he said, smiling.

"Okay, I get it," she said with a smirk. "Enough about them. So what about me and you?" Katie said in a more formal tone. "I know that this is forward but I have a different view on relationships than most people. I like to get the sex out of the way as soon as possible. That way, I know for sure if the guy just wanted sex or if he's really interested in me," she said, looking up at Michael for his reaction.

"Whoa. I've never heard that one before. I can't say I agree with it but I do see the logic," Michael said, trying to be polite as he considered how many guys Katie must've already slept with after adopting this view on relationships. "I actually have someone I'm already interested in. And honestly, just meeting with you girls tonight makes me feel a little guilty."

"That's so sweet. But she's not your girlfriend though?"

"No. But that's my goal."

"Well, I'd like to put my bid in," Katie said, with a sly smile.

"What do you mean *bid*?"

"If she's not your girlfriend, then you're still on the market. I'd like to show you what I have to offer before you make up your mind about who you want to be with. I have confidence in my abilities."

Michael had never met a girl so forward. She almost reminded him of a female version of Eric, except that she claimed to be in search of a relationship. He'd never been so intimidated and turned on at the same time in his life. "Katie, you're one of the most attractive girls I've ever seen, but I feel something with this other girl that I'm afraid I don't feel with you. I'm definitely physically attracted to you, and you seem really cool and nice, but if you and I were to get physical, I know that I'd feel more guilt than anything."

"Guilt for having a good time?" Katie asked in confusion.

"No. Guilt for jeopardizing something that could really be special, just for a moment of physical pleasure. I know this sounds like I'm gay, turning down sex with a beautiful girl, but I have to stay true to my feelings. I'm sure this won't hurt your feelings though. I bet a girl who looks like you has guys hitting on her all the time." Michael looked over at Katie to see a lone tear sliding and stopping half way down her cheek. "I'm sorry, I didn't mean to…" Michael didn't know what to say.

"It's okay. I'm just realizing that there *are* good men out there. And I'm out here offering sex when that's not even what good men really want."

"Don't get me wrong, we do want it, but in due time. When we realize that she may be the one who puts all other girls in the background."

"How many guys like you are out there, Michael?"

"I'm not special; I just know what I want. So I try to stay loyal to my feelings and to the people I care about."

"Most men I meet want sex, and then they look to see what other qualities are there. You look for all the qualities you want then consummate the relationship with sex. I never knew guys like you existed. You must think I'm a whore?"

"No, not at all. In fact, I believe the experiences you've probably had, with the way most men are, have most likely made you feel this way. I'm still figuring out how a man should react to certain situations and I'm a man myself, so I can imagine how difficult it is for a woman to figure us out."

Katie dried her moist eyes. "That makes me feel a lot better."

"Good, because I hate to see a beautiful woman cry. And by the way, could we keep this between us. If Eric or any other guys on campus heard about this conversation, I'd be blackballed for life," he said, smiling.

"No problem," Katie said, laughing. "I'll let everybody know how much of a womanizer you are."

"Don't do that. Then you'll give me a reputation."

"That's good for guys, isn't it?"

"Unless you're trying to begin a relationship with someone, like I am."

"Oh, that's right, I almost forgot. What's her name?"

"Lori, she lives in the all-girl dorm."

"You're kidding. We live in the all-girl dorm. And there was a girl named Lori who was almost sexually assaulted a couple weeks back. I wonder if it's the same girl?"

"It is. She told me she was involved in an assault attempt." Michael didn't want to tell Katie that he actually saw Lori socializing with the perpetrator. He still didn't fully understand how someone could be so forgiving.

"Attempt is right. Did she tell you she broke the guy's arm?"

"She broke his arm?" he asked, remembering the older man had had his arm in a cast with a sling.

"Yeah, it was in the school paper and everything. I can understand why you like her. She's a beautiful girl. Obviously strong and in good shape, but she seems super nice and sweet too. I don't know her too well but she spoke about her assault attempt to all the floors in our building. She gave us tips on how to prevent an assault, and what to do if you become a victim."

"Do you know where she's from?" Michael asked.

"No. But like I said, I don't know her that well. She doesn't look like your average American. Then again, what does your average American look like nowadays anyway? She does speak really proper English, though. I mean, you'd think her mom teaches grammar or something."

"Yeah, I noticed that too. And she definitely knows a lot more words than I do," he said, smiling playfully. "I don't know what to think. She doesn't have any accent, but she avoids the subject of where she's from when we talk."

"Well, if that's your only problem with her so far then you guys should be fine. You're obviously a good man and she seems to be an adorable person."

"Thanks. I hope it works out."

Katie's cell phone began to ring. "This should be good, it's Monica. I wonder what happened on their end?" she said, smiling.

Michael was happy to see Katie smiling. She was really a good person with a couple of issues, just like himself. He wondered for a second, had he not met Lori, what could've been between them. But then he pictured Lori's face and those thoughts quickly faded.

"You'll never guess what happened," Katie said as she brought the phone down from her ear with a look of disbelief.

"What?" Michael answered, with a hint of worry in his voice.

"Eric didn't try anything. He was a perfect gentleman and they hit it off."

"You're kidding," Michael answered with a similar look of shock.

"She said they talked for a while and then, just like us, they laughed about the footsies thing. They have a date on Friday."

Michael wondered if Eric was really trying to turn over a new leaf, or if this was all some kind of scheme to seduce Monica.

"They certainly would make an odd couple but you never know," Katie said, trying to sound optimistic.

"Well, I had a nice time talking with you. To be such an attractive girl, you have a lot of substance. I'm sure you'll make some guy very happy."

"Thank you. And even though you're the first man to ever reject me, I'm happy I met you. Believe it or not, in a small way, you've changed my life. There are very few people that I can say I care about. Especially someone I've known for less than a day."

Michael felt good about the way he'd handled the situation. It was a deep down good feeling that made him smile without trying.

"Oh, here's Monica coming now. Again, it was nice to meet you, Michael. I'm sure we'll see each other again," Katie hugged him tightly.

"You guys have been walking around here, hugged up all night?" Monica asked in a sarcastic tone.

"Time flies when you're with good company. Goodnight, Michael." Katie waved goodbye as her fashion twin accompanied her down the sidewalk.

Michael couldn't wait to get upstairs to get Eric's side of the night. He was so anxious that he missed a step and tripped. He sat on the stairs for a moment to laugh at himself. After taking a quick look around to make sure no one saw, he finished his quick dash to their room. When he opened the door, he saw Eric, sunk back on his bed with a concentrated look. "You okay?" Michael asked softly. "I heard you were a perfect gentleman, so I figured you weren't feeling well."

"You knew, didn't you?" Eric asked with a smile.

"Knew what?"

"You knew that Katie was playing footsies with me by accident, and not Monica."

"Yeah, but I didn't have time to tell you before they got back to the table."

"It's cool," Eric said, still smiling. "I'm glad it happened like that."

"Why?"

"I don't know. I just feel like if any of this had happened any other way, I wouldn't feel the way I do now."

"And how is that?"

"I feel like I finally see your side in a lot of the things we've talked about now. I feel like a lot of what I was saying made sense but the truth is, I look down on women. I was just lying here thinking about it. I don't believe I consciously look down on women, but nevertheless I do. And it's because I've learned to use them. I've become so good at using women that I've begun to look down on them. Man, it sounds really bad when you say it aloud. Think about it. How can you fully respect any group of people when you've trained yourself to use them?"

"That's super deep. What made you even take your thoughts in that direction?" Michael asked.

"Monica. I respect her. And since I respect her, I can't simply use her for her body like I normally would. This made me ask myself why. So, after a little self-analyzing, here I am."

"What is it about her that makes you respect her more than other women?"

"I mean, you saw her. She's super sexy, but she wasn't trying to use it as a weapon. Most women use their sex appeal to get men to do whatever they want. This is no secret. But she was genuinely nice, funny, and just so gorgeous that I didn't want to do her wrong. This is the first time I've ever felt this way. What's the difference between respecting someone and being in love with them?"

"There shouldn't be much of a difference," Michael said, laughing. "They go hand in hand. If you love someone, you have to respect their mind and body."

"But what if I just respect her and I don't love her?"

"It's still early, youngster," Michael said, with a big grin, happy to finally turn the tables on Eric. "You two may know each other from the track team but you're just getting to know each other intimately. Give it time. You can't stress. If you're falling in love with someone on the first night, you become interested in her. I'm trying to teach you a little bit about women. It's up to you to soak up the knowledge, or just let it slide off."

"See, this is why men don't talk about things like this with each other," Eric said, laughing. "We just *have* to hear the jokes."

"That's right, because you would do, and have done, the same with me."

"Okay, you're right. How did you say it before? Touché."

"All jokes aside, I hope it works out for you," Michael said with sincerity.

"Thanks, man. Oh yeah, how did things go with you and Katie?"

"Cool, I mean we talked a lot and I found out she kind of knows Lori."

"Well, it's good you didn't try anything," Eric said, chuckling.

CHAPTER 4
LORI'S TRUE IDENTITY

Michael figured if he was late for his psychology class then he could find Lori and sit next to her. He arrived and was surprised to see his plan had a chance at actually working. He spotted her in the crowd of students and saw there was no one on either side of her. She wore a blinding white blouse and sat with her legs crossed in tan khakis and perfect white sandals. As he made his way to her, she looked up and smiled at him. He tried to play it cool and just nod back, but his face wouldn't cooperate. He ended up smiling so hard that he felt his dry bottom lip almost split down the middle. He licked his lips and searched pocket after pocket for his lip balm. Just as he was giving out a sigh of defeat, he saw Lori's perfectly-manicured fingernails holding her own cherry Chap Stick.

"Is it that obvious?" he whispered.

"A little."

"You know if I use this then it's just like we've kissed," Michael said, just before he smeared the fruity gel on his lips.

"You can have it," Lori said with a semi-disgusted look.

Michael's face dropped.

After a few moments of awkward silence, she held her hand out and said, "I'm just kidding."

Michael's appreciation for Lori's sense of humor was interrupted by the professor.

"You. Young lady, can you answer the question?" The elderly man's proper voice rang throughout the lecture hall. His cold stare at Lori made other students turn to see who he was addressing.

Michael hadn't heard the question or even the subject they were on. He felt embarrassed for Lori, and guilty for taking her attention from the class. With half a giggle still in her lungs, Lori began her answer. "A simplified way to describe the law would be to say anything that can go wrong will go wrong," she said, still smiling.

"Correct," the professor replied then casually continued as if Lori hadn't just got the best of him.

Michael wrote, "that was so cool," on his notebook and turned it towards Lori for her to see.

She smiled and scribbled on her notebook the words, "Thank you, now pay attention before he calls on you." It was a difficult task, but he managed to focus on the professor's lecture for most of the rest of class.

As the auditorium began dispersing, Michael remembered a favor he needed to ask of Lori. "Do you have any plans right now?"

"I have a few things I need to do, but they can wait a while," Lori answered.

"Well, my roommate, Eric, believes I need to find a girlfriend. So when he dates, he keeps trying to get his girls to bring a friend for me."

"Really? Are they cute?" she asked.

"Yeah, but I'm honestly only interested in you." Then before Michael knew it, he felt a sharp pain shoot through his arm. He saw Lori's fingers balled into a fist and realized that she'd punched him. "Ouch," he said, laughing. "They're not cute compared to you, though."

"Well, you should've said it like that first," she said, laughing. "Now what do you want?"

"An icepack. You're pretty strong for a woman."

"For a woman!" she said, squinting her big brown eyes.

"Everybody knows men are naturally stronger than women."

"Really?"

"Hey, don't get mad and hit me again. It's just factual science," Michael said, still rubbing his arm.

"All right, I accept."

"Accept what?"

"Your challenge. Whatever you choose, I'll do it better than you," she said.

"Well…what if it's not me?"

"Then who?"

"My roommate. First of all, if he met you then he'd get off my case about getting a girl. Second, and this is a plus for you, he'd stop bringing girls over for me," Michael said, smiling.

"All right, but what does all that have to do with our challenge?"

"I'm getting to that right now. See it just so happens that my roommate also runs track."

"So you want me to race your roommate who runs track?"

"You're right, it wouldn't be fair. Every world record set by a man is faster than that set by women. It's just factual science."

"You know what? I will race him. And when I beat him, I don't ever want to hear you say anything about factual science again," she said in a playful but stern voice.

"Fair enough."

As they started their way to the track, Michael began to doubt if Lori was actually serious. "Aren't you going to stop by your place and grab some workout clothes?"

"This won't be a workout. I'll just run faster than him."

"But you're wearing cute little sandals."

"So your roommate should have no excuse."

"You sound way too confident. You must never have watched any Olympic games," he said.

"Everyone is different, Michael. Remember that."

"It would only be fair to tell you that Eric is also on a track scholarship."

"What's the matter? Are you trying to back out of this?"

"No, just giving you the facts, ma'am. Just the facts," he said, smiling.

"I'm getting tired of you and your facts," she said, laughing. "You're making this so much worse for your friend."

When they approached the track, everyone was once again grouped into their different cliques as they stretched and joked. With Lori on Michael's side, Eric spotted them easily. "Michael...is that you?" he shouted from one of the small clusters of uniformed athletes. Eric left his group and headed towards them.

"Finally, this is Lori." Michael introduced them as they shook hands.

"I was beginning to believe you were a figment of Michael's imagination," Eric said, surveying Lori with approving eyes.

"No, I'm real, but his imagination is leading him to believe that you can beat me."

Eric smiled and looked over at Michael. "Beat her in what? Checkers, pool, chess, video games, I mean what? Don't tell me in racing."

Michael smiled and looked at Lori.

"No. I'm sorry, I wouldn't want to embarrass you and hinder Michael's only chance at a decent girlfriend," Eric said, glowing with confidence.

Without saying another word, Lori looked away from Eric to study the track. She then walked to the starting line and looked back at Eric. By this time, the rest of the track team had recognized the challenge by this young girl in sandals.

"Don't be scared, Eric," a voice came from one of his teammates.

"Yeah, don't be scared to get beaten by a *girl*," Michael added.

Eric glanced around at his teammates then took his sweatshirt off. "Is this what you all want?" he cried, thrusting his hands in the air. A small round of applause was heard as Eric stepped up to the starting line.

"Let me say go," a small familiar voice came from the audience. Katie walked out of the crowd and Lori recognized her. They gave each other a quick hug. "Go get him, girl," Michael overheard Katie tell Lori.

Katie stood behind them and gave formal instructions for the hundred-yard dash. As they began to set their toe to the line, Eric stepped back about ten feet to give Lori a head start. Lori looked at Eric and boldly walked back to where he was starting from. Eric's teammates rumbled with all kinds of 'oohs.' "On the clap of three, you go. One, two…." Katie clapped and they both exploded from the line. Eric was in full stride within four steps. Every muscle in his body was visibly flexing and bulging as he pushed off the ground beneath him. Lori took three or four steps jogging. Michael began to hear the audience smacking their lips in disappointment.

On Lori's fourth step, it looked as if Eric had begun moonwalking. He was still laboring as he was before but Lori's effortless jog was beginning to show its real power. For every step Lori was taking, Eric was taking three. By her fifth step she was neck to neck with him. His face began to show his struggle. If he wasn't running at full strength before, he definitely was at this point. Lori looked over at Eric in the heat of the battle and smiled. She shortened her stride and seemed to be slowing down. Eric regained the lead, making his vigorous effort seem less foolish. After they crossed the finish line, Michael was the first to meet his two friends.

"I don't know. That was pretty close for sandals," Michael joked.

Eric was bent over with his hands on his knees. Lori bent down to dust off her sandals. "You're not even breathing hard," Eric said in between his hard, fast breaths. "I thought I burned you out half way through."

"You did. I'm just taking deep slow breaths," Lori said with a slight grin.

"You don't know about that, track star?" Michael continued bragging on Lori. "What are they teaching you guys out here? She looks like she just came from a walk in the park while you look like you were running for your life."

"Michael, he beat me. You make it sound as if I won," Lori said humbly.

"Seriously, why don't you try out? There's a coach around here somewhere, and I'm pretty sure you could get a scholarship," Eric said, just beginning to catch his breath. "You must've run track before?"

"I do enjoy working out but I'm not into athletic competition. I'm sorry, Eric. Congratulations, though, you *are* very fast. At least for a boy," Lori said, smiling.

"Hey, Lori," Monica said. "It's too bad you didn't beat him, he needs to be humbled a little bit," she added with a smirk.

"You see how popular you've become since you've raced me? Now everybody knows your name," Eric said.

"Monica actually lives in my building, but I'm sure that people will recognize me more on campus after this," Lori laughed with sarcasm.

Michael couldn't help but realize how Eric was right about Lori's breathing. It didn't even appear as though she was taking deep breaths anymore. She was speaking completely normally. Eric's chest was still rapidly pumping and pushing hard breaths between his words. Even during the race, Lori seemed to be toying with him. Michael found this to be very odd. He was about to ask about it but then he thought if he brought it up, it'd be even more awkward. "I believe you're the same as a six foot ten athletic guy who just doesn't like basketball. If the guy doesn't want to play then you can't teach that passion. But if he did have the passion, he'd go pro for sure. It's the same here," Michael said, moving his thoughts on.

"Okay, Michael. Everyone knows you like her. We get it," Eric said, laughing.

"That's good," Lori said, looking over at Michael with a smile that tingled his insides.

"Well, ladies and gentlemen, unless he messes it up somehow, I'd say my man Michael is on his way out of Singletown. And it's about time too," Eric joked.

"Everybody warmed up and ready to go. Let's get some sprint lines going, up and at 'em." The voice of the impatient track and field coach echoed and moved each team member.

"Well, it looks like that's our cue. Plus I have to get Lori out of here before they find out she almost beat you. They might kidnap her and make her run," Michael said.

"Yeah, they probably would. You guys do know I wasn't running at a full hundred percent though, right?" Eric asked, smiling.

"Oh yeah, we know," Michael said, with strong sarcasm.

"Of course you weren't," Lori chimed in.

"You two are made for each other," Eric said, laughing. "You're both delusional. I'll see you later. Again, it was nice meeting you, Lori," he said, running off to join the rest of the team.

Walking with Lori made Michael feel complete. Being with her made him feel a way he'd only heard of in love songs. At first, he felt she was so far out of his league that he was insecure. Now he was finding the more time he spent around her, the more he felt comfortable with her beauty. The fact that she even found him desirable made him feel better about himself.

A few weeks passed and Michael felt their relationship was growing. Unlike his ex, Rachel, Lori hadn't shown any signs of a hidden personality. He wanted to tell his parents about her, but they always asked about Rachel. He decided to let Rachel fade in their minds a bit before presenting Lori. Michael could understand how his moving on to Lori may seem pretty quick but in reality they hadn't even kissed. He was totally fine with taking it slow though; and after thinking about it, he even preferred it.

One sunny Sunday morning at breakfast, Eric and Michael were sitting in their routine seats, catching up.

"So, I've been trying to respect your relationship and everything, but tell me, what's going on with you and Lori?" Eric asked.

"We're doing good," Michael said, trying to think of something perfect to finish his statement with. Instead, the moment passed and he knew that wouldn't float with Eric.

"Aww, man. Don't tell me you're falling into the friendship zone," Eric said in a disappointed tone as his shoulders dropped.

"The friendship zone?"

"Yeah, it's like the *Twilight Zone,* because you wake up one morning not knowing when, why, or how you got there. This is the place where men have often found themselves when they were too patient with a woman. This is when women find that the relationship as friends has become so valuable that it wouldn't be worth the risk of going further. See, most women don't have any male plutonic friends to talk to. Of course, this is because most men don't want to be plutonic friends with a woman, which is also why a lot of women become such good friends with gay men. So when a woman sees an opportunity to have a male plutonic friend who isn't gay, she jumps all over it. Then she starts asking you every question that she ever wanted to know about men. Even asking you about all the *other* men she may be interested in. And all this because you tried to be a gentleman. Then one day you're sitting there, remembering when you were on her list of men she was interested in. Thinking when, why, and how…did I ever enter the friendship zone."

Michael sat and just stared at Eric for a moment. "Some woman, somewhere, must've really done you wrong, huh?" he said as Eric burst out in laughter. "No, I'm serious. Have you ever thought maybe girls hurt you so bad in the past that you take vengeance on women you date now?"

"Actually that's probably true, but I believe every man is like that. I believe every womanizing man out there was once deeply in love as a young boy. Then when whatever girl broke his heart, he felt a pain that he never wanted to feel again. Therefore, he builds up that wall to protect his feelings. You know, the wall that women constantly try to break down to get close to you."

"Don't you think the exact same process happens with women? Yet they still put their hearts out there for us," Michael argued.

"Man, whose side are you on?" Eric asked with a look of disgust on his face. "What do you mean they still put their hearts out? You mean to tell me that women don't have walls? Superman couldn't see through all the walls women have put up. That's why Lois Lane always made him nervous. Their thick prison walls make ours look like little picket fences. Their walls are built and tested before we even develop body odor."

"Okay, okay, you've made your point," Michael conceded.

"You sure? Because I can keep going."

"I'm sure you can. But I got it. Women have emotional walls," he said, laughing. "Anyway, what's going on with you and Monica? While you're asking me twenty questions."

"We're doing good," Eric said and just quietly stared at Michael for a few moments.

"Okay, point taken, you're getting me back. Now since I had to listen to all that, what's up with your personal life?"

"All right," he said, chuckling. "We went to the movies yesterday and we held hands. Man, I tell you, I never thought I'd be so contently turned on by just holding hands with a girl. Seriously, after all I've done, holding hands is making me feel that good. I'm not even stressing anything else. When and if it happens, then fine. But right now, I know this doesn't sound corny to you, but I just like being around her. I couldn't just say that to any guy but I know you understand. The only difference is I won't fall into the friendship zone."

"Again," Michael added, laughing, "I don't believe I'm asking this, but how do you stay out of the friendship zone?"

"Well really it's kind of simple. I mean, it's important to be friends, so keep doing that part, but flirt. Flirt like you did to let her know you were interested in the beginning. Once we get the girl, we sometimes stop flirting because that was a part of the hunt. Now that the hunt is over, so is the flirting. In our minds, it's sometimes like bargaining with a salesman for something that's already ours. But women need that. It can be fun for us too, if we make it."

"That surprisingly makes sense. Once again, you've amazed me with something that just might work from your odd theories."

"So just imagine how advanced you'd be if you followed all of them," Eric said, smiling. "I could be your mentor."

"You yourself just said that you're still learning new things with Monica."

"Leave it to you to bring reality into guy talk. Speaking of Monica, she suggested a double date. How about it?"

"That sounds cool, but what about Katie?" Michael asked. "Isn't she roommates with Monica? Won't she feel left out, knowing we're out having a good time while she's at home?"

"Relax. You know how thoughtful Monica is. She already talked about it with Katie, and she's fine with it. After talking with you that one night, Katie has decided to just be by herself for a while."

"Is she okay?"

"She's fine. From what Monica says, it sounds like you really helped her," Eric said, looking over at Michael. "She's just re-evaluating herself before she starts dating again. She won't have any problem finding a man when she's ready."

"Yeah, no kidding."

"There are a lot of men on campus who'd be very upset with you if they knew you were the reason that Killer Katie is off the market."

"Well, those guys don't deserve Katie anyway. She's a good girl."

"Yeah, she is," Eric said in reflection. "So, are we on for dinner?"

"I'm supposed to see her tonight to study. She missed another class and she needs to go over my notes with me. I'll ask her, but it's a good idea so I don't see why not."

The rest of that afternoon Eric and Michael relaxed. Mondays were hard days for practice so Eric stayed off his feet on Sundays. They spent most of the day watching football and yelling at the big screen plasma mounted on the wall of the student lounge. This particular student lounge was connected to their dorm building on the first floor. It was very convenient for Michael and Eric, who knew most of the other guys watching the games. The lounge was also connected to a recreational area where students played pool and bought snacks. Here, the boys could be as loud and obnoxious as they wanted.

While normally he would be cheering or yelling with the others, this afternoon Michael was deep in thought. He was really happy with the way things were unfolding with Lori, as well as his friendship with Eric. The double date on his mind just made him really appreciate how well this first year of college was going for him. His classes were going great. He was on the verge of being in a relationship with the perfect girl. And his best friend was finally settling down with a good girl. And they were all friends. He never imagined having such a near perfect transition from high school to living on his own in college.

That night, while walking up to Lori's building, he saw the same older man who assaulted her. He was coming from the direction of the door to her building. His arm was still cast in a sling; this made Michael feel a little better. He figured the man couldn't assault anybody with a broken arm. Although he couldn't understand just why this guy had to keep coming around. Michael called Lori on his cell phone to let her know he was downstairs. While he was waiting, he tried to think of a way to casually ask about the older man. When the door swung open and he saw her face, all his thoughts cleared and he was just happy to be with her again.

"Come on in." She welcomed him, wearing an oversized sweatshirt and some worn out jeans that comfortably fit her every curve.

Lori seemed a little agitated when they reached her room. She was still smiling and in a good mood but Michael could sense something was a little off. He took a seat on the side of her bed while Lori sat at her desk that was built into the wall.

"Everything alright?" he asked.

"Yeah, I'm just a little frustrated."

"About what?" Michael asked, expecting to hear something related to the older man who had just walked off into the night.

"You," she answered.

"Me? What did I do?"

"It's what you're not doing. Do you like me?"

"Of course. You know I do."

"Like me like a girlfriend?"

Michael's face looked as if he'd been the one called on in class while not paying attention this time. "Yeah, I do," he confessed.

"Then why haven't you asked me to be your girlfriend, or even tried to kiss me?" she asked with a perfectly innocent face. "Are you still in love with your ex-girlfriend?"

"Rachel? No. It's not that at all. I told you I was over her."

"Then what is it? You give me all the compliments that a girl could want. Weren't you supposed to ask me to be your girl by now? Isn't that how it works?"

Michael laughed a little as she smiled. "I honestly don't know how this works. Truth is, I've never met anyone like you before. I couldn't really tell if you were being nice to me because you liked me, or because you're just nice to everybody. I certainly didn't want to make a move too soon and make the entire relationship awkward." He sighed and took a deep breath. "Look, when things or people are important to me, I tend to overthink the details. It's as simple as that."

"So what now?" she asked.

"So this," he said as he stood up and walked over to her without any more hesitation to engage in the softest, most tender kiss he could ever remember having.

"Wow!" Lori said, smiling. "That was worth waiting for."

"Well, hopefully there will be many more to come," he said as he sat back down and smiled back.

"Not to downplay what just happened but if we don't get to this studying right away, I don't think we ever will."

"Don't say ever. We can pick it up tomorrow."

"We have an exam tomorrow. You didn't know that?" she asked.

"Tomorrow?" Michael flipped through the rustling pages of his notes until he found what he was looking for. "Oh yeah, tomorrow. I knew we had an exam tomorrow...you didn't know?"

"Don't try to use reverse psychology on me about psychology class," she said, laughing.

"That was *not* reverse psychology."

"Not in the traditional sense that people speak of it, but look on page three hundred and thirteen and you can see in paragraph three…" Lori slowed her words to a pause. "Well, never mind. I don't know, but anyway that is a type of reverse psychology." Lori quickly looked away and into one of her drawers.

"Wait a minute." Michael took another deep breath and exhaled an even longer sigh. He rubbed his hands over his face and built the courage to continue. "If we're truly taking this friendship to the next level, then I have some questions."

"O-kay," Lori said cautiously.

"I just feel that not asking these questions would be like lying. Like I'm pretending that everything's cool through my silence. You understand?"

"Totally," she said, with a renewed energy in her voice that inspired him to proceed.

"Well, first of all, how did you just know that specific topic would be on that specific page? I already know, without looking, that there's a subject related to our conversation on that page and in that paragraph. And we aren't even on that chapter yet. In other words, why and how could you have memorized an entire psychology book in two months? Next, how did you break that man's arm? I shook his hand, and even though he's older, he still had a pretty strong grip. And how did you almost beat Eric? I've seen enough track meets on TV and have been to enough track practices to know when someone is pushing themselves. And I don't care what Eric says, he was definitely pushing himself. But to me it looked like you were toying with him. I even saw you look over at him right before you slowed up to let him win. And Eric is probably the best athlete on our collegiate track team. The deep breathing thing was cute, but you weren't even winded from that sprint. It seemed more of a light jog for you. And finally, where are you really from? You don't have any kind of accent that I can hear. You speak perfect English. And why have you avoided this topic every time it came up?"

While listening to himself speak, Michael realized he may be coming off a little harsh with all his questions. "Lori…please understand that I'm only having these thoughts because I see a future with you. But when I try to picture this future with you, I just feel like I don't completely know who you are. The more I learn about you, the closer I feel to you. On the other hand, the more I feel left out of your life, the less important I feel I am to you."

Lori sat quietly and listened with a humble stare. The twinkle in her eye was still there, but it was distant.

"For the most part, this has been the reason I've been slow to move our relationship forward," Michael added.

Lori looked away for a moment then back at Michael. "I don't believe I'm about to tell you this, but they say you do stupid things when you're falling in love."

Michael's eyes widened and his heart skipped a beat. "With me?" he asked.

"I think so. It's just that I can't stop thinking about you. It started just a couple times a week when you'd occasionally cross my mind then it grew to a couple of times a day. Now, I just want to be around you all the time."

"This better not be some cute trick to get me off the subject of all my questions." For the first time, Michael saw Lori's face twist into an unpleasant emotion.

"Are you serious? I'll answer all your questions. But it's disappointing to know that you feel I'd try and trick you."

"I'm sorry, but you have to know I think about you all day too. I also have strong feelings for you, but I don't know if I'm falling in love yet. It just seems a little sudden," Michael said.

"That's because this society has trained you to keep your guard up and be careful who you trust your heart to. I come from a place where love and deceit do not coincide. I understand your hesitation and suspicion, but it hurts nevertheless."

"I'm sorry, I never meant to hurt you. But please understand that men don't use those words unless they're one hundred percent sure, or they're trying to take advantage of someone. So yes, I feel the same way you do. But I *think* that I could be falling in love with you. This strong feeling I have deep inside me for you very well could be love. As a matter of fact, odds are that it probably is. But until I was certain, I hadn't planned on bringing that subject up."

"I can understand that but you will not understand the explanations to your questions."

"Try me. I'm a pretty open-minded person."

"Well, open up and buckle up," she said, smiling.

"You make it sound as if you're about to tell me that you're an alien from another planet or something."

"Actually, that would probably be simpler than the truth," Lori said.

Michael's eyes widened and her words sat him back in his seat a little. He braced himself for something he thought he wanted but hadn't anticipated the caliber of.

"First let me ask you, have you ever wondered what happens to the souls of babies that are aborted or stillborn? Or even infants that perish in tragedies?"

"Yeah." But what could this possibly have to do with her, he thought. "I guess I just assumed they all went to heaven."

"Well, listen close, because from here on, you'll need that open mind of yours," she said, looking him directly in his eyes. "It is written that there will be a New Heaven and a New Earth after the apocalypse. Of course, the souls of the impure humans will occupy the New Heaven-"

"Wait a minute. You mean impure people will inhabit the New Heaven? Then why even try to be good?"

"No, that's not what I meant," Lori said, chuckling. "Let me come back to that part. Okay, let's just say human souls will inhabit the New Heaven. Who do you think will inhabit the New Earth?"

"Is that a rhetorical question, or do you want me to answer? Because I'll tell you now I don't know."

"Put it together," she said in a playful tone. "The souls of the babies who didn't have a chance will be given their opportunity in this New Earth."

Michael's head tilted to the left, as it does when he begins to understand a concept.

"Now these babies are still human but they're from pure blood. Their bodies are made from the hands of the Supreme Being Himself."

"You mean God?" he asked.

"The Creator has been given many names. And just as the first man who walked this earth, the Supreme Being creates their new bodies and breathes His breath into them. The next truth is that they walk the earth as we speak."

Michael's mouth was wide open. He didn't recognize the dryness of his mouth until he spoke. "Where are they now?"

"Well, most of them are in a protected area believed to be the geographical location of where the first man took his first step."

"You mean Eden?" he asked, as innocently as a child. "The actual *Garden of Eden*?"

"Again, this place has many names."

"Wait, wait. So does God make these bodies there? Or does He make them then place them in Eden?"

"Do you remember the music I told you about? The beautiful melody that I didn't know the words to, but just knew the sounds?" she asked.

"Yeah, I remember."

"Well, first that sound is heard in the distance. As it grows louder, a bright light can be seen in the sky. The beautiful sound grows even louder and the light softly falls to a special area. At this point, the light becomes so intense that no one can even look directly at it. When the music begins to fade and the light rises again, there's a crying infant in the area where the light touched down."

"How many of these babies are there?"

"Babies don't stay babies forever. They do grow older, you know," Lori said, laughing. "I don't know how many. Only the Elders know that."

"Who are the Elders?"

"These are the first pure humans to be reborn so they're the oldest."

"How old?" Michael asked, continuing his line of questions with wide eyes.

"The oldest Elder is said to be over seven hundred years old."

"Does he look it?" Michael chuckled. "Although I don't even know how a person over seven hundred years old would look."

"He looks like he's in his late fifties, in impure human years. You see, since the first man and woman were made by the Creator, of course their blood was pure as well. But as the generations continued, the blood became more and more diluted. Mankind was slowly becoming weaker, slower, and dying younger and younger as the centuries passed."

"So impure humans are all of us who have diluted impure blood? And since pure humans are made with God's hands, they have pure blood?" he asked.

"You're getting it," Lori said, then paused and took a deep breath. "Now there are a few of these *pure humans* that are allowed outside the protected area, and into the outside world."

"What do they do?"

"They do what I'm doing. Scouting the earth to note the mistakes we should make sure not to repeat when it's our turn. The Elders have said this mission is essential in guaranteeing a harmonious New Earth."

Michael had been so intrigued by the fascinating tale that he'd forgotten what had sparked the conversation. He should've picked it up a while ago. She was saying that she was one of these pure humans. This was not possible, he thought.

Just when the silence was beginning to become awkward, Lori stood up.

"Do you know what it means to have a body that wasn't born of mankind?" She asked, lifting her shirt to expose her flat tummy.

Michael was speechless, staring directly at a smooth area where her navel should've been. She was never connected to a mother and fed through an umbilical cord, he thought. He didn't know what to say. He tried to think of a phrase or a word to respond with. Instead, he continued to sit dumfounded.

"Are you disgusted?" Lori asked, with a look of vulnerability that Michael had never seen her with.

Finally snapping out of his short daze, he took a deep breath and tried to ease the situation as best he could. "Nice abs, you must do Pilates."

She pulled her shirt down and smiled until she leaned in and kissed him. "It's the moments like this that make me believe I'm falling in love with you."

"I've never had a moment like this one," he said, chuckling to himself.

"I know there's more you want to ask me."

"Of course, I have so many questions that I don't know where to start. But I imagine this must be hard for you so I'll try not to overwhelm you. We have time. Don't we? The world isn't coming to an end any time soon, is it?" Michael asked with a newfound sense of concern.

Lori's face took a form of seriousness that demanded respect for her words. "Only the Supreme Being knows the Day of the End although the Elders have told us that the stage is set. The world is hanging by a thread of the Creator's mercy. This is why I've been given my mission."

"Okay, that's enough for now. I mean I do want to know more but right now I have to let this sink in a little. My brain just needs some time to process all of this. Although, speaking of brains, do you remember the lesson in psychology about how we only use about ten percent of our brain?"

"Yes. I wasn't in class that day but I've read about it," Lori replied with a smile as if she knew where this question was heading.

"Well, you being a pure human and all, how much of your brain do you use?"

"No pure human has ever been examined by a physician to confirm any percentage of brain activity. But I do know we use far more than ten percent."

"How much more? I mean, how fast did you read our psychology book?"

"I read all my books in about two hours the night I bought them."

"And you can remember every word on every page?"

"Memorizing a three hundred-page book is probably the same as you memorizing a new address or phone number," Lori answered casually.

"Really?" Michael said, with a look of astonishment painted across his face. "So you really didn't need to study? You just wanted to spend time with me, huh?" he said, smiling.

"Actually it's just that professors are known for including information from their lectures on their exams and sometimes those lecture topics are purposely not found in the book." She paused for a moment, and then laughed. "Okay, I wanted to spend a little time with you too. I can't help it. I admit you're kind of cute and just genuinely amusing."

"You almost make it sound as if you want me around to entertain you."

"I do. And hopefully I entertain you as well. Isn't the purpose of mates to entertain and enjoy each other's company?"

"Well, when you put it like that, it doesn't sound as bad. But you're probably just playing mind tricks on me because you're so much smarter," he said laughing.

"Your sense of humor, honesty, friendship, and compassion are the qualities that attract me to you so please don't ever feel as if I don't respect you," Lori pleaded.

"I admit that you being perfect and all is a bit intimidating but if I really don't have to put forth a super effort to be above average because you're attracted to me for me, well that takes a lot of pressure off. As if I'm almost worthy of you."

"Would you stop," she said. "I'm not perfect, I still make mistakes. For example, I made the mistake of talking too much and now we might be late for dinner with Eric and Monica."

Michael had forgotten all about their double date that night. He couldn't blame himself, considering how he'd just learned of a secret super society that will inhabit the world when his kind is gone. "You're right, we should get going. I'll call Eric and let him know it's your fault we'll be a few minutes late."

"Yeah, and make sure you tell him the truth about me letting him win the race while you're at it," she said joking.

The four of them decided to leave campus and eat at a real restaurant. Monica drove her black and tan 1998 Ford Explorer. Michael and Lori sat in the back seat while Eric sat in the front. The truck drove fine, except the air conditioning didn't work. It was about eighty-six degrees so they to rode with all the windows down. The wind occasionally blew Lori's hair in Michael's face, but he didn't care. His mind was elsewhere.

While holding Lori's hand, Michael wondered how he'd get through this date. He was worried that Eric and Monica would notice he was being distant. He tried to put Lori's words out of his head for a while, but her story was just too overwhelming. He told himself she was just delusional, but then remembered how she has no navel. Michael's last option was to wrack his brain for topics to spark conversations that would disrupt his thoughts. "So it's official," he said, forcing the words into the air.

"What's official?" Eric asked, turning around in the passenger seat.

"What do you think? Lori and I are officially a couple," Michael said with pride, tightening his grip on Lori's hand. Lori looked up at him with such gorgeous big eyes that he could almost see himself in them.

"What happened, she broke down and asked you?" Eric questioned through his signature chuckle.

Lori and Michael couldn't contain themselves. They erupted into such a thunderous duet of laughter that proved Eric's joke was obviously true. This ignited Eric into another laughing frenzy.

"Really, Lori?" Monica asked, trying to contain her giggles.

"It was a frustration for me not knowing what was going on with us. So I basically asked if he wanted to be with me or not," Lori admitted.

"I applaud you," Monica said, finding Lori in her rear view mirror. "Women need to be strong and go after what they want, no matter what it is. So many women lose out on good men because they're afraid of being aggressive, or they believe a man just has to come to them. You shouldn't be embarrassed, you should be proud."

"What do you mean? I heard you over there giggling too," Eric said.

"That was a contagious laugh. I was laughing more at the sound of your laughter than at what was said," Monica replied.

"I was going to get around to it anyway," Michael said, trying to defend himself.

"I was just waiting for the perfect moment because she's the perfect girl."

"You're something else," Lori whispered to Michael.

"Man…that was real Eric-ish. You've been hanging around me a little too long, son. You're starting to pick up on my charm," Eric said with a grin and turned back around in his seat.

Monica looked over at Eric. "You know, sometimes I can really see the reasoning behind lesbianism," she said, looking again in her rear view mirror at Lori. "I'm kidding, Lori," she said, still laughing.

"I didn't know Monica had jokes," Michael said.

"She didn't. That's another thing she's starting to pick up from hanging around me too," Eric said.

"Oh, brother. You're impossible," Monica said, pulling into the restaurant parking lot.

Michael's plan was working. He realized it would be much easier to get through the night than he thought. He just smiled and kept talking. He credited most of how well the night was going with the good company he was in. Eric, Monica, and, of course Lori, all had qualities that made them special and exciting people. He soon found himself enjoying the night without any thought of Lori's extraordinary tale although he understood that after the conversation he had with Lori, his reality would never be the same.

CHAPTER 5
WHO AM I?

Michael couldn't wait to see Lori again. He found himself tossing and turning at night with so many thoughts and questions. He pictured the world as he knew it actually coming to an end. What was going to happen to all the people, he thought. The more he reflected on their relationship, the more he tried to put himself in Lori's position. He was sure it would be annoying to ask her several questions at once. Instead, he decided to inquire here and there when the moments were right.

A hard knock on the door snatched Michael from a deep sleep the next morning. He naturally assumed Eric had locked himself out again. Dragging himself to the door, he twisted the knob and turned back for his bed without even looking. When he pulled the blanket over him, he was shocked to hear Lori's voice.

"You think it's that easy to get me into bed?" she asked, laughing. "You thought I'd just follow you into bed and get under the covers with you?"

"Yeah, actually. Come here," Michael said, extending his arm.

"Michael!" Lori sang, posing with her hand on her hip.

"I'm serious. Come over here and lie with me. I won't try anything."

"So you just want to cuddle?"

"No, I don't want to cuddle. I'm a man, I just want to lie here and hold you. Is that bad?"

"You know that doesn't sound so bad," she said, and set her book bag down. "I don't mind cuddling," she whispered with a grin.

Michael felt Lori dig her head up under his chin to rest on his chest. He pulled the blanket over her and kept his arms around her back. Holding her close, he was captivated by her scent. When he closed his eyes, the aroma took him to a grassy field full of daisies. He saw them under a tree, peacefully still in their exact positions. The smell of summer rain as it drizzled, while the sun refused to hide its shine behind the clouds. "What's that you have on that smells so good?" he finally asked, interrupting the sound of his fantasy droplets dancing off leaves.

"Deodorant," she said.

Michael burst into a roaring laugh that he instantly regretted. The entire mood that he'd set was now compromised by her innocent humor. "It's moments like this that make me think I could be falling for you," he said, trying to pull her close again to resume the moment.

"I thought you were much more original than that. Using my own words on me."

"Well, most women would be impressed that their boyfriend listens close enough to repeat something like that."

"Obviously I'm not like most women. And if you were like most men then we wouldn't be lying on this bed together."

"Well said. And not to change the subject but was there a reason you came by or did you just want to see me?"

"The reason is because I wanted to see you," she said.

"I find myself wanting to be around you too but I can't just come up to your door. You can just walk right in here but the all-girl dorms are more secure than Fort Knox for me."

"I've found if you really want something or want to do something, there's always a way. The question is, are you willing to do what it takes to get it?"

"You make it sound so simple," Michael said, trying not to sound too impressed.

"I think people sometimes let all the gray areas in life confuse the simplicity of it."

"Okay then, Einstein, what's the answer to the age old question?"

"What question is that?" she asked.

"What is the meaning of life?"

"This age old question is also the easiest question to answer," she said, leaning up on her elbow. "We must realize we're not here for ourselves. We're here to love and help one another. That's the test. To earnestly put others before yourself. To love the Creator first, to love each other, and *then* love yourself last. If this love is truly applied to every thought, conversation, and decision that's made, then life becomes simple. There's sublime peace and order in the midst of the worldly chaos."

As Michael listened to words that his heart knew were true, he began to feel as though he could trust Lori. He felt as if there were no secret he ever wanted to keep from her. But how could he even bring up his sleeping disorder? What if they fell asleep right there and he hurt her during one of his episodes? He knew he'd tell her, he just had to figure out how. In the meantime, Michael still had some questions of his own.

"Why are you so quiet?" Lori asked.

"I was sitting here thinking if the Elders are around, six or seven hundred years old, you said?" He thought quickly. "Well then how old are you? Because when you speak, it's as if you can break down sophisticated concepts into a couple of lines that a professor and textbook would take an entire semester to explain. And yeah, I remember you use much more of your brain than us impure humans, but I can hear years of experience in your words too. Then I look at you and wonder, how old could she be?"

"I'm one hundred and forty-seven years old," she said. Silence fell across the room as if someone had muted the scene. "Aren't you going to say anything?"

"Well," Michael said, trying to gather himself, "I guess I was right about your words having experience behind them."

"I guess," Lori responded and sat up on the bed.

"I'm sorry, I don't mean to seem awkward. It's just that I can't help but think there's no way I'd make it to that age. So if we were to get married and made it to our thirtieth anniversary, I'd look fifty and you'd still look as if you were in your twenties. Of course I'd like that, but would you? Eventually I'd grow old and die, leaving you young and alone. And all of this only if the world doesn't end first. I was just thinking the other day how well my life was going. I should've known there was a catch. There's a catch to everything. If something seems too good to be true, it is. Whoever made that up, really knew what they were talking about." Michael felt himself becoming hot. He took a deep breath and got up from the bed to open the window for some fresh air. He took another deep breath and sighed. "I'm sorry," he said as he tried to relax and cool himself down. "Things were just going so well, I…I don't know." He looked out the window.

"Do you always become hot like that when you get emotional?" Lori asked.

"Pretty much. I guess that's another reason I have to stay so cool all the time," he said, smiling. "Seriously though, if I become frustrated, I can feel my entire body begin to heat up so I almost have no choice but to stay calm."

"Have you ever been to see any doctors?"

"They all say I'm fine, but I've never had a frustrating moment in a doctor's office for them to really understand what happens. They've checked my blood pressure and other tests to ensure I won't have a heart attack or a stroke. Why? Have you heard of anyone else who's had this problem?"

"Kind of, but there were other symptoms as well."

"Like what?" Michael asked anxiously.

"Problems in their sleep," Lori said as they both stared at each other. "The person would leave a heavy imprint where they lay. An imprint of their body that would be impossible to make from the weight of the person. And he'd wake up coated in sweat from dreams he couldn't remember."

Michael sat in bewilderment once again as she described his most intimate secret. He'd told no one. Could Eric have told her, he thought. He didn't think Eric would jeopardize his chances with Lori. He seemed genuinely happy for Michael's new relationship. Maybe she really does know someone with this condition. Maybe she could help, he thought. "What happened with this guy? Was he treated or cured?" he asked.

"He was just fine after a while. It was just a phase. Kind of like his own personal phase of maturing into manhood. Why, do you believe you may have the same condition?"

"Maybe. Well, yes," he admitted. "Since I can remember, I've broken my beds, and awakened covered in sweat. Not every night, but enough that I worry. I even wondered while we were lying here a minute ago, what would happen if I fell asleep with you in my arms and I had an episode? I've never remembered any of my dreams, and I don't know how I break my beds. I've always believed it was from the rough tossing and turning during my nightmares. But just how could someone become heavier in their sleep?"

"I don't know all the details, but I can tell you that even though it was weird, he was just fine."

"So that's it. There's no explanation. That sounds almost as crazy as your story. At least not having a navel brings proof and understanding to your situation. My predicament has no reasoning to its weirdness."

"Faith, Michael. The Supreme Being has created us all different. He has given us all different roles to play, and the tools with which to perform these roles. Faith is believing the Creator has power over every situation. So no matter what happens, we can find comfort in knowing the outcome of every event we've ever seen or heard is in His plan. He wouldn't have created you like you are for no reason. He would also not have taken you through every hardship you've ever faced without reasoning. Now you or I may not understand the reasoning, but who are we? The Creator does not have to explain Himself to anyone. He is infallible. Who are we to question Him? Our job is to have faith in Him and to simply understand that He's in control, not us. We may not see where this road is headed but since He made the road, we just have to believe He's taking us to where we need to be."

"So that's why they call it blind faith?" Michael replied, looking through the window out into the distance.

Lori stood up and walked over to Michael. "You're special. Don't ever forget that," she said and kissed him.

"So how'd you know this other guy with the same condition I have?" Michael asked, totally ignoring the comment Lori made but not the kiss.

"In some ways you *are* just like the average man," Lori said, with a soft laugh.

"What's that supposed to mean?" Michael asked in a defensive tone.

"Now don't get yourself all hot again. I'm just saying that I'm trying to comfort you, and you seem to only care about who the guy is in the story," she said, still giggling.

"I'm just curious about the guy," he said, smiling. "Our conditions are obviously related, I'm just asking how'd you know him."

"Okay, whatever," she said, smirking. "I just heard stories like how we're talking now. In fact, the story even goes on to say that the guy was a much stronger person after he'd outgrown the phase. But again, I never met the guy."

"I wasn't saying that anything was going on. I was just curious about how you actually knew about his sleeping habits and how he woke up, that's all," he said, sounding as serious as he could.

"Right. Like I knew, firsthand, what his sleeping habits were."

"Is that so wrong for me to want to know?"

"Michael, you should know from the time we've spent together that I'm a virgin," she said.

"Well at first I did but then I found out that you were one hundred and forty-seven years old and I said to myself, there's no way," he said, chuckling.

"Seriously," she said, laughing, "if I was the type of girl that had casual sex then we would've already crossed that bridge. And, unlike what we see here every day, we mate for life back at home."

"So why haven't you?"

"Well, we have certain rules about marriage back home, but I've been too busy on missions to consider marriage anyway."

"So what about me? You're on the mission right now yet still you say you could be falling in love with me. Am I a part of your mission? Are you trying to see what people do wrong in relationships so you guys don't mess that up too?"

"Michael," Lori said in a voice that instantly made him feel guilty for his accusations, "what I feel for you is genuine. And if you know me at all then you should know that. Second, there's nothing you could do to hinder my mission. It's important to understand that. Even with the differences in our age and aging, I have faith. The Supreme Being is love, pure and simple. Love cannot exist unless He is present. So He must approve of this relationship, because what I feel for you is love. Everything else is minor details. I believe that in true love, faith in Him can make all things possible."

"This is just a lot to digest but I'm trying hard," Michael said.

"You're doing fine."

"I'm sorry for questioning your intentions. It's just that I woke up one morning and found myself investing so much so fast. And I'm trying hard to play it smooth, but this is both exciting and overwhelming at the same time. It's kind of like being in a dream that you haven't realized is good or bad yet."

"Looking from your point of view, I can totally understand. For me it's a little more like watching a movie that you've already read the book to. You already know good triumphs over evil. So while the rest of the crowd is raving in suspense, it's pretty calm in my reality."

"In that case I guess I should look at it that way too," he said.

"Now you're finally getting it. It's just good old-fashioned faith. Believing that whatever happens, you're on the winning side."

"When you really think about it, it's really a peaceful feeling," Michael added.

"Yes it is. Now I know you understand. Now you just have to hold on to that feeling when times get really hard. Like most things, it may be a little more difficult than it sounds, but it works every time."

"One day I'll return the favor and teach you something."

Lori smiled. "Every day you teach me how understanding and courageous love can be."

"Come back and lie with me," Michael said, walking back to the bed.

"Awww, he wants to cuddle some more."

"Okay, fine, call it whatever you want, just come here." Michael had more questions, but didn't want to talk anymore.

She came gently, flying in like an angel that morning, effortlessly easing his worries. He was once again content with his entire being. He hoped to somehow hold on to this peace so the feeling of serenity would never totally leave him.

In fact, Michael was so caught up in thought he didn't hear the rattle of keys or the doorknob turn. He had no clue that Eric was in the room until he heard his voice.

"I promise you I know exactly how a proud father feels when he looks down on his son in his finest moment. I'm fighting back tears right now just so I can remain a man in both your eyes," Eric said, turning his back and pretending to dry his eyes.

"Is he always this dramatic?" Lori asked, trying to hold her laughter.

"When it comes to him feeling responsible for any romantic moments I may have, yes. He's always that dramatic."

"Why would you be responsible for any of his romantic moments with me?" Lori asked Eric.

"Here we go," Michael said under his breath.

"Well, Ms. Lori, I'm glad you asked," Eric said as he took a seat in the chair at his desk, posing for his conversation.

"You see, our friend Michael here is a very nice guy with a lot of good qualities. But even Superman has his weakness, and Michael's kryptonite is women. Now when I say women, I obviously don't mean his taste, but how to initiate the romantic aspect of a relationship. We already know this because you basically had to ask him to be your boyfriend."

"Isn't there anything else we can talk about? Why am I the center of attention?" Michael said with a hint of humor and a dash of sincerity.

"She asked a question and I'm just trying to satisfy her curiosity. Besides I'm just about done," Eric said, and turned his eyes back on Lori. "So I noticed this, months ago, and since I have extensive experience and success in this area, I've been trying to assist our subtle friend. Now I can only assume my assistance has been effective when you came into the picture shortly after I began to influence him."

"I can understand that," Lori said, smiling.

"What do you mean, you understand?" Michael asked in amazement.

"I'm not saying I believe every word, but I can see how he's come to that conclusion." Lori smiled.

"Okay. Let's all just agree that people grow and learn from friends and experiences every day. I think that's a fair enough statement to close this conversation. So, is anybody hungry?" Michael asked.

"But before we do get off the subject, it would only be fair to humble myself. It's possible Michael would've learned everything I've told him on his own, but I would never have discovered what he's taught me. This guy showed me how I was missing out on so much with the way I was living. I never would've been able to discover the emotions I feel for Monica if it weren't for my man here. I mean that," Eric said, looking Michael directly in the eyes.

"See, that's why I love you," Lori said, turning to hug Michael.

"The *L bomb*. You guys are that deep? Woooh, man that's special. I'm happy for you guys," Eric said with wide eyes.

"Actually this is something we both *think* we're feeling. Until we're sure, we're being careful," Lori said quickly. "We've known each other less than six months, but it feels like much longer. That was just a slip of the tongue."

"Freud said there were no slips of the tongue," Eric said. "But that's really a smart thing you guys are doing. You should take it slow. Things that are meant to be, will be."

Michael noticed that Lori looked up as if Eric had said something that jolted her. "What is it?" Michael asked.

"Nothing, there was just something familiar about what he said," Lori said, still looking at Eric in bewilderment.

"Well, I'm actually headed right back out. I just came by to get my track sweats. After class, Monica and I are going to hang out before practice so you kids have fun and don't do anything I wouldn't do," Eric said, throwing his bag over his shoulder and heading out the door.

"I'm actually glad he left; I need to ask you something very important," Lori said.

"I knew there was a reason for you coming over this morning," he said, smiling.

"Well, I've been thinking about this for a while, but I really just decided to ask you since I've been here this morning."

"Okay, what's so important?"

"I want you to come home with me," Lori said, then once again, the familiar silence fell on them both.

"Would I even be allowed? Didn't you say this is a specially protected place?"

"Yes. Protected from anyone with a wicked heart. Yours is pure."

"Do I need to take any shots?" he asked.

"No, my village is free of diseases."

"Have any impure human ever been there?"

"Very few have been invited that I know of, but you're different."

"How am I different?"

"I can't fully explain it but there's a definite connection with your heat sensations and sleeping condition to the prophecy of my people."

"What kind of connection?" Michael asked.

"I'm not sure, but if you come home with me, I'm certain the Elders can provide you with all the answers you've been searching for."

"How soon are you talking about?"

"We have spring break coming up," she said with a hopeful expression.

"That's pretty soon. It leaves me with less than two months to get a passport, visa, and clothes. Not to mention running this across my parents."

"Don't worry about passports and such. We have friends in that department who can expedite the process for us."

"When you say we, you mean the pure humans?" he asked.

"Yes, like I told you before, there are pure humans in many high positions performing different roles for the Elders. And as for your parents, I understand. Just talk to them and see what happens. I don't want to pressure you," Lori said with a confident smile.

"This is definitely the opportunity of a lifetime, to say the least."

"This will also help you to understand everything even more. The future includes everyone after the Day of the End, not just me and my people."

"Yeah, but what'll happen to me and my family?" he asked.

"That's a question you may ask the Elders yourself."

The thought of speaking with the oldest beings on earth made Michael's heart beat a little faster and he felt overwhelmed by the entire relationship once again. But strangely, there was a feeling of excitement and adventure as well. And even a sense of relief that life wasn't as mundane as he'd come to know it over his past eighteen years. "Let's try and make this happen," he said, with a new sense of enthusiasm in his heart that he'd never felt before.

"You mean it?" Lori said, with the light of a thousand watts in her eyes.

"I don't know if everything will work out by spring break, or what my parents will say, but I'll do what I can to make it happen," Michael said in an assertive voice.

"If you're not the one then I don't think I want to be in love," she said, tightening her grasp around him.

Michael gave thought to what his life would be like had he not met her. He considered the suppressed loneliness he'd still feel, along with the ignorance of Lori, pure humans, and the apparent reality of the world's fate. As he lay there holding her, he assured himself that if he could do it all over again he wouldn't change a thing. Michael was ready to face his fears of the unknown.

CHAPTER 6
SUPER FRIENDS

After the stress of midterms, Michael and Eric decided to take Lori and Monica bowling. There was a bowling alley in the Student Union Building but it was always too crowded so they decided to go off campus to a larger bowling alley where they wouldn't have to wait for lanes.

The sun was setting and painted the sky fiery orange over the fading blue horizon. Riding in Monica's car was beginning to feel routine on their outings. This made Michael wonder if he'd always be confined to the backseat.

"If I was to get a new car, would you all ride with me like this, or are we too used to riding with Monica?" Michael asked.

"Why? Do you have a problem with Betsy? She's never left me stranded, and she's an SUV so she has plenty of room for everybody. What's wrong?" Monica asked, defending her Ford Explorer.

"Your car's name is Betsy?" Lori asked with a giggle.

"It has nothing to do with Betsy, sweetheart. My youngster is becoming a man. He just wants to know if he'll ever be able to get up here in the grown people's seats," Eric said with a sigh, reclining his seat.

"Is that true, Michael?" Monica asked.

"Well not the way that he said it. I was just thinking of asking my parents to buy me a car," Michael answered.

"Yeah, it's pretty much like I said," Eric said with another sigh.

There was a half second of silence before Michael gave himself away with a burst of laughter. "You're a silly individual."

"A silly individual who's right though," Eric said, turning to look back at Michael with a sly smile.

"I just have a sophisticated woman now who's worthy of a front seat," Michael said, looking at Lori.

"My goodness I have taught you well. Not that he's wrong about you, Lori, but yeah it's still pretty much like I said," Eric said, sighing once again, while turning back around.

Lori chuckled and then looked up at Michael.

"Really?" Michael said, smiling.

"I'm sorry, he's funny." Lori confessed with that vibrant smile that Michael just couldn't resist.

They soon reached the bowling alley, which had more people than the facility on campus. They wanted to complain, but the space made it less crowded. They were also pleasantly surprised to have a lane by the time they rented their shoes.

"Are you any good?" Eric asked Michael as they sat down to change their shoes.

"For someone who's never bowled before, I'm very good," Michael replied.

"Okay that's it. We're playing couple verses couple," Eric belted.

"That's fine with me," Michael said, smiling at Lori.

"I've never bowled before either," Lori leaned in and whispered to Michael.

"That's fine. Just concentrate and your pure humanness should do the rest," Michael whispered back with a wink. Reflecting back on all the superhero movies and cartoons he'd seen growing up, Michael felt he had a secret weapon in Lori.

He'd just have to coach her on when to tone down her perfection.

"Okay, looks like the computer recognizes who should show you guys how this is done," Eric said as he walked up and began his search for the perfect ball. "You beginners might want to pay attention to the professional form I'm about to display."

Eric brought the ball up to his chest and took a deep breath. After a pause, he took two steps and flung the slick ball on his third. His right foot curled behind his left ankle. Then after his release, he planted his right toes back on the floor and twisted himself around towards Michael and the girls. Showing no interest in how the ball was rolling down to the pins, Eric smiled and began his stride back to his seat.

Michael was paying so much attention to Eric that he almost missed the ball curve into the pins with a crisp clatter. Eric calmly took his seat while the last pin simultaneously dropped. "You know I actually feel a little guilty when I talk trash, but the silence is so boring when I don't," he boasted with a look of pure honesty.

"You know I have to truly say I'm impressed. You really backed up all your trash talking. Can you do that on every roll?" Michael asked.

"No, I'm kind of surprised I did it that time to be honest. Don't get me wrong, I'm good, but I can only do that about half the time. The entire walk to my seat, I was imagining how embarrassing it was going to be to have to get back up and work for a spare," Eric admitted with a chuckle.

Michael was again struck by Eric's honesty. He expected Eric to brag how he could bowl strikes all day. His respect for Eric had increased one notch.

"Okay, you're next, Lori," Monica said with a smile of confidence.

"Already? I have to follow that," Lori replied.

"You'll do fine," Michael said, walking her up into position. "Just find a ball that's not too heavy and not too light. Relax and try to roll the ball straight up the middle. Don't worry about putting a spin on it like Eric did."

"Okay, this ball feels comfortable," she said, bringing it to her chest. She then positioned herself on the middle of the line and took three steps back. "Does this look about right?"

"That looks perfect. Take a deep breath and on the third or fourth step, release the ball right down the middle," Michael repeated.

Lori's torso slightly expanded, then deflated the air from her deep breath. She began her three steps and Michael watched in amazement. It was as if she was moving in slow motion. On her third step she effortlessly released the ball but Michael was still focused on her. Before he could even turn his head to see the progress of the ball, he was snapped out of his gaze by a deafening crash. It sounded as if there had been a small explosion down at the end of their lane. Michael turned to see Lori had rolled the ball so powerfully that the only pins she hit were straight up the middle. The pins were struck so violently, they had no time to knock any other pins down before they were cast back. Even more astonishing was the alarming bang her ball made, which now had the attention of over half the facility. The noise and conversation level of the entire bowling alley dropped to a whisper. Everyone was looking down Lori's lane, where it seemed there was actually some dust floating above the pins.

Lori slowly turned around with her hands over her mouth, and tried to retreat back to her seat.

The silence was broken by a voice from the next lane. "Who pissed you off, little cutie?" the middle-aged man said in an intoxicated accent.

There was a laughter that erupted throughout the building from the man's comment as the noise level began to resume. Lori tried to give a little smile to show she was a good sport about the joke. Michael stood up and met Lori at her seat to comfort her obvious embarrassment. But before he could speak, he heard the man's voice again.

"Oh, that's who's got her all pissed off. Man, you can't keep that little sweet thang happy? Baby, you'd never be that upset if you was over here in this lane with me," the man said, showing even more hints of heavy boozing in his speech.

"She's happy right here," Michael said, beginning to feel a little warm inside. Then he heard another voice behind him.

"I'm the manager, is everything all right over here? Is this where that loud crash came from? One of you guys trying to show off in front of your girlfriends? I don't see any alcohol over here, what' going on?" the well-dressed man asked.

"Sir this is my friend's first time bowling and she picked up a ball that was too light for her," Eric explained. "It's our fault, we told her to roll the ball as hard as she could. We just didn't know she was so strong. I'm sure it won't happen again," he said. "But now it seems this guy in the next lane has had a little too much to drink. He's been making comments to my friend and his girlfriend. He's the problem now," Eric said, looking over at the middle-aged man.

The manager looked over at the man that Eric had nodded to, who'd thrown his arms up into the air. "I didn't do nothing, Jim," the man said to the manager.

"Sam, I don't want to have to put you out of here. You behave yourself. How've you been?" As the manager walked over and greeted his rude, but regular, customer, Michael turned to Lori.

"You okay?" he asked.

"Yeah, I'm fine. I'm just sorry I embarrassed everybody," Lori said, looking back at Michael with the eyes of a young fawn.

"As long as you're fine, we're fine. Don't worry about us. We're your friends," Michael said with his arm around her. "All right, who's next?" he said, looking up at the monitor, trying to move the night along.

"It's supposed to still be Lori's turn, but she can sit this one out and recover for the next one," Eric said.

"Then it looks like me," Monica said.

"You got this, baby?" Eric asked.

"This isn't my first time, and what did I tell you about calling me baby in public?" Monica replied with a playful sternness in her voice.

"Just checking, sweetheart," Eric said, smiling.

Monica turned and smiled before she rolled her ball and knocked all but two of the pins down. "That was good," Lori said.

"If you get this spare, then I promise you for as long as we're together, I'll never have a spare girlfriend," Eric said.

"And what if I don't get it?" Monica asked as her ball rolled back.

"Well then it depends on if we win or not," Eric said with a chuckle.

"Sometimes I wonder if we'll make it," Monica said before taking her steps and rolling the ball right into the two pins that were almost lined up one behind the other.

"Good job," Eric said, clapping as she headed back to her seat.

"I was picturing your face down there in front of those pins," she said, right before she punched Eric's shoulder.

"Ouch, come on. Now does it make sense to injure your star player?" Eric said, rubbing his shoulder.

"Okay, looks like they saved the best for last," Michael said.

"Remember, I backed up my trash talking," Eric said smiling.

As Michael walked up to the lane, he heard a familiar voice. "You're gonna try to get the manager to shut me up when you can't even get your sweet little girlfriend to stay calm." The middle-aged man started again, looking right at Michael.

"Sir, what's your problem? We're just trying to have a good time. We haven't been rude to you in any way. Why are you trying to start trouble?" As Michael spoke, he realized he was becoming warmer.

"You kids come into our town thinking you're better than us because you're in college. I was born here. You punk kids think you can take our women, our jobs, and take over our bars? I'm not having it," the man said, staggering closer to Michael. "Now, tell your little sweet girl to come over here and let me show her how to properly roll a ball."

Michael felt himself getting even hotter the more the man spoke. He was trying to calm himself but he felt the heat overtaking his body. He just knew he was about to pass out or maybe even have a stroke. Michael noticed the man coming closer, but he couldn't move. He saw the man's mouth moving, but the words were fading. He even thought he heard Eric ask if he was alright, but he couldn't turn and respond. Michael felt whatever sense of consciousness he had left was hanging by a thread.

As the man began to move closer to Michael, he saw Eric stand up. Just as the situation was approaching its climax, a stern voice interrupted the scene. "That's it, Sam. Goodnight. You've had enough," the manager scolded as he looked at Sam in disappointment.

"Now, Jim, I told you I wasn't causing no harm. Just trying to show the young lady how to bowl, that's all. Come on, Jim, now don't start not being fair."

"Sam, I've known you a long time, but if you don't leave in the next sixty seconds I'll have you physically escorted out. You're welcome back tomorrow, when I'll be very open to all your apologies. Down to fifty-five seconds, Sam; I'm not playing and the clock ain't stopping."

Jim suddenly turned towards Lori with a totally different facial expression and tone. "I'm so sorry about this, you and your group are welcome to enjoy a complimentary lane after this game, or whenever you choose to come back." He then turned back to Sam. "Forty-six seconds, Sam. I see someone is just going to have put their hands on you."

"Alright, alright. I'm outta here. I see townies don't get no more love here," Sam said, walking towards the exit.

The manager just shook his head in further disappointment when he noticed Sam was bowling in his tennis shoes. "Like I said, the next one is on us," he repeated, and disappeared into the crowd of the bowling alley.

"Are you okay?" Lori asked.

"I think I just need some air," Michael said, trying to downplay the severity of his disorientation.

"You guys, we're going to get some air. We'll be right back," Lori told Eric and Monica.

"If you want to meet up with that Sam guy in the parking lot, I'll go with you," Eric said, leaning forward.

"You're not going anywhere," Monica insisted as she grabbed Eric's arm and pulled him back into his seat.

"Yeah, you can relax, Eric. He went out the front. We're going out the back for a quick second. And if that guy does come around, I'll pull Michael in here and get security," Lori said, leading Michael through the crowd.

Michael was beginning to feel a little better, but now he could feel a deep pulse within him. He also felt his skin tingling all over. I'm going to have a heart attack right here, he thought to himself. As they made their way through the crowd and into the night air, Michael felt as if his vision was becoming crisper. Crickets and other insignificant background sounds of the starlit night were becoming more noticeable to him.

"Is that better?" she asked, holding his hand.

"Much better. I don't know if I ate something bad or what," Michael said, trying to make sense of his nauseous episode.

"You look different," Lori said, with a confused look on her face. Her eyes scanned him as if she were meeting him for the first time.

"Different how?" he answered, also making a concerned expression to check his facial muscles for stroke symptoms.

"I don't know. I mean you look fine, but just different. I can't quite put my finger on it, but there's definitely something different about you," she said firmly while continuing to examine him.

"Have you noticed this all night, or just now?" he asked.

"I've just felt it since that incident inside, and on the walk out here. You seem totally different to me than when I first met you, or even from earlier tonight."

"That sounds kind of strange for someone like you to say. I'm not trying to be funny, but with your mental capacity and all, I figured there weren't too many things you couldn't figure out."

"Well, this is almost as if your aura has changed. It's so weird."

"Okay you're officially making me paranoid now," Michael said.

"I'm sorry, but like I said, it's not anything bad. Trust me. It's just that I feel I'd be lying if I didn't say when I look at you, I see and feel the same you, but just different."

"Oh, okay. I totally see what you're saying now. I mean, you just cleared all that right up," Michael said, with heavy sarcasm.

"Well, you actually look great, so as long as you feel fine then I guess I won't worry about it," Lori said, smiling.

He did feel better. A lot better. He almost wanted to say that since shaking off his dizziness, he felt like a new man.

"You ready to go back in? They're probably worried," Lori said.

"Yeah, I'm ready to bowl now," Michael said as he playfully raised his elbow for Lori to put her arm through.

She smiled and hooked her arm around his. "Now you're behaving like a boyfriend," she said, looking up at him.

"I think maybe it's just taking me a minute to get comfortable with being a boyfriend again. Especially to someone like you."

"Would you stop talking like that?" Lori said with a subtle squeeze of his arm.

As they walked up to the lane's booth, Michael noticed Eric and Monica were deep into what seemed to be an intellectual conversation.

"I see you didn't run into that guy," Eric said with a smile.

"How do you know we didn't? You're trying to say that since I'm not all beat up, we must not have seen him?"

"You said it, not me," Eric said with a snicker.

Michael noticed Lori gave a suppressed giggle as well. "Oh, that's funny?"

Lori gave a full bellow of laughter this time. "Baby," she said, pausing to finish her laughter, "I'm not laughing because it's true." She pausing again to clear her throat. "I'm laughing because it was funny."

"And that makes it better?" Michael asked, which just caused more laughter from everyone.

"I like hanging out with you guys. Even after the episode with that drunk guy, you all still keep me laughing," Monica said.

"Yeah, but mostly at my expense," Michael said, although he secretly cherished this moment as it was the first time Lori called him 'baby.' After leaving this quick but pleasant thought, he turned to see Monica gazing at him.

"Michael, are you sure you're alright?" she asked.

"Why does everyone keep asking me that? I'm fine," Michael responded, trying not to sound offended.

"You just look a little different. Did you go and wash your face or something?" Monica asked.

"I was telling him the same thing outside. Not bad different, a kind of good different," Lori repeated.

"Right. I mean, no disrespect to you Lori, but better different is right. It's just because you needed some air that we're still asking if you're okay," Monica said. "But you really do look good."

"C'mon, I'm sitting right here," Eric said, throwing his hands up in the air.

"Awww, Alpha Male Eric is getting jealous," Monica responded in a playful voice.

"I promise you I'm just kidding. It's actually pride that I'm feeling. Like watching a son grow and mature before your very eyes," Eric said, sitting back with his arms folded.

"You can just take anything and twist it to your benefit, huh?" Michael asked.

"It's one of my gifts. And another one is bowling, so are we doing this or what?" Eric asked.

"Bring it!" Lori said, followed by a few moments of awkward silence. A short burst of laughter followed the quiet pause as Lori looked on with a smile of confusion.

"This little episode was your first official belittlement by friends. Now you know you're part of a clique," Michael said.

"So let me see if I understand this right. In this country, the more you joke and belittle one another, the closer you are?" Lori asked, looking even more baffled.

"When you say it like that it sounds crazy, but it's pretty much how it is," Eric answered with a smile.

In that instant, Michael thought he was becoming nauseous again when he felt a slight vibration within himself. As the vibration became a rumble, he simultaneously became relieved and more worried when he noticed everyone else had also felt the growing rumble.

"It feels like an earthquake. Get down and grab hold of something," Eric shouted over the crowd of people who had begun to panic and run towards the exits.

There was immediate chaos in the bowling alley. The power went completely out for a few seconds before the back-up lights kicked in. Screams could be heard as bottles had begun to fall and shatter behind the bar. Bowling balls were heard dropping and rolling everywhere. Smoke could be seen bellowing from the double doors to the kitchen as they swung back and forth. Michael looked around while he and the others were kneeling down under the tables in their lane. He could see people falling and being trampled on as they tried fleeing to the parking lot. The rumbling lasted about forty five seconds. Then there was sheer silence.

"Is everyone alright?" Michael asked, tightly clenching Lori's hand.

"Yeah, we're okay," Eric answered.

"What are we doing having an earthquake? I mean really, when was our last earthquake?" Monica asked.

"Evidently about twenty seconds ago," Michael answered.

"You know what I mean though? Hey, where did Lori go?" Monica asked as she looked around the smoke-filled air.

The moment Monica spoke, Michael felt a slight tingling in his hand as he looked around to find his fingers holding themselves in a tight fist. He couldn't believe she was gone.

"There she is," Eric said in a voice of relief.

Michael turned to see Lori bent down with her cell phone in hand, helping a woman who'd been trampled in the stampede to the exits. Without saying a word, Michael also began to see if anyone needed any help. Eric and Monica followed right behind Michael in helping people to their feet, and trying to comfort those who couldn't stand.

After doing a complete round of the bowling alley, they heard the paramedics begin to pull up outside. The four of them regrouped and headed for the parking lot. There was only the sound of sneakers grinding the small rocks of gravel and sirens as they walked to the car.

"Lori, I just wanted to say that my first thought was getting out. Seeing how you just instinctively began to help those people shows the kind of heart you have," Monica said before opening the car doors for everyone.

"Monica is right," Michael said, smiling. "My first thoughts were also about which was the fastest route out to avoid people. I actually feel ashamed."

"I'd have to agree with them both, Lori. No disrespect to you, Monica, but there's something special about her, Michael," Eric said.

"Now I feel like I belong in a clique. See, you guys are also nice to those close to you as well. Thank you for the compliments, but I find it hard to believe you guys would've stepped over those hurt people to get to the parking lot. Maybe I noticed them before you, but I believe you all would've still helped those people without my influence," Lori said.

Michael felt proud of Lori. He felt this part of her moral personality must've been what led her to accept and help the man who assaulted her. Although he knew he had a long way to go, he was beginning to understand her more.

CHAPTER 7
END OF THE WORLD

As they approached the campus, Michael noticed there was something occupying Lori's mind. She'd been engaging in conversation but he could see her gazing out the window in her own independent thoughts.

"Well that's a good sign. You can see from here the power is on in our building, Lori," Monica said.

"Good," Lori answered.

"Are you sure you're alright?" Michael leaned over and asked her.

"We'll talk about it later," she whispered back with a comforting smile.

The reflective silence that had fallen amongst them was broken by the sirens and flashing lights of more fire-trucks and ambulances racing past them.

As they rode up to Lori's dorm, she leaned over to Michael. "Actually, do you have time to talk tonight?" she asked.

"Sure, you know I'm here for you," Michael answered. "Hey, Eric, I'm going to stay with Lori for a little while in case we have any aftershocks. I'll be back a little later."

"Yeah okay, you just want to leave me to clean up any mess this earthquake did to our room," Eric said.

"I didn't even think of that. Just when I thought spending time with Lori couldn't feel any sweeter," Michael said as they stepped out of the car.

"Goodnight, Eric, and thanks for the ride, Monica," Lori said.

Goodnights sang in harmony back and forth before the door closed and Michael began to become concerned with what was on Lori's mind. He thought their relationship was progressing just fine. What could it be, he thought.

"It's not about us so you can relax about that," Lori said, without even looking over at him.

"You pure humans can read minds too? You never told me that," Michael said, trying to quickly review all the thoughts he'd had around her.

"No I can't read minds. You don't have to be telepathic to know that was on your mind. If you weren't thinking that then it would mean you have no fear of us not being together. But anyway, I need to check out something and I need you to see it with me."

"Well, that's simple enough," he said.

"If this is what I think it is then there will be absolutely nothing simple about this situation."

They reached Lori's dorm, where there were a couple of books and papers scattered, but no real damage. He automatically began to help with the clutter.

"My biggest fear has always been to have feelings for someone outside my home. I'd always wondered how I'd explain my situation, and how that person would take it," she said slowly.

"I admit I did feel hesitant in the beginning. I couldn't figure out what I could possibly bring to the table that would compare to everything you are. But then I decided to put my insecurities aside and realized there must be something in me

91

you see. And if a woman of your being sees something in me, then what does that say about the person I am? In fact, I can say this entire relationship has actually boosted my confidence quite a bit."

As he finished, Michael could see his words had painted the happiest expression on Lori's face that he'd seen thus far. She turned her back to him for a moment. After gathering herself, it took her another moment to begin speaking.

"That was really, really sweet. And I don't mean to downplay it at all, but I actually need to change the subject right now if that's all right?" she said and paused for another moment.

"That's fine, take your time."

She grabbed the remote control to the television. "Well, I told you on the way in here that this wasn't about our relationship. This is what it was about," Lori said, turning on the television to a news station.

The news anchorman spoke of how there had never been as many earthquakes recorded across the earth as there had been today. The news crew was on location in Mississippi, where entire swamps had been swallowed by the cracks in the earth. She changed the channel to another news program. The story was the same, with another news crew in a different location. This reporter spoke of thousands of birds that had simply dropped dead from the sky. She changed to yet another news program that reported thousands of dead fish, washed up on the beaches. The stories of natural disasters continued as she turned and looked at Michael.

"Remember I asked you about this before? It's beginning," Lori said.

"What is?"

"The end," she said in a somber voice.

"The end?" Michael repeated. After a second of reflection, he remembered how she'd oddly brought up the apocalypse a while back. As he realized what she was saying, Michael felt the rollercoaster feeling that left his heart beneath his stomach. He quickly grew tired of this sensation. An irritation began to build in him that he wasn't familiar with. He identified this frustration as his helplessness. He'd become aggravated with feeling powerless in so many situations. His emotions pushed words too far out his mouth to pull them back. "Is there anything that anyone can do?" he asked.

Lori looked over at him with bulging eyes. "Are you asking me how you can save the world?" she said and began laughing before she could even get the question out. "I'm sorry, this is not a laughing matter," she said, clearing her face of humor.

"You're right, it isn't funny. I understand your people are waiting to inherit this world, but what about everyone that I've ever met, known, and loved who live in this world *now*."

"I'm truly sorry, it's just that it was so cliché-ishly sweet. But the Elders would know if there is any way to stop it."

"Okay, but wouldn't that be a conflict of interest if they've been waiting for centuries to claim this world? And how could they stop it if this is God's will?" he asked.

"Michael, understand that these natural disasters have been occurring for years. Now granted, this is the worst it's ever been, but the true danger is in the Elders believing that now is the time for the end although the Elders' only interest is in the will of the Creator. So if you feel you can explain the will of the Creator is for the end to be delayed, then you'd have an audience. I say this only because I've heard very old stories of a powerful being that would convince the Elders not to wage war on impure humans."

"War! You never said anything about a war. Who are the soldiers? People like you? We wouldn't stand a chance. This is the will of the Creator?" he asked in total disbelief.

"This is what the Elders are interpreting as His will, yes."

"And so now you're suggesting that I could be this powerful being who stops this war and saves the world?"

"Michael, all these situations that you've been describing to me are just too similar to the story of this being. His love and mercy for the people were so strong that the Creator found him worthy to be granted the opportunity to give the world another chance. You may not like it, but this being really may be you."

"Stop, stop, just stop." Michael stood up and covered his face with his hands. "This is way too much. Are you saying that I'm like you? Because I'm not. Except for being adopted, I've lived a pretty normal life. So there's no way I'm some being or whatever you think I am."

"Except for your dreams, remember? We had that conversation before, when you told me about waking up on broken beds. And having the heat flashes like a woman in menopause when you become emotional," she said, smiling.

"I'm glad you can find time to throw humor in the middle of all this," Michael said with a stern face.

"I apologize, you're right this is pretty serious."

"You think?" he said with a short laugh. "So why didn't you tell me all this when I first told you about my little disorder? It's like you're telling me little things here and there, instead of just giving me the whole story."

"I can see your point, but please understand I did tell you about how you were related to the prophecy I'd heard."

"Yeah, I do remember you saying how the story related to me but you never said you actually thought I was him."

"Again, I understand your frustration, but please hear me out. First of all, if I was to tell you too much at once, it would overwhelm you for sure. You told me how you've felt that way already. Second, I haven't been as confident that you could be the Prophesized One until now. I was thinking, just as you were. You're an average person, living an ordinary life. So what you've broke a couple of beds in your life during your sleep. I mean, what were the odds that I'd stumble upon you, the Prophesized One?"

"So, according to your stories, what am I supposed to do? Just persuade them. Do I fight them?" he asked with a sarcastic laugh.

"I wouldn't try that. The Elders are very strong and very fast. In fact they're the most powerful of all the pure humans. The older we are, the stronger we become. So we're at our peak just before death. And like I said, we have Elders that are over seven hundred years old. So no, I don't believe you're meant to physically fight them but I do believe in the power of simple diplomacy. Though you may not be of this world, you're a pure- hearted being who has been loved and cared for in this world. And with your supposed status, maybe you can persuade them to see the time is not yet at hand for pure humans."

"Has the Supreme Being given the Elders authority to annihilate us?"

"Think about all of the natural disasters over the years. I mean seriously think about them. There have been many tragic deaths, by the thousands, sometimes hundreds of thousands. I don't have to list them for you. You've read books and watched the news growing up, I'm sure. Within the last ten or twenty years, even before you were born, there have been natural disasters and wars between mankind. The Elders have believed for years that the stage was set for the exchange of power. Arrogant impure humans warring with one another over wealth, power, and even in the Creator's name, while other men in high positions profit from the weapons and artillery sold. For some, war has become a business. The rich become even wealthier while they disregard the countless deaths they're responsible for. The only thing that has saved the world time and time again has been the mercy of the Supreme Being. He's always given the impures more time to turn from their ways, even though the stage was perfectly set for the end of them."

"I can imagine the Elders have become a little impatient?" he said.

"Some assume so. Others have faith that the Elders are incapable of such self-absorbing emotions."

"But even though they're the oldest of the pure humans, they're still human? Don't they still feel the same emotions that all humans feel? Jealousy, impatience, or anger?"

"I'm sure they do. But after so many years of living, Elders are believed to have managed their physical emotions. They're believed to operate totally in their spiritual consciousness in order to make precise decisions. The words and decisions of the Elders have never been successfully challenged. It's by the grace of the Creator that the Elders do not order the obliteration of impure humans each year. Yet the impures ignorantly take all these chances in vain. They just continue in their arrogant ways of greed, vengeance, and murder. It never stops. And now, all these unprecedented natural disasters are signs that the Elders are finally beginning their preparations."

"I've never told you this, but when you speak of impure humans in that way, I take a little offense," he said in a serious tone. "Before you met me you had to have felt this same way. And you said in your own words that I had a pure heart so all of us aren't wicked. But you pre-judge impures with what some, or most of us, are. There are a lot of good people in the world."

"Again, you're correct. But you must have faith that the Creator's mercy will comfort them."

"But what about those who are becoming better people as we speak?" he argued. "There are people who are doing things today that they'll eventually turn from. Impure humans grow into better people, better beings. They, I mean, we, grow spiritually and emotionally. So many people are just on the verge of making that change."

"This may be exactly what you may need to be telling the Elders to persuade them. I don't have the power to stop all of this. But, like I said, maybe you do. Are you willing to come with me and try?"

"Do I have a choice? It sounds like I either try this, or your kind will try and kill everybody. I feel like I've learned too many secrets about the mafia so now I can't just walk away."

"That was wrong on so many levels to compare my people to the mafia," Lori said with disappointment in her voice.

"I apologize; it's just from all the movies I've seen."

"I can understand this is a lot to take in. Pure human or not. Or whatever you may be. That sounds almost like I'm calling you an 'it.' I apologize for all this, but please understand this isn't easy for me either," she said with a half-smile. "I'm right alongside you, feeling your curiosity and overwhelming fears of the unknown."

"You said you thought it was odd that you'd stumble upon me. I believe there is no coincidence, only the Supreme Being's will. So it had to be His will for you to find and help me on this hard road I have ahead." Michael noticed Lori put her head down as he finished his heart felt statement. "What's wrong?"

"Nothing, it's just that you can be so sweet sometimes," she said, re-engaging herself back into the conversation. "You will need to call your parents," she said, looking away.

"And just what do I tell them?"

"This is the toughest part for me." Lori somberly continued. "We have affiliate locations around the world which you can choose from. This is how a secret society stays secret. We are able to sync your GPS signal with the travel route and location of your choice."

"So if I tell my parents we're going to a small town in France, then that's where my phone will show it is. That's so James Bond."

"If France is your choice, then I will e-mail your parents an address, contact person, and land line phone that will reroute to your cell phone."

Although Michael could see the necessity in deceiving his parents, he could plainly see that it made Lori uncomfortable. At that instant, he pulled her to her feet and kissed her passionately. There was no telling how long the kiss was. The feeling he felt was so right that he didn't want to let go of her soft lips. When they finally released each other, he looked down on her face. Her eyes were still closed and her tender mouth was slowly closing.

"That kiss was definitely not that of an ordinary impure human. I felt chills I can't explain," Lori said.

"Well, that's probably just because you're a virgin. I'll try to hold my power back until the time for us is right," Michael said, with a wide smile across his face. He'd finally found something about her perfection that could be an advantage to him. When the time was right, this could be the one thing he could have the upper hand on her with. She'll have had no experience with sex, leaving him to play the dominant role. Michael felt this would finally give him the opportunity to be more of a man to Lori in his own mind. He decided to put that mental note in his back pocket for the future.

"If that's anything like making love is then I really can't wait," she said with a seductive smile. "I love how you make me feel."

"Even if I could get used to how unbelievably beautiful you are, you've made me feel ten times the man I was before I met you."

"You could make any woman fall in love with a tongue like that."

"Well, I only say things I'm inspired to say. It's that simple."

"I love simplicity. It's so pure," Lori said, then leaned in and kissed him. This time she put her arms around him and pulled him close to her.

"Okay, I think it's time for me to go," Michael said, leaning back from the kiss.

"Why, what's wrong?"

"Look, I honestly don't want to take your virginity on this cheap bed in a dorm room. If your first time is with me, then I promise you it'll be special."

"What if I just like kissing you and had no intentions of sleeping with you tonight?"

"Well, to be honest, I can't take too much more. Any more kissing and I might want to cross that line. That'd be bad. I mean, it would be good, but I'd feel bad. Afterwards I mean I'd feel bad, not during. Look!" he said, stumbling over his words and becoming frustrated. "I need to go because I love you and I want to do this right."

"I just wanted to kiss a little more but I understand if you're too turned on to keep kissing right now. I totally agree with everything you just said, and I feel even more comfortable with you knowing you value my virginity. But also understand I just wanted to kiss," she said, smiling.

"I admit, it kind of felt good when I was saying that," Michael proudly stated. "I didn't really know if I was that strong."

"Oh trust me, when I choose to be with you, there's no strength you'll be able to muster that'll save you then," Lori said with playful, but firm eyes.

"That could possibly be the most sensual thing anyone has ever said to me. I accept your challenge."

After another short kiss and a goodbye, Michael headed back to his dorm. The night air was refreshing on his face although thoughts of what Lori had told him were weighing on his mind. He thought it was best to just let everything sink in overnight and think about it tomorrow otherwise he'd never fall asleep.

Michael's steps slowed when he tried to hold the heavy reality that the world as he knew it could possibly cease to exist. He thought about his parents and how they'd react to him going overseas. His more immediate problem became clear when he approached his building. He wanted to go right in and tell Eric everything. But he couldn't. No one would believe him anyway. Plus, he'd have to expose Lori, and Michael didn't even allow that thought to even set before he quickly forced it out his brain. So the decision to remain silent was easy for him.

There was still a feeling of guilt deep within Michael he couldn't ignore. He sat on a bench near the entrance to his dorm to clear his head. He thought of all the people who wouldn't have the chance to be with or even speak to their loved ones before the end. Or what of all the people who would've forgiven their family and friends of petty quarrels if they knew the end was near? How could he not tell Eric that he needed to go home and spend these precious days with his family? This is too much, he thought to himself. He looked down at his hands and wondered what power he could possibly have.

It didn't matter anymore to Michael. He made his mind up to go to see the Elders. That's the only path he could see. Michael laughed to himself when he considered having some great power of persuasion. He wasn't sure he could even persuade Drake and Debra to let him go.

Up in the dorm, Eric had selected clothes for the next day and was lying them over the back of the chair at his desk. "Back so soon?" Eric asked.

"I'm not like you. I actually respect women. I don't try and go all the way at every opportunity," Michael replied, closing the door behind him.

"Son, one day I'll sit down and tell you what it is that I've actually done with all these girls. I promise it'll amaze you."

"There's no doubt in my mind that it would."

"Besides, I've already told you I'm a changed man. And it's all because of you. Anyway, Lori is so right for you. Do you love her? I mean, I know you probably tell her that you do, but do you really?" Eric asked, looking at Michael.

"Why? Are you her big brother now? Since when do you care about a girl's feelings?"

"It's actually your feelings I'm worried about."

"My feelings? You think Lori would hurt me?" Michael asked.

"Look, man, I honestly don't know. All I do know is you went from being lonely and on the rebound to head over heels in love in a couple months. And with good reason, like I said, she's an awesome girl. But how well do you really know her?"

"I know things about her that nobody else will ever know," Michael said, changing his clothes.

"You'd really be surprised if you found out what I know about women."

Michael didn't even hear Eric's comment. He was deciding when he'd speak on leaving with Lori. He chose to just get it all out now. "Well, you're going to find out anyway so I might as well tell you now. I'm going overseas to visit Lori's village."

"Village! She lives in a village? Like huts and bathing in the river...village?" Eric asked in confusion.

"You've seen her. I don't think she's from a village like that."

"Well, where is this village and how long has she been in the States?"

Michael wrinkled his forehead and flipped through his mental files for the how long she'd been here.

"See, now that's what I mean when I ask how well do you really know her. It's nothing personal. I think she's a great girl. But you wouldn't invest a million dollars in a stock that you don't know everything about."

Michael interlocked his fingers behind his head and lay back on his pillow. "Maybe you're right. Maybe I haven't known her that long, but she's more than everything I ever wanted. And I feel this bond...without sex. If I lost her now, I'd always wonder what could've been. And I'd probably end up hating myself for the rest of my life."

"That's understandable, but I really don't believe you'd be in jeopardy of losing her if you just slowed down a little and checked your feelings. Trust me, the last thing I want to see is you two break up. But I don't want you to get hurt from doing too much too fast either. That's all, man."

Eric turned off the light and Michael began to hear his friend's sincere words echoing in his head. He even saw the logic of Eric's proposal, but he trusted Lori. He felt free to invest whatever feelings he desired into her. After all, he thought, she'd entrusted him with her dearest secrets.

The next morning, during his shower, Michael decided he wasn't going to be timid about whatever his role would be. He'd made up his mind to boldly walk the path that lay ahead of him.

Michael still felt amazing from the strange rebound of his nauseous episode the night before. He noticed girls on campus smiling at him. Maybe they always did and I just never noticed, he thought. Then he thought maybe they'd been seeing him with Lori, making him more desirable. After a while he didn't care about the reason. He was just having a good day.

He was having such a good day that he decided to call his parents after classes and ask them about his upcoming trip. The phone rang until he heard the familiar sweet sound of his adoptive mother's voice.

"Oh, this caller ID makes you sound silly to say hello when you already know who it is. How's it going, sweetheart?" Debra, answered.

"Pretty good. Well, actually, living away from home out here in the real world is a little crazy."

"I bet. Michael, you sound different. Are you alright?" she asked.

"I've been hearing that a lot lately. People have said I look different too. Different in a good way though."

"I was just about to say you sound really good. Have you recently lost your virginity?"

"Mom! How can you ask me that?" Michael replied in disbelief.

"Hello, son," Drake said as Michael heard Debra in the background, still apologizing.

"What are you doing home, Dad, you're usually working? Did you just take the phone from Mom?"

"Yeah, I don't know what's wrong with her. What's she thinking, trying to do my job? You do sound different. Now, do you love this girl?"

"No, Dad, I'm not having sex, okay. I was just telling Mom how everyone's been saying I sound and look different since the earthquake the other night. And I'm sorry I didn't call to check on you two, but why didn't you guys call me?"

"Well, son, see we didn't want to treat you like a little boy anymore. We know you're a grown man now with friends and we just didn't want to embarrass you."

"Thanks, I guess. I've just had so much on my mind lately it's been a little hard for me to focus. The other night, right before the earthquake hit, I was all nauseous and needed some air. I felt like I might even pass out, but since then I've felt much better. I mean, even better than before. And everybody says I look and sound better too. All kinds of girls have been smiling at me today. It's like I have a new glow or something."

"Well, that's good to hear, Michael, I couldn't be happier for you," Drake said.

"Thanks, but I actually called to talk to you guys about something very important to me."

"Let me put you on speaker phone, hold on…okay, there it is. We're both listening, Michael."

"Okay, you've heard me mention Lori before. Well, she's invited me on an all-expenses paid trip to visit her small hometown in France."

"France?" Debra asked. "That sounds like fun."

"Yeah, Lori said she'd e-mail you her home address and other details. I don't remember the name of her town, I just know it's not a big city like Paris." Michael felt uneasy telling these lies, but he kept telling himself he had no choice. There was no way they'd even believe the truth, much-less agree to it.

"How long you two planning on being gone?" Drake asked.

"About a week, this is sounding like it's going to be a yes. Am I right?"

"Ok, just as long as we get that e-mail from Lori," Debra replied.

"Really?"

"It's like your father said earlier, you're a grown man now. We trust you, Michael."

"Plus the all-expenses paid part is good too," Drake said.

"This was a lot easier than I thought. I really appreciate you two treating me like an adult."

"Michael, you've always been a good kid. Now you've grown to be a good young man. If it's important to you, then we trust you," Drake said. "You must really like this girl?"

"I do. I really like her a lot. I think the best word to describe her is pure. In every way, from her beauty to her personality. She's just pure."

"She sounds like a virgin, I like that." Debra chimed in.

"Mom!" Michael sang. "Dad, has she been drinking?"

"Now you know your mother doesn't drink. We are just missing you and want to know about you and your life away from us, that's all."

"I understand. But that doesn't mean I'm comfortable having sex talks with you guys," Michael said with a disgusted face. "Actually, I don't know anyone who enjoys having any kind of conversation with their parents about that. I mean, I guess I understand you two being interested, but, please, guys."

"Okay, as long as you know it's all out of love. You know that, right?" Debra asked.

"Of course, Mom. Look, I've got a couple of things to do before it gets too late. I'm sorry to cut it short but leaving the country takes a lot of preparation."

"We understand. Give us a call back again before you leave though," Drake said.

"Or whenever you need to talk," Debra added.

"Okay, love you, guys."

"We love you too. Goodnight," they said in chorus.

Michael couldn't believe how easy that was. He took it as a sign he was walking the path he was supposed to be on. He found himself feeling more and more confident with this unbelievable scenario he'd found himself in.

Michael soon noticed his focus was slipping in his classes. Part of him figured that if he truly believed Lori, then school shouldn't matter in the midst of Armageddon. He found it difficult to concentrate, with all the anxiety involving the upcoming events. He kept telling himself anyone would have trouble keeping a clear head in his situation. His reality had taken such a strange and sudden turn.

Michael decided to hold himself to different standards. He never wanted the world's norms to determine his attitude or actions. The more he visualized an average person folding under the pressure that he was bearing, the more he felt he had to persevere. Michael was excited to discover this characteristic within him. He felt this quality would give him a strong edge in becoming the man he wanted to be.

He called Lori and told her he'd be hitting the books pretty hard for the next couple of days. He was thankful she understood. She even offered to bring him over some Chinese food. He respectfully declined, knowing how much of a distraction she'd be. As important as she was to him, Michael figured, end of the world or not, school was still an important responsibility.

CHAPTER 8
INTO THE RABBIT HOLE

Buried in work, the next several weeks flew by for Michael. Before he knew it, the morning of his big day was upon him. With all his exams and papers completed with confidence, he could focus on his upcoming adventure although, deep within him, he still feared the end of the world.

Approaching the airport, Michael felt like he was entering the ring of a heavyweight championship boxing match. He chuckled at the rest of the metaphor, in which he had extremely high expectations without a single day of training. There was no turning back now. All the talk was over and he was heading off to save the world. This was real. His anxiety was being replaced with inflated confidence. All these people don't even realize if I pull this off, they'll owe me big time, he thought to himself. Michael looked over at Lori and her smile put the icing on the cake. He had no regrets or second thoughts about his trip.

"Have you flown before?" she asked.

"I've flown out to Florida and California for family vacations as a kid."

"So you're not afraid?"

"If I was going to be afraid of anything in this entirely unbelievable scenario, trust me, it wouldn't be the flight," he said, laughing.

"Well, what would it be?"

"My only real fear is not knowing if I have the words to convince the Elders."

"Don't rely on the words. Rely on your passion. Passion speaks louder than any words, no matter how loudly they are spoken," she said with a tender look.

Michael looked away for a moment to digest her words. "What happens afterwards with you?"

"What do you mean?"

"Just for argument's sake, let's just say I'm successful and the world remains as it is. Won't you just stay home and wait for your next mission?"

Lori stopped and looked up at Michael. She let her head fall to the side with a smile, then reached up and caressed the left side of his face. "Let's cross that bridge when we get to it. There are many mountains to conquer before we get down into that valley."

"You're right. I need to focus on the task at hand." He agreed aloud, but really wanted to continue the conversation.

They continued through the baggage check, where they were just given plastic tabs with the gate number on them.

"I've never seen any kind of boarding pass like this," Michael said.

"These flights are extremely exclusive. By Elder order only," she whispered. "There's a private airport we normally use, but it's another two hundred miles away. There would be no baggage check or crowds, but we're in quite a hurry."

When they reached the gate, Michael began to understand the power of pure humans. He saw the departure time was six fifteen, but there was no destination posted. He wondered how there could be an active gate in plain sight without displaying any destination.

There was no one else waiting when they walked up to the counter. The woman at the desk was middle-aged with long blonde hair. She was busy typing very fast and loud but looked up and smiled as they approached her.

"You must be Michael and Lori," the woman said and smiled even wider.

"Yes ma'am," Lori answered. They both handed her their identification and plastic boarding passes.

"Okay great, just follow me. You're going to love your trip. We just got this jet two weeks ago. It's the smoothest flight I've ever taken," the woman said, walking away from her computer in mid-key stroke.

Michael was still a little confused as they followed the woman through a door and down some steps. Those steps lead to another door, which led outside. Michael exhaled a deep sigh as they headed towards a brand new, shiny, pearl white private jet. He still wasn't sure if the jet was for them but there was no other aircraft in their path.

Michael felt Lori must be accustomed to this kind of elite treatment. She showed no reaction or emotion after seeing the jet. There was only the sun on her beautiful face.

"Do you have faith in me," he asked.

"Of course I do."

"Do you have faith in us?"

She looked at him and hesitated. "Yes."

"Then smile. And I don't want to see some artificial smile you put on for me just for the moment. I want to see the smile that lets me know you truly believe in me. And us," he said.

She looked up at him and gave him exactly what he wanted to see. Her eyes even seemed to be smiling. Michael noticed a tear struggling to hang on the corner of her curly eyelashes. It finally lost its grip and slid down her face, leaving a sparkling path.

"You're truly something special, Michael," she said, wiping her eye.

Stepping into the jet, Michael saw the interior was lavishly decorated and furnished. He tried to contain his amazement as they took their places in large soft leather seats. There were multiple controls for any seating options he could think of.

"I've seen pictures, but I've always wondered just how different flying in commercial planes is to flying private like this," Lori said with an innocent smile.

"You mean you've never flown commercial?"

"No. Only private like this."

"Okay, listen close. First, you have long slow lines and you're arranged by your seat number. Then it takes forever to get to your seat because people have to put their carry-on bags in the overhead compartments while you wait. Next, you squeeze into your mini-seat that gives you about a fifteen-inch space from your face to the back of the seat in front of you. Then comes the stewardess to show you how to use all the equipment on the plane, in case you crash and die. Finally you take off, and the seat in front of you reclines. This brings your face-space to the back of the seat in front of you from about fifteen inches down to about ten. So, of course, you recline your seat to accommodate for the lost face-space. But just as you do, you hear a groan from the person behind you. Now you can practically feel their knees in your back. Finally, you land and have to wait for everyone ahead of you to get their carry-on bags back out of the overhead compartments, and slowly shuffle out behind one another."

"Wow. Is it really that bad?"

"Compared to this…" Michael said, outstretching both his arms and looking around at all the luxuries provided for them, "…it's worse than it sounds."

The blonde-haired woman from the counter returned with a menu and casually explained the flight instructions.

"About how long is the flight?" Michael asked, as he and Lori fastened their seat belts.

"Not long at our speeds, just relax and enjoy yourself. I'll be back after we're in the air to take your orders," she said, smiling at Michael, then turned her eyes to Lori with an almost awkward stare before walking away.

"How long is *not long*?" Michael asked Lori.

"Michael, you have to understand this is a very sensitive situation. The location of my home is protected on many levels. Did you notice there was no destination displayed for our flight?"

Michael nodded in understanding.

"If a person had a compass, knew about how fast we were flying, and how long the flight was, he or she could come close to an estimate of the location. As a result, all of these variables are changed at different points throughout the flight. She really doesn't know how long the flight will be. That's why we're made as comfortable as possible. I probably should've spent more time preparing you for small things like this. It's just you have so much to deal with already that I've tried to spare you some of the smaller details."

"Well, first of all, I don't think I could be any more overwhelmed than I've already been in the last few months. So it's okay, don't be afraid to drop anything else on me. Second, I understand all the precautions. And the more I begin to understand, the more I can see how your people have remained unknown for so long."

"Actually, there are probably more people involved than you may think. I don't know exactly how deep it goes, but you don't just get to rent out part of a major airport, and be excused from posting your destination if you're just *unknown*. We actually are known to a few groups of select and powerful people."

"Why would any impure humans help pure humans? I mean, how could anyone aid in the process of their own extinction?"

"I'm sure you understand that most people won't even ask any questions if compensated enough," she replied.

"And what if they do ask questions?"

"I'm not sure, that's not my area. These are questions for the Elders."

Michael began to feel as though these Elders weren't as righteous as he'd first thought them to be. Using impure humans to bring about their own demise isn't what he'd expected from the leaders of Lori's people. Michael felt, in this scenario, that the exchange of money and secrets behind closed doors couldn't be for anything positive.

At that moment, Michael's skin began to crawl with chills. Maybe that's it, he thought. Just maybe my purpose is to show them how they've gone a little off track. It seemed that in all Lori's perfection, even she didn't recognize how wrong it is to benefit from the greed of such shallow individuals.

Michael felt the plane began to move slowly and, within seconds, the jet picked up enough speed to lift off. The airport and other buildings along the highway all became part of an organized grid pattern as he watched their ascension from the window.

"I hate this part. When a plane crashes, it's usually a problem during the take-off or landing, " Lori said.

"You ever wonder what it would be like if you were an angel? The feeling of the wind beneath your wings. To float amongst the clouds and look down on the earth," Michael asked, gazing out the window.

Lori began to giggle a little. "I'm sure angels do a lot more than just fly around and lounge on clouds. In this day and age, I'm sure they're very busy," she said, still laughing.

"I know, but if flying around with big magnificent wings is part of being an angel, I'm sure it's cool so please don't ruin my little fantasy moment with reality," he said, smiling.

"You know this flight will probably be the most time we'll have spent together alone since we met so I thought we might learn a few details about each other. I know I've wondered a few things about you, and I'm sure you still have some questions for me. By the time we land, hopefully, we'll know even more about one another. I don't want there to be any limit to how close we become," Lori said.

"There is something minor that's been in the back of my mind for a while."

"What is it?"

"Well, the man who tried to assault you several months back. Do you remember who I'm talking about?"

"Richard. Of course I remember. A woman doesn't forget a thing like that. What about him?"

"Sure you haven't forgotten. That was a silly question. But I remember his arm being in a sling. And I just couldn't imagine an injured person trying to assault someone."

"And you think I hurt his arm?" Lori impatiently added in a guilty tone.

"Please don't think you have to explain yourself to me. You do have a right to defend yourself. I mean he had it coming if you did do it. But if you don't mind me asking, just what happened that night?"

"You think I would hurt you, don't you?" she asked, with a concerned face.

"I mean if I dumped you, I wouldn't want you to come kicking in my door, ripping me limb from limb," he said, laughing. "No, really I guess I am a little curious about just how strong you are."

"Don't dump me and you won't have to worry about it," she said, smiling.

Michael figured she was avoiding the question. "You really don't have to tell me if you don't want to. I can imagine how hard it would be to re-live those moments. I wouldn't want to put you through those horrible thoughts again just to satisfy my curiosity anyway."

"It's alright. And I appreciate your understanding but truthfully, the worst part of the entire situation is that I did hurt Richard. I should've known better, looking back. But I turned to walk through the bike trail for a shortcut after a late workout."

"How late?"

"It actually wasn't too late, but it was just getting dark. I never checked my watch through all this, but by ten-thirty I was home, showering. Anyway, I saw him jogging towards me and I didn't think anything of it. The next thing I know, he reached over and grabbed me, trying to cover my mouth. Well, when he quickly saw that he wasn't overpowering me, he tried to run. I grabbed his wrist…"

"I'm sorry to interrupt, but why did you grab him?" Michael asked in confusion.

"Because I remembered hearing of other female students who'd been assaulted. I figured if I just let him run back into the night, he'd just get the next passing girl."

"Okay, so you grabbed his wrist."

"Well, then he tried to twist away. So I tightened my grasp, and he turned with so much force that my grip injured his arm. Since then, I've felt so much guilt that I've done everything I could to help him."

"I guess I can understand that. What happened next?" he asked.

"I told Richard I'd let his wrist go after I walked him to the campus hospital to treat his arm. He really had no choice. I told him either he let me put his medical bill on my school account and allow me to walk him home to see where he lived, or I'd walk him to the police station by his injured arm. Again, he had no choice," Lori said, with a smirk.

"So you walked all the way to the campus hospital, holding him by the wrist of his injured arm? And you said you didn't believe in punishing people," Michael said sarcastically but with a smile.

"I've already told you how guilty I feel about his arm."

"I know, I'm just kidding. Please finish."

"So by the time we arrived at his apartment, we'd talked enough for him to realize I was genuinely trying to help him. He invited me in and we began to talk further about his past. This was the first time he'd ever attempted an assault on anyone. He said he'd often had the urge and even went out with the intent to go through with it, but he just never had the nerve until he passed me. He said there was an innocence he felt from me that was taken from him at a young age. An innocence so precious, he explained through his tears, that his twisted thoughts lead him to believe he could somehow take my innocence as his own."

"Now that's some deep psychological *Silence of The Lambs* type sickness," Michael interrupted.

"Maybe, but no one should be given up on. Any and everyone can be saved if one person gives them the chance…the one chance they won't even give themselves. I asked Richard about his plans for the future and he had none. I told him the terms of me not pressing charges consisted of him meeting with a therapist of my choice, enrolling in courses next semester, and also meeting with me once a week. He told me no one had ever put so much effort or interest into his success. Since then, he hasn't missed a single meeting with me or with the therapist. He's expressed a genuine passion for art and writing. He even wrote an anonymous letter to the editor of the campus newspaper about the entire scenario. After it was published, almost everyone in my dorm knew it was us. They'd already seen us meeting, and his bandaged arm really gave it away. A few students made it clear they didn't feel comfortable with Richard around an all-girl dorm. And I can understand their concerns, so I've agreed to meet with him at the library from now on. Of course there were no names used and I wouldn't press charges, so there was no case against him. The last time you saw us, we were making the final preparations for his enrollment."

"Wow. I mean that really puts a lot into perspective. Do you remember the conversation we had before about the meaning of life? How you said our purpose was to put ourselves aside and help one another?"

"Of course," she said.

"Okay, well, you perfectly applied that concept in this situation. Obviously, the average woman isn't physically strong enough to do what you did, but it was the intent. Your intent wasn't to make him pay for what he tried to do to you. Instead of a vengeful attitude, you chose to help him by whatever means you could. In this day and age, that concept is so foreign."

"That's because it is. It's so foreign in fact that it's not of this world. It is written that we are in this world, but not of it. Therefore, our ways should be foreign to this world. Our actions and thoughts shouldn't coincide with the ways of the world. This is how we stand out and bring attention to our lives. This attention gives us opportunities to spread the good news of the Creator. Think about just going through life on an everyday basis. We shouldn't be walking around blindly, trying to only benefit ourselves. Nor should we believe these are coincidental situations which we daily find ourselves in. Every moment of our life we're on call. Any circumstance that we encounter should be considered a test from the Supreme Being; a test to see how we can put ourselves aside and help someone else. Like you said, this may sound foreign, but that's what we were created for."

"So basically we're supposed to live our lives in a constant effort to help others instead of ourselves?" Michael asked.

"What if you were on a commercial flight seated next to a child, and the plane began to lose cabin pressure? The oxygen masks drop from overhead and now you have a decision to make. Do you put your mask on first, or do you put the child's mask on first. Of course you'd want to help the child first, but that would be a mistake. Suppose, as you're trying to reach over and help the child with their mask, you pass out from lack of oxygen. Now you are both unconscious, with no help. The correct decision would be to secure your own mask first, so you're able to ensure your safety as well as the child's. This same line of reasoning can be related to life. If you give all you have to charity, then you'll need charity. Give whatever kind of help in any way you can, but don't foolishly forsake yourself in the process. If you do, then how will you be able to help the next person tomorrow?"

"I know I may have mentioned this before, but it would seem that someone using one hundred percent of their brain would use complex ideas and words. Instead it's just the opposite. It seems to me with your higher intelligence, you just explain the most complex concepts so simply."

"Truth, purity, and simplicity all go hand in hand. Now if you don't mind, I believe it's your turn to talk," she said, smiling.

"Well I guess you did put it all out there. I'm ready for whatever you got."

"Okay, I'm curious about what kind of upbringing made this unique young man I see here before me. You've told me a little, but how was your childhood? Are you very close with each of your parents?"

Michael smiled. "That's easy enough. I'm much closer to my mom. I still love my dad, but it seemed like she just put a lot more effort into raising me. But in my dad's defense, he works a lot so he's rarely able to spend time with me. Overall, for an adopted kid, I can't complain though. Of course, every adopted child wonders about their biological parents. Who are they, where are they, and why didn't they want me?"

"Did you ever try to find your biological parents?"

"I tried on my own a few times, but the agency never seemed to help or take me seriously. I thought about asking my adoptive parents for help, but I didn't want to hurt them. They never volunteered to help, even when they knew I was searching. Now I feel like searching for my biological parents would be insinuating I'm not happy at home. As childish as it may sound, that's just how I feel about it. It's kind of a sore subject."

"Fair enough," she said.

"I guess the only thing I can complain about is not having any siblings. I always wanted a brother to play with. Older or younger, it didn't matter. I would've liked to learn things from an older brother that a father wouldn't understand. For example, how to talk to girls with the current lingo for this decade. And watching an older brother grow up before me would give a preview of experiences that I'd have coming. Maybe learn from his successes and mistakes. On the other hand, I would've passed down those same jewels of knowledge to help a younger brother."

"So you were pretty lonely as a child?" she asked.

"I had casual friends, but it always seemed that as soon as I was becoming close to anyone, we would have to leave. My father works for the government, so we frequently moved around to wherever he was needed. It worked out well with my mother being a high school teacher. She never had a problem finding a job in whatever new town we moved to."

"So your adoptive father was never home?"

"I wouldn't say he was never home. I'd say about two nights during weekdays, but he was there almost all weekends and holidays."

"How did you and he get along?"

"There's no doubt we love each other but it always seemed as though our few good moments were forced."

"Forced by whom?"

"Sometimes I could actually hear her telling him to spend time with me. Then when he and I were doing things together, it felt as if he'd rather be doing anything else. Or it seemed as though his heart just wasn't in it. But, on some occasions, he'd become lost in the moment and we actually had a genuine good time together."

"You have a nice body; did you work out with him?" Lori asked.

"He always wanted me to be bigger and stronger, so I worked out a lot. But I never got to be as big as he wanted me to be. He always said I had girl muscles."

"Did he want you to play football or something?"

"Yeah, he'd take me to try-outs and then pull me out right in the middle and take me home. He'd tell me I had to try harder and start training that night for next year. We did that for about three years until he finally gave up. He always made sure to take off work for the try-outs. Then one year he had important work that day and we didn't go. And we haven't been since, but I saw it coming. Every year I could tell he was more disappointed. Disappointed until he gave up…that's what hurt the most."

"You didn't try and get your mom to take you to try-outs?"

"I guess when he didn't want to take me anymore, I gave up on myself too. Looking back, I think I often fell short of the man he envisioned me to be. He would always say that I was aggressive, but in this world I needed to be brutally aggressive. But like I said, we've had other good times as well. He taught me how to shave and drive. He never missed a birthday. And he's never raised his voice in anger towards me. At times I thought he just didn't care enough but he probably never wanted to scare me. He's pretty big and stays in good shape for someone his age," Michael said.

"What about your adoptive mom?"

"My mom always says I'm her most important child, but she considers her students her children as well. She often has to leave and council a student. She's the kind of teacher that'll come to your home in the evening and have a parent-teacher conference after dinner."

"So you didn't see your mom every day either?" she asked.

"I saw her more than my dad; she'd only have to leave for a couple of hours. Sometimes she would just come home late, with dinner in hand. But she was there for every cut and scrape. I was never really sick as a kid, but she always checked my temperature for a fever. And every night she knew my dad would be home, we had good home-cooked food."

"That's sweet."

"See, pretty normal. Almost boring," he said, smiling.

"Well, I think it's sweet."

"You know with all the other fascinating things about you, I've never even thought about your childhood."

"We're not raised by a couple as you are here. After our creation and arrival, we're taken to a place where all the young are cared for. At this place we live and are trained in our fields. Our instructors are pure humans who have mastered their various disciplines. We're educated in all curriculums, including different languages and cultures."

It almost sounded like a high class, super foster-care system, or supernatural military school to Michael. He figured if there were an army of pure humans waiting to take over the world then it'd make sense for them to be trained in a military school setting. The more Michael learned of their system, the more logical it became to him. Even Lori's role as an intelligence officer seemed to fit perfectly.

"What did you want to be as a kid?" Lori asked, snapping Michael out of his daydream.

"An astronaut," he said, without thinking.

"An astronaut, now that's interesting. So are you planning to major in astronomy or astrophysics?"

"You said as a kid. Back when you're a kid, no one tells you how hard it is to be what you want. Everybody just says you can be whatever you want to be."

"But you really can," Lori said, full of energy.

"Easy for you to say, Einstein. I think you've become so accustomed to using your complete brain that sometimes you don't think about us ordinary impure humans using our little ten or fifteen percent."

"I actually do think about it a lot. I wonder how you can keep my interest the way you do. It's true I've met some nice impures, but most are so simple, arrogant, and predictable. You're none of those…except nice. On my first mission, I expected to feel as if I was around children all the time. Which isn't that far off, considering I'm older than any living impure human. But I never feel that way around you."

"I'm glad to hear you say that," Michael replied with a smile. "I've had the same thoughts. Wondering if I bore you or if I'm keeping your interest."

"Well, since that's all cleared up and you feel being an astronaut is too hard, what do you want to be now?"

"I guess I don't really know. I think I'm a late-bloomer, like I'm just now finding myself. It's kind of hard to explain but I just know I'm on the verge of realizing what I really want to do. The best way I can describe it is like when you feel a sneeze coming."

"I think your sneeze is coming too," she said, smiling and trying to hold back her laugh.

"What?" Michael asked in playful confusion.

"I just love the way you express yourself, that's all," she answered, still smiling.

The flight attendant returned with two menus and took their drink orders. This is where it became fuzzy for Michael. He remembers a little more conversation with Lori, then waking up feeling extremely groggy.

"Did I fall asleep?" he asked, feeling embarrassed, checking his face for drool.

"Yes and no." Lori answered with an aggravated look on her face. "There's been a change in protocol that I was unaware of. New visitors to my home are to be gently sedated until they've been sanctioned by the Elders. Your drink was drugged. I'm really sorry, Michael. If I knew anything about this, I certainly would've told you. I hope you're not upset with me."

"No, I 'm not upset, I believe you. The flight attendant could've given me some kind of warning though."

"After you fell unconscious, I spoke with her and she assumed I'd already told you. She apologized and asked me to apologize to you for her."

"She could at least have let me eat first. You know, brought me the drink after my meal. Why even bring me a menu if I'm about to be sedated?" Michael complained.

"You did eat. You said you were feeling a little air sick after you ate, then you immediately fell asleep. Are you still hungry? I can have her fix you up something else."

"No, I'm not hungry, I just don't remember eating. Besides, even if I was hungry, I wouldn't eat anything else served to me on this plane," he said with a smirk, to let Lori know he was serious but not upset. "Plus I have wake-up breath now so I can't kiss you."

"Trusting that I wasn't involved is reason enough for kissing a smelly mouth," she said as she slowly moved in and kissed Michael passionately. "Yeah, that was a little sour, but worth every second," she said, smiling.

"How long was I asleep?" he asked, still yawning.

"Long enough for us to have begun descending. Even I'm not allowed to wear a watch on the jet. Like I said earlier, no one could tell you how long we've actually been in flight. The Elders have made sure only the pilots know the true path to my home for our safety. There are fears that one of us may be taken and interrogated for information leading to the location of my home. So the less we know, the safer we are."

"Why would the location of your home be such valuable information to impure humans?"

"Well, I've already explained how the Supreme Being made our bodies with his own hands, so we live a lot longer because of our pure blood."

"Right," he said.

"Well, as you know, we're also in league with powerful impure humans. Of these impures, several don't believe the Supreme Being created us at all. Instead, they believe the fountain of youth actually exists in my home. So you can imagine if impures think they could have the abilities of pure humans by drinking from a fountain in my village, then my home's location has been relentlessly sought after for many years. Can you believe it's easier for some to believe in this fountain than the Creator?"

"As crazy as it sounds, it seems totally normal for the people in the world I know. People believe in themselves before God so a fountain of youth is easy to believe in. Oh yeah, before I forget, if the pilots of this plane know the location of your home then what of their safety? You spoke of the fear for you or I being taken. Is there no fear for the pilot's safety?"

"Actually no. The pilots are considered the strongest of all the pure humans who aren't Elders. They also have a very high rank in the pure human military. And although very powerful, they don't like conflict. Their battles usually end with a death, so they choose to avoid combat unless absolutely necessary. In fact, being a pilot is so high an honor that some even become Elders. On a different note, I'm actually surprised to see you conscious so soon. The flight attendant told me the sedative would keep you asleep for at least 24hrs. This way, you wouldn't even be conscious for the ground transport either. But here you are, bright-eyed and bushy-tailed."

"Does this mean I'll be sedated again?" Michael asked with concern.

"I don't believe so, but if that's the case I'll make sure you're well aware of it."

"Thank you."

"I promise all this will be worth it once we reach my home."

CHAPTER 9
LORI'S GIFT

Michael felt the plane's descent but was yet to see any land when he looked out the window. He thought of how privileged he was as the wooziness from the drug had begun to fade. Very few people in the history of existence had experienced the kind of adventure that was unfolding before him. "I know you've told me the Elders said this was where the Garden of Eden was, but what exactly do you call it? I've only heard you refer to your home or your village."

"When I was in training, I was taught the Elders felt the Village would be more secure if it was not identified. The logic was that it'd be even more difficult to locate a place if it didn't even have a name to begin with. One of the reasons that cities and states are named in your society is because you have to navigate between them. The average pure human has never left the Village. There are no questions of where a person was born or is from. Even pure humans like me who do leave on missions just simply call it home."

"Okay, but it's still awkward to me how a place can exist with no name."

"Does the house you grew up in have a name?" she asked.

"Of course not, but that's my home."

"Exactly my point. You probably feel safe inside your house but when you step outside then you're not in your home any more. You're on your street, where you don't feel as safe. The difference is that my entire village is like the house you grew up in. We feel as safe anywhere in the Village as you do in your home. Leaving the Village is like stepping out our front door. So just as there's no need to name your home, there has been no need to name our village."

As the plane descended even more, Michael became both excited and a little nervous to see land. He could see hulking trees in the most beautiful shade of green that he'd ever seen. It was almost like seeing trees for the first time in high definition. In fact, the plane had descended so much that soon after Michael began to see land, they were touching down. "I can't believe we're here."

"Not exactly," Lori said.

"What do you mean?"

"Like I said earlier, we do have a ground transport as well," Lori said with sympathy in her voice. "Nothing worth having is easily attained. I'll give you a kiss if you can tell me what famous person said that."

"How about you give me a kiss for flying across the globe, being drugged, and trying to somehow save the world? All on the trust of your words." As Michael playfully said the words, he himself felt a little in over his head. He'd known Lori about six months, and here he was in some unknown, unmapped location with her.

But his heart was sure where his head hesitated. He believed he was exactly where he should be, even if the facts of the situation seemed risky.

"How about I just kiss you because I want to?" Lori offered.

"Even better," he answered, but their kiss was quickly interrupted by the flight attendant.

"Oh, you're already back with us. I do apologize you weren't notified of the new protocol. Although I must say I'm surprised to see you conscious. Every other passenger hasn't wakened for at least 26 to 32 hours."

"I understand, Lori explained everything to me and I feel fine. No harm, no foul. But I am curious. Now that I'm awake, will I be shot with a tranquilizer dart for the ground transport?" Michael was joking, but listened seriously for the answer.

"I'll tell you what," the flight attendant said, laughing. "Since I feel so bad about how this happened, and since Lori is very highly ranked and trusted by the Elders, I'll look the other way on the ground transport. Fair enough?"

"Sounds good to me. I like being conscious," Michael said, smiling.

"All right, fine. I hope the flight was comfortable and please, enjoy your stay."

As they prepared to leave the plane, the doors opened and Michael smelled air like he'd never smelled before. He felt as if he had had asthma his entire life, and didn't really know what it was like to use his full lung capacity until now.

"You smell that? I hadn't realized how much I've missed the fresh air here," Lori said, tilting her head back.

"I was just thinking it almost feels like breathing pure oxygen."

"I remember the first time I came to America. I thought the first few breaths I took were filled with exhaust coming from the plane's engine. Then after I was away from the plane, I figured maybe the entire airport was just engrossed in the stench of airplane exhaust fumes. It wasn't until I was miles away from the airport that I realized just how toxic the air is there compared to here."

Michael couldn't help but to feel a little defensive after Lori's repeated comments on impure humans and how he and his people were destroying the earth. After all they live in a village, he thought. "You know there are some advantages to living in an industrialized…" Michael's words abandoned him as he stepped off the jet. He looked around and saw no buildings, no airport, or even any other planes. The only clue of civilization he could find was the small landing strip they used, which lay perfectly in an open field. After further inspection, he noticed an original model *Hummer* SUV in near perfect condition. "Where is everyone and everything?" he asked, trying not to sound too disturbed.

"I told you there would be a ground transport," she said, nodding at the SUV. "We should make it just before sundown."

"I didn't mean that. I was talking about the airport. There's no commercial airport? This jet is the only way on and off this place?"

Lori smiled as if to try and comfort Michael. "If there were a commercial airport, then why would there be a need to be so discreet about the location? A commercial airport is just that, commercial. We're a civilization unlike the world has ever known."

They walked over to the SUV and began loading their bags.

"What about the pilot and the flight attendant. Will they be traveling with us?"

"No, they'll rest on the jet then fly back. Either there are others who may be headed out, or the pilots will return to resume their duties back in America."

"So we can't leave whenever we want? Our scheduled time to be here is edged in stone, huh?" Michael repeated in disappointment.

"You make it sound as if you're trapped here."

"I've just always been able to leave any place if I wanted. Even if I never wanted to, I always had the power to. And technically, not being able to leave someplace when you want to, means that you're trapped," Michael said with a chuckle.

"Do you want to leave?" Lori asked as she opened the door and stepped up into the driver's side of the SUV.

"No, not yet," Michael said, hopping up into the passenger side.

"And you'll probably never want to. People have literally killed to get information leading to the location of my village. Believe it or not, you're truly in a privileged position."

"I know, and I don't mean to sound ungrateful. But it's just a little intimidating to go across the world to a place almost no one has been, having no knowledge of where you are, or even if you're able to leave at any time." Michael paused when he saw an unpleasant look began to grow on Lori's face. "Look…I do trust you and I'm sure I'll have a fascinating time. I'm just trying to get a grip. I've jumped head first into a situation I've never even dreamed of experiencing. I just really don't know what to expect. I'm sure you've felt the same way in America at times."

"Sure, it's human nature to fear the unknown. But I just have faith I'm doing the right thing. And since the Supreme Being sees all, I know I'll be fine."

"Again, you almost make me feel silly with your simplicity. But what can I say, you're right again," Michael confessed.

He sat back to enjoy the scenery of the ride as Lori drove off when he realized there was no road. "Let me guess, if someone did somehow find this place, then a road might lead them straight to your village. So, as children, everyone had to learn the way here with no maps or roads."

"You know you actually aren't that far from the truth. Except everyone in my village isn't made to learn the path here. It's part of the training that one must complete in my village if chosen to leave on missions."

"Well, if there are no roads then that explains the Hummer."

The grass was greener and taller than he'd ever seen. He was impressed with how well Lori navigated her way through the bulking vegetation, which grew almost five feet. Michael had seen various nature shows on cable television where he'd learned scientists were still finding new species of plant life every day. He wondered if these species had been discovered yet, or if they were indigenous and confined to this secret place. He heard birds all around him, but was yet to see one up close.

The ride was bumpy, but not uncomfortable. He couldn't see a single cloud in the sky. "Does it ever rain here?" he asked.

"Of course. Mostly during your winter season, we have rain to replenish our needs and feed the plants."

"How cold does it get during the winter?"

"There's really no change in the temperature, just the rain."

"Paradise. It's so funny. Everyone in my world is looking for your paradise yet everyone in your world wants to leave it. I guess the grass really does seem greener on the other side."

"I was thinking of what you said earlier also," she said, casually looking over while managing the restless steering wheel. "About when you spoke of not being able to leave a place whenever you want to. I've never considered anyone would ever feel trapped here, but I do understand your point."

He couldn't help but notice Lori had been a little preoccupied in her own thoughts since they'd arrived. He considered asking her about her periods of distance, but then decided against it. He didn't want her to try and fill the silence with meaningless words for his benefit. Maybe she was just overjoyed to be back at home. Or maybe she was mentally preparing herself for their meetings with the Elders. The more he thought about it, he didn't really know what he was going to say to them. He'd become so intrigued with just being in this majestic place that his purpose for coming had slipped his mind. He imagined the disappointment of failing at the only chance to stop a massacre of the entire impure human race. He felt the pressure began to build and his heart rate began to climb.

"Michael I've met a lot of impure and almost all the pure humans as well. Of all the beings I've met, both young and old, I must tell you if anyone can do this, you can. I have complete faith in you," she said, smiling.

Michael couldn't believe Lori's words. It was like she could read his mind and knew exactly what he needed to hear to calm his anxiety. This was just too much of a coincidence for

Michael to ignore. "Tell me, honestly. Can you read people's minds?"

Lori smiled. "No, I can't read anyone's mind," she said, still smiling as if she were hiding something.

"But..." Michael added.

"But I can read emotions."

"What?"

"Please don't feel violated. It's really no different than how your mom or dad can look at you and just know there's something on your mind. They may not know exactly what your thoughts are, but they can sense your mental frustration or concern. The biggest advantage to my ability is sensing someone's intentions. This is how I always knew you were a genuine person with a pure heart. It's also how I just knew you were becoming a little edgy a second ago. "

Michael was still a little confused but believed he was beginning to understand. "So you can sense fear, sadness, jealousy, and all that?"

"Yes, if I give just a little effort, but your anxiety a second ago was almost like a scent."

"A scent like a fart," he said chuckling.

"No, silly, it's neither a pleasant or unpleasant scent. But when the emotion is intense enough, I can sense it without trying."

"Can you sense when someone is lying."

"Yeah, that's what I meant when I spoke of people's intentions," she said.

"Does it take a lot of concentration?"

"It takes about as much effort as mentally doing elementary arithmetic. My ability only becomes challenging when it comes to simultaneously sensing multiple emotions."

"Okay, so what about this guy Richard then? Why couldn't you sense he was about to try and assault you? Or if you did sense what he was feeling, why didn't you just avoid the entire situation?"

"That's a good question with a simple answer. Fear. All I felt was fear from him before he grabbed me. I was actually expecting someone to need help when I sensed him."

"What did he have to be afraid of if he was about to commit the crime," he asked.

"Richard knew better. That's how I later came to realize he had a good heart. He knew of the pain he was about to try and inflict, because he'd been a victim himself. The fear came from the depths of his heart, where he knew the Creator was watching him."

"That didn't stop him though," Michael added.

"No, it didn't, but there's hope for those who fear Him. To fear the Supreme Being is to show that you believe in His power. Not only in the power of His wrath, but also in the power of His love. The fear of Him ever removing His watchful eye from over you, or His merciful protection from seen and unseen dangers. After a short time, I realized Richard had this fear."

"I see. Do all pure humans have this ability to sense emotion?"

"No. Just like impures, we all have our different talents. For example, someone may have the talent of speed so he or she trains and becomes a track star. Although there are some pure humans who, just as impures, have not yet found their talent. For whatever reasons, they're just not yet able to do anything special. Of course they're still stronger and faster than impure humans, but without any abilities. If you have a talent and it's discovered here, you're not put on television or become a rich and famous icon. You're given the privilege of being trained to carry out the righteous missions of the Elders."

"So being on a mission from the Elders is basically like being on a mission from God?" he asked.

"Exactly, the Elders are as close to the Creator as any being can be."

"Really. Who chooses the Elders?"

"The current Elders choose who will become an Elder."

Michael's face wrinkled up, trying to understand. "So what you're saying is that the Elders choose who will be close to God?"

"When you say it like that it does sound manipulative although you have to realize the Elders were the first to inhabit our village. They were given instructions from the Creator Himself."

"I don't mean to sound disrespectful to your beliefs, but I personally feel your own personal relationship with God, the Supreme Being, the Creator, or whatever you want to call Him, determines how close a person is to God. It's just a little difficult for me to understand the concept of believing I'm closer to God or not because another sinner says so. I prefer to fully put my trust and belief in Him, with no mediators."

"So you don't believe in the concept of priests?" she asked.

"I believe God has given purpose to every life. I also understand there are many people who rely on priests, and I won't judge anyone or any institution that promotes a relationship with God. I even personally know people I truly believe have been completely changed through their counseling with priests. But I personally prefer a direct and personal relationship with Him. Some people may see that as arrogant. I feel if God knew me before I was born and knows every hair on my head, then he must know and love me enough to speak back to my heart when I pray. And maybe priests help people to reach that personal relationship; I don't know God's plan. I can only speak on what I feel in my heart."

There was silence. Michael kept expecting Lori to say something back at any moment. The silence continued and Michael began to feel a sour twist in his stomach. He wondered if he'd said too much. Had he really insulted her entire way of life? Was this a perfect example of how he'd heard Americans called an arrogant people who try and force their beliefs on the rest of the world? His stomach twisted even tighter when he thought of how awkward he'd made it between Lori and himself.

Just when he thought he couldn't take it anymore, Lori broke her silence. "You're truly something special, Michael," she said, smiling.

"Really?"

"Really. I've been sitting here thinking about what you've said. My first reaction was how thought-provoking you are. Then I quickly told myself the enemy may use anyone and anything to shake your faith in the Creator. Although after a third thought, I realized you weren't trying to shake my faith in the Creator at all. You were actually trying to strengthen my faith in Him, while shaking my faith in man. Now I'm thinking of how surprised I am that someone with a fraction of my intellect could make me wonder as much as you do," Lori said as she looked over and smiled at him.

"Oh, I get it. I forgot just that quickly about your ability with emotions. You must've sensed I was feeling bad about what I said, and now you're trying to make me feel better about it."

"True," she said, smiling. "That's why I made the little joke about your brain's horsepower."

Michael found himself beginning to invest one hundred percent of his trust in Lori's every word. He felt her intent was always righteous. This gave his heart a feeling of security he'd never known in any past romantic relationship.

He tried to shake his emotions for the moment and focus on the task at hand. Learning whatever he could about the Elders from Lori was his only option. The more I understand them, the better I can communicate with them, he thought. "Has there ever been any bad pure humans?"

"You mean bad like super-cool, or do you mean like immorally bad?" she asked smiling. "Your culture is so funny."

"I guess that's a legitimate question." He couldn't help but to give a little chuckle. "But yeah, I meant immorally bad, like criminal."

"The Supreme Being did create us with His own hands, but that doesn't mean we're without sin. We're no different than the first of the pure humans you call Adam and Eve, who obviously both sinned."

"Okay, so how are pure humans punished?" he asked. "Is there a special prison built to hold them in your village?"

"No, actually the Elders have designed the military around them."

"What!"

"Anyone convicted by the Elders must be highly trained and used as sparring partners for the current soldiers," she answered in a lower voice. "Those who survive the training are given the privilege to fight on the front lines when the war begins. Those who survive the war will be given a pardon with a second chance to live in the New Earth."

"Of course I don't agree with war being waged on my people, but the concept is interesting."

"This has given us the fiercest, yet controlled, military in the world's history."

"Yeah, I'm sure, but how is that something to be proud of when there's already such a difference in speed, strength, and intelligence?" he asked.

"You have to understand, Michael. The pure human military doesn't use any tanks, battleships, aircraft, or any other type of machines."

"Then what are their weapons?"

"Like I told you earlier, I can sense emotions. There are many other pure humans with more offensive abilities. And as you just said, along with the difference in speed, strength, and intelligence, it won't be much of a war. Trust me, if pure humans used military machines instead of abilities, the odds would be much more in the favor of impures."

"This just keeps getting better and better."

"Really, that's good news?" Lori asked in a confused tone.

"No. That's just a sarcastic expression."

"Oh I see. Well I've tried to inform you as best I can, as it becomes relevant. Hopefully this helps you understand one piece of this puzzle before I move to the next."

"Yeah, this whole thing can be a little intimidating at times. And I thought this whole time I was just taking everything so well. Now I see it's really been your ability to sense when I'm becoming overwhelmed. So I guess when you feel I have a peaceful understanding, you hit me with the next piece of info?"

"For the most part, yeah. But after years of training and experience, all that has become mostly instinctual." She paused for a moment." You know you pick up on things pretty quick."

"Yeah, for an impure," he said, looking over at her.

"Michael!" Lori answered smiling.

Michael had been a little intimidated when she had first told him of her ability, but now he was beginning to believe it would be an asset in a relationship. If she could sense his frustrations and what made him happy or sad, then she could adjust. If all women had this ability, then there'd be fewer problems in relationships, he thought. Although some females he'd met enjoyed pressing men's buttons of anger and frustration. He considered women may feel if a man argues back, that shows if he cares or not. At any rate, he was relieved he'd never have to experience that with Lori.

CHAPTER 10
TERROR

After trailblazing for a while on no path, Michael was curious about how much longer they had before reaching her village. "Are we about halfway there?"

"We're almost to the point where we can't use a vehicle anymore."

"We have to travel on foot?" he asked.

"Yeah, there's a bit of a hike. We have to travel through a thick forest that surrounds my village. I'm sure I told you. That's why I reminded you to pack light."

"It's fine. I'm looking forward to stretching my legs a little after the flight and this ride."

After a short while, Michael could see what looked like thick black smoke reaching its way to the sky. As they rode closer, he could now see this was the dense forest Lori spoke of. The woods seemed to just keep growing and growing as they approached. Soon the sunlight was eclipsed by the massive trees and the edge of the forest looked like a bleak wall of darkness.

"Well, we're here," Lori said as she pulled up alongside what looked like the border of day and night. The grass was still high enough that it just about reached the bottom of the window on the SUV.

"This sure is dramatic," Michael said.

"What do you mean?"

"I mean this thick forest that almost completely blocks the sunlight. It's almost cliché-ish. Like you have to go through hell to get to heaven."

"It was once said angels stood watch here, protecting the purity of the Supreme Being's most beloved creation," Lori said, gazing into the forest.

"Do you think they're still here?"

"I'd like to think so, but the Elders have taken precautions just in case."

"What kind of precautions?" Michael asked as they climbed out the vehicle and unpacked their bags.

"Don't worry, as long as you stay one step behind me, you'll be fine," she said smiling.

"I don't like the sound of that. What if I was three or four steps behind you? What would happen? Are there booby traps?" he asked looking around the ground.

"Noh there are no booby traps," Lori said, giggling. "Just relax and enjoy our little journey together."

"Yeah, that's easy when you already know what to expect," he said, smiling.

"Just come on."

As they stepped through the tall grass and into the forest, again he couldn't really understand it but he felt as if he was doing exactly what he was supposed to be doing. He felt as if he was truly beginning to fulfill the purpose of his life.

The time seemed to go from afternoon to dusk within seconds of entering the woods. Other than the huge trunks of the overgrown trees and the greenest leaves he'd ever seen, Michael saw no other differences from any other forest.

He thought about asking Lori if he could carry her bag. Then he remembered how strong she was and flirted with the idea of asking her to carry his. He quickly decided against the joke. He figured he didn't want to take the chance of planting a seed of inferiority. He was fine with accepting her abilities, but he never wanted her to feel as if she *had* to protect or help him with anything a man should be able to handle.

About half an hour had passed and Lori hadn't said a word. Michael began to wonder if she was lost. He then noticed it had become very quiet. There was only the rustling of their feet crunching the dead leaves and twigs beneath them.

Listening even closer, he couldn't hear a single bird chirping in the trees. He looked up, distinctively remembering hearing a symphony of cheery tweeting when they first entered the forest. But now they alone were breaking the silence of the woodland.

"Where have all the birds gone?" Michael asked.

"What?" Lori answered as if she were pulled from a deep thought.

"I asked where all the birds are. There's not one chirping. I've never heard a forest this quiet before."

"You're right," she said and slowed her steps until she came to a complete stop. Carefully turning her head from left to right, Lori then circled around and looked behind them without saying a single word. Finally, she looked up as if she were expecting a storm.

"What's wrong?" Michael asked, searching her face for any sign of worry.

"Shhh," Lori replied before he could even finish his last word. She had a disturbed look on her face he hadn't seen before. The fact that she was uncomfortable on her own turf made him instantly alert. Michael could actually feel his fluids pulsing through him. He wondered if the flow was blood or adrenalin. Either way, he was more concerned with not looking frightened in Lori's presence than whatever it was that had her attention.

"Michael, before we take another step on this journey, you must realize something very important. And you may already know it, but right now you need to believe it. Just as clear as I can see your face right now, I can see that you have a pure heart. With that, along with your belief in the Creator, you must understand you were chosen by Him before you were born. Michael, I've said this only as a reminder that you are in this world but you are not of it. Do you understand?"

"Kind of, but why are you telling me this now?"

"Because right now you need to abandon all the influences this world has over you. Right now you need to open your mind to the fact that man cannot fully understand the extent of the Creator's power, or His plans."

"Lori, what are you saying?" he asked, feeling even more confused.

"I'm simply saying that you may see things here that defy the laws of man's nature. Just remember that man did not make this world, so don't consider everything you've ever heard or read as fact. Now, don't move," she whispered. "And don't speak."

It had now become so unnaturally quiet that he felt a sense of inevitable misfortune. He finally heard a faint sound high up in the trees. Michael looked up again to see a large dark shadow that seemed to be growing downward towards them. Before he could alert Lori, he felt a violent tug on his arm. His legs instinctively reacted, and before he knew it, he was running full speed to keep from being dragged by Lori. He was ten steps from his luggage before he even realized he left it. He was sprinting so fast that he couldn't draw enough oxygen to speak.

Immediately after they'd begun their dash, Michael heard a lot of loud crackling sounds followed by an earsplitting crash. He wanted to look back and see what was happening but even running at his fastest, he was barely keeping hold of her hand.

Lori finally slowed down and came to an immediate stop. Michael couldn't help bumping her a little coming to his halt. Not even two seconds after they'd stopped, he saw what his brain had trouble conceiving.

A huge two hundred foot tree had fallen out of the sky and crashed about twenty feet ahead of them. To Michael, the entire scene was happening in slow motion. He could feel the force of the crash beneath his feet as the vibrations rattled up through to his chest.

With his hand still in hers, she quickly led him up to the side of the mossy, overgrown tree. Michael noticed the tree's long roots on the bottom end. He shivered at the thought of what could be strong enough to uproot a tree of this size. Even worse, how did this tree get so far up in the sky to fall anyway? he thought. The toppled wooden mammoth gave them over nine feet of shield, yet they still they crouched down, facing one another. Lori brought her index finger up to her relaxed lips. Michael responded with a nod to show he understood the universal sign to not speak. He was waiting to hear more crashes, but again it was silent.

Michael didn't know what to think. His only objective at that moment was to stay alive by following Lori's every command. He totally understood how it was impossible for it to be raining trees but he had no time to quench such thoughts.

After a few moments of sitting in silence, Lori grabbed Michael's hand again and pointed behind her. She stood up and looked around before clearing the cover of the massive tree. Much slower and more cautiously, they began again.

Just as Michael was beginning to feel a little safer, he felt Lori's hand yanked from his. By the time he turned his head, he could just see her face disappear into a tree they had been walking past. Michael just looked at the tree, speechless. He was staring directly into Lori's eyes. Her entire body, except for her eyes, had been covered by the bark of the tree. He could hear her murmuring and knew she had to be having trouble breathing. Michael told himself to move and try to do something but he was too confused.

His body slowly began to respond but he paused again to think of what he was about to do. Do I try and tear open a tree with my fingernails? he thought. He had to try something; the look in her eyes was horrifying. The familiar feeling of heat began to ignite deep within him. Breaking free of his disbelief, he began reaching for the tree but was interrupted by an eerie, bone-grinding sound all around him. Finally deciding to proceed, he jumped to the tree and tried picking at the bark around her nose and mouth.

The bone-grinding sound grew so loud that Michael could no longer ignore it. He turned around to see himself being surrounded by hideous children in dirty togas with elongated heads. Their skin was extremely pale, and for little children they had bulging muscles. Michael saw their dirty lips pulled back, showing yellowish rotting teeth that seemed too big for their mouth. Their overgrown teeth were gnashing, making the intolerable bone-grinding sound. He couldn't help but to stare into their wide open bloodshot eyes that sank deep into their enlarged heads.

He felt the heat within him building. Michael was once again frozen in fright. He could feel his heart begin to beat faster when he saw the ghoulish-looking children began to scurry unnaturally faster towards them. There now were too many of them to count. Just as the young monsters were about to come into arm's length of Michael, he felt as if there were a flame in him about to explode.

"Kur-duh." The strong but calm voice came from beside Michael.

Michael looked over to see a man in a bright white robe, holding his left fingers up in some contorted figure.

The little beasts suddenly stopped and began to line up behind one another. Michael looked back behind him to see Lori standing peacefully beside a young teenage boy. She looked fine, except for the disappointed look on her face. By the time Michael turned back around, he saw the last three little monsters disappear behind a single child. This child's face was as clean and innocent as a sugary cereal commercial.

At that moment, there was a flutter of leaves and a female teenager dropped from the trees. Her face looked clean and harmless as well. She came and stood beside the young child.

"Thank you, Harold," Lori said, in a tone registering failure to the man in the bright white robe.

"English?" Harold asked.

"Yes please. For the benefit of Michael, the Prophesized One," Lori said, forcing a smile.

"Oh, that's right. I almost forgot," Harold said, turning to Michael with an outstretched hand. "Welcome, Michael."

Michael shook Harold's hand in routine reflex. He still hadn't gained enough of his wits back to even form a question.

"I can imagine this was probably a bit much for him," Harold said, looking at Lori, then back to Michael. "Are you alright?"

Michael rubbed his hands over his face and nodded.

"I'll explain everything, Michael, just relax," Lori said, gently pulling him down, inviting him to sit with her.

Harold sat as well then looked over at the youths. "Twenty minutes down time. At ease."

They sat and began to play and laugh as children do.

Michael began taking deep breaths, hoping what he saw were just some aftereffects of the drugs from the flight.

"This was a training exercise," Lori started. "There are no cell phones here, so there was no way to communicate that we were coming through the forest at this time. As I've told you, selected children begin training at a very young age to become agents. This forest is the perfect training field. It allows young pure humans to exercise their abilities without restraint. And as you've have seen, it also serves as protection for the perimeter of the Village. There are many different platoons of children. More than enough to keep the forest full, twenty-four hours a day. To the children, it's the best part of training. Like gym class is for most kids in school. Their target is any adult. High ranked agents are selected as targets by the Elders," Lori said, gesturing towards Harold. "Adult pure human agents are supposed to be strong enough to battle multiple children and still be victorious. This allows the children to push their abilities to their limits, while also exercising restraint in battle for the adult agents. The training helps adults with apprehending in the field without terminating the target. If an agent ever wants to be an Elder, he or she must never lose to any platoon of children. No matter how outnumbered he or she may be. This is because the children's abilities aren't fully developed yet. Of course, the older and more advanced children occupy the forest at night. And I also know how to pause the training, but we were never close enough to Ajanae, who was up in the trees. Then Don covered my mouth and restricted my hand movement. They're good."

"Thank you," Harold replied.

"How?" Michael asked, thinking he was still talking inside his head. Realizing he'd said it aloud, Michael tried to continue with the momentum of his returning speech. "How…how did they attack us? What was all that?" he asked, slowly beginning to recognize reality.

"The youngest one," Harold said, pointing. "His name is Paul. His ability is multiplying himself. We don't know how many he can produce yet, but his ability has matured already. At his age, he's considered a prodigy. The manifestation of his doubles normally match his own physical appearance but now they correspond with his mood. So naturally, when in battle, the appearance of his doubles is just as terrifying as the damage he intends to inflict. Outside the training of the forest, his doubles have never taken that form. When performing his chores, he doubles himself all the time and they all look as pleasant as he does now. So please, don't be afraid of him, he's really sweet. Next we have Don, who tactfully apprehended Lori. He has the ability to become whatever object he's in contact with at the time. He'd fused himself with the tree and pulled her inside his embrace. You should see what he does with boulders and walls."

"What about humans and animals?" Lori asked. "The tree is alive, so does that mean
his ability works on mammals and insect as well?"

"He has been prohibited from such attempts thus far. There's much to be considered before experimentations of fusion with mammals, insects, fish, and such."

"I understand," she replied.

"And finally, we have Ajanae. Most female agents are in the intelligence department, like Lori. But Ajanae's ability is so fascinating, not to mention she's repeatedly requested battle training. She relates to objects, just as Don does, but she can control the size of matter. Her most dangerous attack in the forest is shrinking enormous tress down to twigs then tossing them from the treetops as they return to their original mass. Another attack she's mastered is reducing boulders to pebbles and hurling them. These abilities are very dangerous. I apologize for the misunderstanding, Michael. Target agents are sometimes dressed like you, in plain clothes to see how the children's training will react to intruders. So they either thought you were agents or intruders. They're trained to relentlessly attack, regardless. I understand this is a bit much, but the Prophesized One should be able to handle it."

Michael opened his mouth to speak but his throat was too dry to produce any words. He swallowed and cleared his throat to speak once more. "I don't know if I'm this Prophesized One or not, but thank you for explaining. I'm still a little shaken, but I'll be okay."

Lori grabbed Michael's hand and said, "You'll be fine."

He'd purposely avoided looking at her. He realized why when he felt a tear escape his eye after she spoke. "I froze...I froze when you were in danger. When you needed me most, I just stood there, looking stupid," he said, still avoiding her face.

"No, you-" she attempted, but Michael interrupted.

"I'm sorry, Lori, please let me finish. I have to say this. I looked you right in the eyes and hesitated before I even attempted to help you. From this day forward..." Michael said, finally looking over at Lori with more tears sledding down his face, "I promise I will give my all to protect you. I don't care how much stronger, faster, or however superior you or anyone is to me. I promise if you're ever in trouble, I'll never again hesitate to dedicate all the strength in my being to keep you safe."

"I love you," Lori replied and tenderly kissed him, her eyes glassy with tears.

Harold looked on in astonishment. "I've finally seen it."

"Seen what," Lori quickly answered.

"Pure love," Harold replied. "And not the kind of love we all feel for each other but the kind of true love that two people feel for one another. I know the Creator loves me, but I've never seen that same love shown between two people until now. There's no doubt in my mind that Michael would die for you right now. This is the love that the Supreme Being has for us. You two have just shown me what I never thought I'd live to see. Why would the Creator not want us to show this love between one another? Why would He instruct the Elders to prohibit marriage between our people? I find myself both delighted and deeply confused."

Michael sat in silence beside Lori, with no clue of what to say or how to feel about what Harold had said.

"Thank you," Lori finally said.

"No. Thank you. I won't mention your relationship to anyone," Harold said, standing up and resuming his assertive tone. "It's time for us to recommence our training. I'll alert the other platoons of your presence. You shouldn't have any more incidences before you reach the Village. I hope to see you in the Palace," he said and walked past the children, who immediately stood and followed him.

Michael took a deep breath and sighed. "My brain still can't believe it, even though I can still see those little...ugly little monster kids. And I understand he's a sweet kid. I saw him innocently playing with the others, but those little faces, and teeth were...let's just say they should always try and keep him happy."

"Does this mean you don't want kids?" Lori asked, smiling.

"Please don't ask me that right now," he said, shaking his head. "Anyway, shouldn't we get going?"

"If you're ready. I was just trying to give you a little more time to recover."

"I just don't want to be in this forest at nightfall," Michael said, standing up. "I heard Harold say the more advanced platoons come out at night. If those were the elementary and junior high training sessions, I'd hate to be caught up in the high school and college shift."

"We should make it there well before nightfall," Lori said, smiling. "And even if we didn't, Harold said he'd alert the other platoons. We'll be fine."

"By the way, thanks for the heads up about everything," Michael said, sarcastically. "Really appreciate that."

"I knew that was coming and I am sorry. I tried to think of a way to tell you without your every step being in paranoia and sheer fear. I really thought I'd be able to pause the training. Ajanae was just too far up in the trees to heed to the command. Then I couldn't detect Don fused with the tree because I sensed we were already being surrounded by Paul and his doubles. It was just a chain of abnormal circumstances. And, like I said, they're good."

"I understand your intent but in the future please have more faith in me. Especially after this little episode. I mean, after this, anything else should be a piece of cake...right?" he asked, almost afraid of the answer.

"I will say that after this, you're well prepared for the wonders of my village."

"That's good enough."

"Some things you just have to see for yourself. If I tried to explain all the things in my village without you actually seeing them, it would only confuse you. Just understand there's nothing or no one who will harm you here. We were made to be people of love."

Was she trying to say impure humans were a people of hate and war once again? he thought. Even if she was, how could Michael argue that? Although he could understand the logic of her view on impure humans, Michael still wasn't comfortable with it. He just couldn't find the words to negate anything she was saying. Impure humans have waged war throughout history, he thought. He couldn't ignore the crimes of envy and hatred committed every day. Not even children are spared from such wrongdoings. He had no response for her insinuations.

"This place almost looks like pictures of a forest I've seen in Northern Australia," he said innocently.

Lori looked up at Michael with a stone serious face. "Don't speak like that, Michael."

"Like what?" Michael interrupted, anxious to know what he'd said wrong.

"Don't ever associate anything you see, hear, or smell here to any place at any time. Your words may be taken as

Pure Humans

evidence that you're trying to figure out this location. If it's determined that you have intentions of exposing my village, then you'll be either immediately asked to leave or permanently made to stay. And if you're asked to leave, then the way you were casually drugged on the jet will seem very considerate compared to your deportation experience. Every pure human, including myself, would be prohibited from ever having any contact with you. And that's *if* you're allowed to leave."

"Well, that would've been nice to know before agreeing to all of this."

"I would've told you, but the thought of you ever trying to expose our location never crossed my mind. I know you'd never have that intention in your heart but for those who don't know you and who are skeptical of impure humans anyway, any of those types of questions or comments may spark suspicion."

"I understand," Michael answered. "It would be like warning a foreigner of the death penalty in some of our states. If you don't suspect that person would kill someone then you wouldn't think of bringing it up."

"Exactly. I love how I can just talk to you and you easily understand me."

"Well, we do both speak the same language," Michael said with a chuckle.

"You know what I mean. You actually make the effort to put yourself in my shoes, to see what I see and understand me. Most impure humans are too busy thinking of what they want to say back, or analyzing for inconsistencies to listen with an open enough mind to try and relate to the other person's perspective. I wonder if we stay like this, is it possible we'll never have an argument?"

"Please…you're a woman. We'll argue eventually," Michael said and continued walking as if he'd said nothing wrong. After a moment of feeling Lori's eyes staring at the side of his face, he broke into laughter. "I'm sorry. That was a man-joke."

"So that's how men talk when women aren't around?"

"What kind of question is that? You expect me to break the man-code and tell you the content of our inner circle confidential conferences?" Michael said, laughing. "I'm sorry. I think I'm in such a good mood because I just escaped death."

Lori looked over to him and smiled. "I've often wondered if you were popular in high school. It seems like everyone would've liked you."

"Well, I had friends but I was never really in a clique. Most people were so busy trying to entertain each other, they were never *really* themselves. Kind of like how you'd find an entertainer is in his alter ego on stage. I was only comfortable hanging around a few genuine people in high school. They were good friends, but they also belonged in cliques. Of course they invited me to hang with their groups, but I would've felt awkward in a circle of guys with their own inside jokes and such."

"So you didn't have a group to hang with? That's so sad."

"No, it's not sad. Didn't you hear what I said? I was invited, but I just chose not to be in cliques for my own reasons," he said.

"Yeah, I heard you. But my words meant it was so sad you couldn't find a group of people worthy enough to enjoy your company."

"Boy, that was really good. Imagine the many different ways I could smoothly remove my foot from my mouth if I used my entire brain," Michael said, smiling.

"You manage just fine."

CHAPTER 11
DECEIT

As they continued to walk, Lori fell silent again. Michael wondered how long they'd go without talking. When it seemed to become too awkward for Michael to bear, he broke his silence. "You okay? You've been really quiet."

"There's a lot on my mind, Michael. There should be a lot on yours as well. The decisions we make here may alter the history of the world," she said, without looking at him.

"I understand. I guess a part of me is kind of hoping I'm not really this person that you and the Elders think I am. And then there's the other side of me that's at peace with whatever it is that God, the Creator, or the Supreme Being as you call him, will place in my path. I haven't always felt this way. But since all this has started, I only see two options. Avoid the entire situation and go on with my life as a coward in my heart; or face any obstacle I may come across as a mission that He's put forth for me to accomplish." As the words fell from his mouth, Michael felt himself gaining even more confidence.

Lori looked at him this time. "I can feel your words are coming purely from your heart. It's your heart, Michael. Your pure heart that has brought me to believe you're the Prophesized One."

"And if I'm not, I understand you'll be disappointed. But will you be disappointed in me as a boyfriend too? I guess what I'm asking is will you see me as less of the man you see me as now? And of course I know it's easy to just say no to the question, but please think seriously about what I'm asking. "

Lori turned her head away from Michael as if she were ashamed of her face.

"What's wrong? And don't tell me it's nothing this time," he said in a stern voice.

"Michael, I know what I'm doing is right but why do I feel so wrong about it?"

"What!" Michael said, seeing she'd begun to cry.

"Michael, we know it's you. The Elders have been watching you since birth. So you need to know within yourself that you're not a normal impure human."

"Lori, what are you saying?"

"I don't have time to explain it all now, but understand you are the Prophesized One. There may be ears in the forest amongst us right now, the Village is just ahead. I promise I'll explain it all later, but I couldn't go any further without at least telling you that. Please be patient until we have a chance to talk again in private."

"How can you tell me that and then just tell me to be patient? You expect me to just act as if everything was the same as it was two minutes ago?" Michael stopped walking and looked Lori right into the big beautiful eyes that always captivated him. "I'm not taking another step until you tell me exactly what it is that I'm walking into. These beings, or whatever they are, have been watching me since birth? What are they going to do with me here?" he asked in an aggravated tone. "And what about you? Your mission has been to get close to me so you could get me here? Our entire relationship is a lie. All that, what's the odds that we would meet, was just part of your mission? How could you do this to me when I trusted you?"

Lori wiped the tears from her eyes but they kept streaming. "Michael, I know you may not have much reason to continue to trust me but please understand the feelings I have for you are very genuine. Everything is as I've said before, except that we've known you're the one prophesied to come here. And they've been watching over you since birth, ready to protect you from enemies you weren't even aware of. Please continue as before. No one will do you any harm, Michael. You have my word. But please understand, the fate of impure humans is truly in your hands. That fact has not changed."

As upset as he was, he just couldn't help but to think, what if she was right. Even though he knew he'd just as easily been misled before, he was considering her words. Still, it was a tough hit for Michael to accept that Lori would be a willful participant in plans that included misleading him. "What would happen if I demanded to be taken back home?" he asked.

"As I said before, the pilots will only fly on direct orders from the Council of Elders themselves. I'm sorry, Michael."

"So I really don't have a choice?" he asked, looking away.

"If you could go back home, would you? Could you just go back to school and act as if none of this is happening? You think you could really sleep at night, knowing at any minute an army of pure humans could begin their attack? An attack you possibly could've prevented."

She'd made a good point, he thought. As uncomfortable as this trip was becoming, he couldn't just turn his back now. Not after everything he'd seen although he couldn't help feeling as if he was being played. He wanted to call everything off, but was more curious about just how deep the rabbit hole would go. "Okay, Lori, you win. I'll see this through. But I expect you to sit down and tell me everything you know at the first opportunity. And I mean, everything," Michael said in a firm voice.

"That's all I'm asking. Thank you, Michael," she said as her eyes continued to overflow and sparkling tears streamed down to her perfect chin. "Please don't lose faith in me, or us, yet."

He wanted to comfort her, but he had no idea of how the rest of this would unfold. The more he thought about it all, the more betrayed he felt. His imagination began to race in a million different directions. Questions piled up in his mind, one after another. He couldn't continue like this. I have to have a clear mind to deal with this situation, he thought to himself.

"I understand you're upset with me, but I just have to say you continue to impress me, Michael. I can feel you getting control over your emotions and becoming more focused. You're even stronger than I thought," Lori said, trying to clear the traces of her tears.

"You're right. I am upset with you. But I'm also focused. Perhaps even more focused than I was before. And I'm trying to tell myself you have a good reason for not being completely truthful with me. So it better be good."

"I don't know if it'll be good or not but it'll be the truth. I never want to feel the way I do now again," she said.

"That's enough of that conversation for now," Michael said changing the subject. "It looks as if we're nearing the end of the forest. I believe I can see a clearing ahead."

"You can see the clearing?"

"Yeah, why?" he asked.

"Nothing, it's just that's still pretty far. I can barely see it."

The sun's rays began to shine brighter the closer they came to the clearing. Michael could see the beams of light streaming down through the trees as if golden javelins had penetrated the earth. The clearing was so bright that leaving the forest felt like they were coming out of a dark cave.

They stood at the top of a hill from which the splendor of the inland was displayed. As he took in the scenery of the Village, Michael sighed at the beautiful simplicity of this foreign lifestyle. He saw that even though there were trees scattered throughout the Village, the trees surrounding the Village were much larger. Their massive size and number seemed to serve as an obvious perimeter of protection.

The rippling landscape complimented the largest hill, where a magnificent fortress sat. Beneath the hill sat many huts that were very neatly made. Michael could see these huts were made of dried mud, sticks, straw, and grass. These semi-primitive homes had been so well crafted that the scene resembled an undeveloped tropical resort.

There was a small river flowing right through the middle of the Village. Michael could see through the river's crystal clear water to the white sand underneath. There were trees with some kind of robust fruit Michael had never seen before and the grass was so lusciously soft and green that Michael felt like he was walking on someone's well-fertilized lawn. There was only one thing that struck him as strange about the scene.

"Where are all the people?" Michael asked.

"Again, this is a pretty big deal for my people. I'm sure once Harold spread the word that we've arrived, everyone has gathered to formally greet us."

"Let me guess. We're headed to that fortress up on the hill," he said, pointing.

"We call it the Palace. It's where all pure humans are raised. When a certain level of maturity is reached, we're kept for missions or given a choice; we can become an infantry soldier or a civilian living here in peace."

"Does that level of maturity have anything to do with the pure human's ability, or lack of?"

"Again, you catch on pretty quick. Most of the people living outside the Palace are those whose abilities are nonexistent or just weren't seen as useful to the Elders as the others."

"So everyone who has a *worthy* ability lives in the Palace?" he asked.

"Of course it sounds like a segregation of class when you say it like that, but living in the Palace means you're constantly going away on missions. Some can be quite dangerous, even for pure humans. In fact, some pure humans living in the Palace at times envy the carefree life civilians have out here in the open air of the Village."

"Really. That's like saying you prefer camping in a tent over living in a home," he said, smiling.

"I'm just glad to see you can talk to me without holding anger in your heart."

"It's like I said, I trust you'll have a good explanation and tell me everything later. So until then I'm just playing it cool. I mean, what other choice do I have? Sure, I could get all upset but how would that help. I'd just start heating up again. And since there's no time to go through it all right now, I'll just be patient until I can hear the entire situation."

"Again, I couldn't ask anything more from you, Michael," she said in a very humble tone.

They followed a wide trail that led to the bottom of the large hill, where the Palace sat atop. Michael could hear the birds again. He looked up to see there wasn't a cloud in the perfect blue sky. As they approached the center of the Village, he noticed some of the dwellings were larger and more detailed with structural designs. Some were just a little bigger and then others were impressively massive.

"What determines how grand a person's home can be? Is there a certain amount of space allotted for each person?" he asked.

"Our system is actually quite simple. There's no limit for anything. All that's needed is an agreement with your neighbors on either side. Some people choose to live further back in the outskirts of the Village, where they can have more privacy. Others choose to live closer to the center of the Village, where they have more convenient access to the river and the company of more people."

"So there's no need for currency here?"

"No. The simplicity of the Village is what we plan to bring to the New Earth. There's plenty of food and water for everyone. Only love and honest work are needed here. Someone's home will only be as nice or as spacious as the amount of effort that person is willing to sacrifice. The larger homes take months to finish."

"Aren't women at a disadvantage? I mean, since men are naturally stronger than women, wouldn't they have larger homes?" he asked. "It seems this would cause a separation of class by sex."

"If another pure human female heard you say that, they might believe you were sexist."

"How? I honestly thought what I just said was in the best interest of the women here."

"I understand that, but first let me help quickly explain something else about being here. You should never preface anything you say with words *like honestly, sincerely, or I swear.* This implies you may not be honest whenever you don't preface your statements. It is written and believed here to let your yes be yes and your no be no," she said.

"Point taken."

"And second, you have to understand these are pure human females. They're faster and stronger than any of the impure females you've known all your life. Some women actually have larger homes than some of the men. For example, this one is the home of a female," Lori said, pointing up at a nicely-decorated and noticeably larger home than the others around it. "The smaller homes around it were made by men."

"I stand corrected," Michael confessed.

"Now also understand the men do tend to finish quite faster than the women and probably with a lot less effort but, nonetheless, a woman can live just as a man can if she's willing to put in the time and effort."

"So what's the reasoning behind the prohibition of marriage?" he asked.

"We're forbidden to mate until we've inherited the New Earth. Of course I don't agree with it but it really makes sense when you think about it. Can you imagine how many children a couple can have who live to be over eight hundred years old? Now imagine six hundred couples. The possible exponential numbers would've probably overcrowded the Village long ago."

"So there are twelve hundred pure humans?" he asked.

"That's a rough estimate of the pure humans here in the Village. This doesn't include the number of us out on missions throughout the world. Only the Elders know the total amount of us walking the earth."

"If this is too personal just say so, but if marriage is forbidden until you've inherited the New Earth then every pure human is a virgin?"

"Yes. Every marriage will be overseen by the Elders. This means the marriage isn't truly final until stained bed sheets are provided to show purity. No pure human would dare break this law."

Michael figured this was yet another major reason for them to be eager to inherit the earth. *If I had to remain a virgin then I'd probably be impatient too,* he thought.

Michael noticed an area in the distance, aside from the homes with an assortment of boulders. There were huge chunks of rock, some about six feet tall, others down to the size of a beach ball. They were organized as if they were used in a game of some sort. "What's that area over there?" he asked, pointing to the boulders.

"That's a workout area," she answered.

"With those big boulders? What can they do with those? The *smallest* piece over there has to be a couple of hundred pounds."

"With the larger boulders, the object is to get it rolling pretty fast then run ahead of it and stop it. The mid-sized stones are tossed between two people standing about eight to ten feet apart. The smallest boulders are more for speed and strengthening. The workout with those includes throwing the boulder as far as you can, then running to catch it before the stone touches the ground. I've also seen sit-ups done while holding the smaller stones overhead. I'm sure there are other exercises the boulders are used for, but those are the ones I've seen."

"So that's the true strength of pure humans?" he asked in disbelief.

"Remember, these are the pure humans that the Elders have chosen not to use on missions. Those chosen to remain in the Palace are rigorously trained in ways you couldn't imagine. Those stones are child's play."

Michael couldn't help but to imagine the absolute slaughter of mankind if war was initiated by these beings. So much brute strength, unreal speed, and the highest intellect possible. He remembered Lori telling him of their infiltration on the corporate level. He figured they wouldn't stop there. If true power is in the government then surely they have pure humans in political positions, he thought. This would mean even the military could possibly be compromised.

"We're almost there," Lori cheerfully announced.

Michael could see a courtyard ahead that sat at the bottom of the largest of the rolling hills. Now he finally knew where everyone was. There seemed to be hundreds of people assembled in the courtyard, lined up in perfectly tight rows. They all wore immaculate white robes and stood painstakingly still. No one in the disciplined crowd made a sound. In the midst of so many people, the only noise Michael heard was his own breathing. He could see the steps leading up to the Palace at the back of the courtyard. Looking closer, he saw even more people lining both sides of the steps. He had failed to notice this before because their white robes were camouflaged by the white steps behind them. Their robes seemed to be even brighter than those who in the courtyard. He looked up to see the trail of people lead all the way up to the top of the hill where the Palace sat.

Now even closer, Michael saw each person was holding a small oil lamp out in front of them, and they all stood with their heads down. "Is all this for us?" he asked.

"Actually it's all for you. They've all seen me before."

"How long have they been holding those poses and waiting for me?"

"That's not important right now. Just stay focused. This is a historic event for us," Lori whispered as they approached the first step.

Michael noticed Lori had stopped at the steps. "What's wrong?" he asked.

"Nothing is wrong. You are to go first and I'll follow. This is how it has to be. Don't worry. I'll be right behind you," she said, smiling.

Michael turned around and took a deep breath. He started up the steps and suddenly saw light arise on both sides of him. He looked to see the flames on the small oil lamps had grown to a blue blaze that was almost blinding to look at. He simultaneously heard thunderous cheers, which raised all the bowed heads. He looked back at Lori, who was smiling at him with a single tear that made it half way down her face before she wiped it off.

"That's just confirmation you are indeed who we've been waiting for," she shouted out to Michael over the ovation.

Michael tried, in vain, to hide the feelings of confusion and flattery from his face. He turned back around and continued up to the steps, where the next two oil lamps grew big blue flames, just as the last. The cheers continued with each step he took. He wondered if this could all be some kind of hoax. Maybe there was a switch or something on the lamp which fed an accelerant to the flame. Either way, at this point, he decided to see this thing through. There was no turning back now. Just as Michael began to feel the steps seemed endless, he could finally see they were nearing the top. Amid the continuing cheers, he glanced back to see Lori was still two steps behind him.

At the top of the steps, Michael saw five men awaiting him at the entrance of the Palace. A sizeable pair of magnificent pillars lined each side of the path to the giant golden doors. The faces of these five figures seemed to be just as excited as everyone else. Michael assumed these were the Elders he'd heard so much about. They actually only looked to be in their mid-fifties. He had been expecting long white beards and bent backs. Instead, he was surprised to see their bodies were very well kept. They all had the appearance of retired bodybuilders who'd stayed in shape. Their barely-wrinkled faces gave a wise impression that complimented their muscular stature. The almost deafening cheers began to fade as Michael came closer to the Elders. He noticed their robes were the brightest of all.

Michael expected to be a bit nervous at this moment, but he wasn't. He figured it was because now he was on the defense from what Lori had alerted him to. Although here and now, he didn't care why. He preferred to be focused anyway, rather than the anxiety he was expecting.

"You truly are the one we've been waiting for," one of the Elders said in a friendly voice.

"We've longed for this moment for centuries," a second Elder declared.

"Michael, welcome to our home," another said with a warm smile.

One Elder stood apart from the others. Michael realized this Elder's robe was brighter than everyone else's. When he looked even closer down the line of Elders, Michael saw that all their robes slightly varied in their shades of brightness. The brighter robes didn't seem cleaner, just more brilliant. He figured this must be the head Elder and the ranks must coincide with the different shades of their garments.

"Our language is very ancient," the Elder with the brightest robe began. "Even the true name of the Village, which has been kept secret, has never been translated from our language so for now the Village will do just fine. And our names would take much training with your tongue to even come close to the pronunciation. So, just as Lori has done, we've adopted American names to help us in our interactions. I'll answer to Max. We have all agreed to speak English to make your stay more comfortable. I'll introduce you to the others after you've rested. I understand this may be a bit much to take in all at one time. I hope Lori has been an adequate guide and ambassador."

"Lori has done her job beautifully," Michael said, glancing back at her. "Executed perfectly," he said with a smirk before turning back around. "I feel very privileged to be allowed into this place of wonders. And I look forward to our conversations."

"You must be exhausted from your journey. We've prepared quarters for you to rest and bath here in the Palace. Please, come this way," Max said, extending his arm towards the elegant entrance of the Palace.

As they entered the atrium, Michael was fascinated by the beauty of the fortress. There were obviously no construction machines or even electricity here. How could a civilization completely off the grid engineer such a fortress? he thought. It seemed to be ancient yet there were no signs of deterioration. The ceilings were high and arched. Almost everything was the color and texture of ivory with gold accents. Even the flooring seemed to be an ivory and gold colored marble. "I must say, your Palace is stunning," Michael said as they turned down a long, wide corridor.

"Thank you," Max replied. "We've remodeled over the centuries to reinforce the stability and beauty of the Palace. Piece by piece brought in by plane from locations around the globe. We're very proud of our engineers."

Michael heard something in Max's voice that he just couldn't put his finger on. He thought it was vanity at first, but he didn't feel as though he was being talked down to or treated inferior in any way. Although he appreciated the warm welcome, he wouldn't let his guard down.

There were small torches set on each wall of the luxuriously spacious hallway about twenty feet apart from one another. It reminded Michael of streetlights in the city.

"I apologize for any inconveniences you may have experienced on your journey here. Our village is sought after by so many that precautions, which were never even considered in the past, have become necessary. I hope you understand," Max said.

"I may not have agreed with the sedation but I do understand it. Although I do have one concern about that," Michael said, as he came to a stop and looked Max right into his hawk-like eyes. "I don't know if I feel like a guest or a threat to you. I've been received with such a warm welcome, but what has changed from my sedation till now? I mean, how has your trust grown for me? There may be people present right now who may feel I could somehow expose this beautiful place. And at the same time I'm being told that everyone has anxiously awaited my arrival. I'd just really like to know where I stand with everyone."

Max looked over to Lori, then back to Michael. "I'm very impressed. That's a very sharp analysis. Of course I'd expect nothing less from you, Michael. And to answer your question, you're correct. Until now, we didn't know for sure if you were the Prophesized One or not. There are a few of us who've insisted that you were, but we had to know for sure. Of course you saw the small flames grow into a blue blaze when you started up the stairs of the Palace?"

"Yes, I did," Michael said, anxious to hear the explanation.

"It has been prophesized that there will walk amongst us a being so powerfully favored by the Creator that when a murderer's blood is in his presence, it becomes flammable. The oil that fed the flames you walked by was mixed with droplets of blood from the fiercest murderers who have never shown remorse. The blue flames were the confirmation we needed. That's why you heard the cheers. This isn't the first time we've welcomed in a stranger but it is the first time we have not been disappointed. Our intentions are nothing but honorable. We have indeed awaited your arrival for centuries and now that you actually stand before us, we need a moment to gather ourselves and prepare for the next step. Which also gives you time to rest and relax before your destiny is unraveled."

Michael slowly turned and continued down the corridor. "So a murderer's blood becomes flammable in my presence?"

"Yes, but of course the catalyst is the oxygen in the air. The blood must be exposed to air, then it'll react to even the smallest spark," Max responded.

"Of course," Michael said sarcastically, as if all that made perfect sense. But there weren't any smiles in response, except for Lori. Michael's peripheral vision caught the partial smile that could still give him butterflies, no matter how hard he tried to fight them off. "I didn't mean to sound rude, Max. Thanks for taking the time to explain that to me."

"And everything else will also be explained to you very soon, Michael. And from what I've seen so far, I believe you'll indeed be strong enough to handle the information and application. Until then…" Max said with a smile as they came to a stop. He opened the door to Michael's quarters and gestured for him to enter.

Michael smiled and thanked him again as he walked into the room prepared for him. It looked like a room out of some Disney fairytale movie, but he was okay with it. The closer he looked, he thought maybe the Disney vibe was just from a vale that hung from the bed's canopy. There was a mounted mirror above a large basin that looked to be for bathing. Michael figured he'd seen enough clips of old western movies to figure it out. He was surprised at how comfortable the Palace was in comparison to the upscale huts of the rest of the Village. They even have big fluffy pillows, he thought.

He turned to see if Lori would be available to stay a bit with him, but just as he was turning around, the door was shutting. His tattered luggage stood neatly against the wall just inside the door. I figured my luggage was crushed by those giant falling trees, he thought. The footsteps outside the door quickly faded, leaving him alone in silence.

He turned back to the glowing light of dusk from an arched window. The window was positioned between the basin and the bed, and had no glass or screen. He figured the canopy was a net for the insects. The hilltop view of the Village from the window was magnificent.

Michael felt this was truly a beautiful place, better off without all of the technical advances he was accustomed to. There were no power lines or sounds from car engines and horns. The air was incomparable to what he'd smelled and breathed his entire life. And for all his suspicion, Michael couldn't help but admit to himself this was a much more peaceful and modest society than his own.

Michael hadn't realized how tired he was until he approached his bed. He took a seat and sank into a comfort that put the bed in his dorm to shame. Maybe even his bed back at home as well.

Michael had been playing it so cool with everyone but now, finally alone, he began to wonder what was really going on. Is this real, he asked himself, lying back with a long sigh. Are they trying to manipulate me for some reason?, he thought. He figured if they wanted to harm him, there was no need to be so polite now. He was already in their possession. Michael searched himself for what they might want from him. But he didn't have anything. These people can obviously get anything they want. He wasn't important. He had no abilities. And he still just couldn't figure out why Lori didn't tell him the full truth from the beginning.

He felt himself beginning to panic and took a deep breath. He closed his eyes and reassured himself that if he hadn't come, he would've regretted it for the rest of his life. So let's just hang on for the ride, he told himself.

CHAPTER 12
A NIGHT OF CELEBRATION

Michael opened his eyes to find Lori standing over him.

"Hey," she said with her signature smile.

"What's going on?" Michael asked, wondering how she had just appeared out of thin air without a sound.

"I thought you might want to talk now. Unless you need more rest."

"More rest?" Michael asked, realizing he was in a totally different position than he was in, what seemed to be, just a second ago. It was completely dark outside and there were torches lit on both sides of his room.

"Yeah, you've been asleep for the past nine hours."

"Nine hours?" he said in disbelief.

"Yeah, silly. I've come to check on you twice. You look so boyishly cute when you're sound asleep."

"Are you insinuating that something happens when I wake up? Like as soon as I open my eyes and expression falls on my face, I'm not attractive anymore?" Michael asked, checking his face for dried drool.

"That's exactly what I'm saying. If you were a sleepwalker, you'd be the perfect boyfriend." She smiled just a little, then looked down. "Can I still call you my boyfriend?" she asked, without looking back up.

Michael's thoughts were so focused and clear now; he didn't realize how mentally fatigued he must've been. He was happy to have his mind so sharp when he needed it most. "By my definition of a girlfriend, no, you're not. I lost my girlfriend in that forest, where I left those feelings."

"Michael-"

"No, please let me finish." Michael interrupted her in a low, but direct tone. "My definition of a girlfriend is someone that I can trust. Someone who confides in me, as well as I in her. A woman I can laugh and joke with while dropping all my guards. These things should be present in the friendship stage and grow even stronger at the next level. You've destroyed our foundation. I feel like you had this motive to get me here before we even met while the entire time, I was just looking so foolish. Falling for that adorable face, fully equipped with the angelic smile. And let's not forget those innocently seductive eyes; I mean I never stood a chance. You were perfect for this mission. What man could say no to such apparent purity? And now…now, I'm trying to tell myself you must've had your reasons. So, depending on this conversation, maybe we can rebuild a new foundation. I don't know. It's in your hands now. But a really good start is telling me everything. I mean, total disclosure. Even things the Elders may not want me know." He looked up at Lori to see her eyes were glassy, and about to erupt into a waterfall of tears at any second.

"First, let me say I totally understand your feelings and I appreciate your honesty."

"I promise you honesty, even if it hurts you," Michael replied.

"I see. And for some reason that attracts me to you even more…despite the pain."

"That's just guilt, it'll pass," he said, smiling.

Lori smiled back. One of her eyes had reached its limit and tears began leaking down her face, but she paid them no attention. "My mission was to bring you here, this is correct. I was also told to befriend you. Not to seduce you. The feelings that I have for you, I have of my own volition. I have not had feelings for any of the others."

"Others. What others?" Michael asked in confusion.

"Remember earlier, when Max said this wasn't the first time we'd welcomed in a stranger. He said your arrival was the first time we haven't been disappointed?"

"Yeah, I remember that."

"Well, I've brought three potential candidates here from America. There was no problem like this with any of those guys. Of course my ability allowed me to feel their attraction to me, but I never encouraged those feelings. Even if they were physically attractive, there was nothing in any of them that mentally stimulated me. You've made me smile from the first day I caught you looking at that girl in class. I can read your emotions, yet you still say and do things that incite me. Pure or impure, I've never met anyone like you. And for those reasons, I'll tell you everything I know."

Michael looked over her shoulder to see if the door was completely shut.

"Don't worry about privacy. I'm still your designated guide. Besides, I can sense anyone's emotions well before they would enter. Now listen carefully. It has been prophesized that a being from outside the Village will come and usher in a new way of life for pure humans. It is also said that the blood of those who have murdered will ignite in his presence and his power will be unmatched by any mortal."

"How would I have any power? I'm telling you this guy can't be me."

"The Prophesized One is also of human and spiritual blood."

"Human and spiritual blood? What does that mean? A spirit had sex with a human? So now I'm half spirit and half human?" Michael said with a chuckle, though he could see Lori was very serious.

"A spirit in the flesh," she answered.

"How can a spirit be in the flesh?"

"There's been at least one written account of a man wrestling with an angel. If a man can wrestle an angel, then why can't an angel fall in love with a woman and consummate their love?"

"You've been saying that all this has been prophesized, but by whom? Where is all this coming from?" he asked.

"There's a very powerful Elder who has the gift of prophecy. Her ability has been challenged many times, and has never failed. This is how we knew the blood in the lamps would ignite the flame."

"Well if that's her ability, then why have you gone through so many others before you found me? Wouldn't she know exactly when I'd show up?"

"All of our abilities have their limits. She can only see what the Creator allows her to see. Nothing more, nothing less. Now if she's telling us everything that she sees, we may never know but she is yet to be wrong," Lori declared.

"You said she, but all I've seen are male Elders."

"There are seven Elders, but two are out on missions. There's the army general, and though he's hardly ever here, he's the most powerful Elder of all. And then she's the only female Elder amongst the pure humans. Her ability of prophecy was too powerful for her to not be given an Elder seat."

"So, according to her, my biological father is an angel?"

"The actual prophecy was that the chosen one would be of spiritual and human blood. The child of an angel and a human is our interpretation," she answered.

"I'm sorry, but considering angels and people having sex just seems like wrong thoughts," Michael said, confusion on his face. "I mean, how can a spiritual being have sex with a physical being? It just doesn't sound possible."

"I know you're not calling anything impossible after what you've been through today."

"Good point," he said.

"And like I said, if angels can make physical contact to wrestle, then why can't they be physical for love?"

"I would guess the angel was probably under orders. I'm sure angels have never just gone around wrestling random people," Michael said, grinning.

"So, maybe your spiritual parent was ordered to love your human parent. I don't claim to know the Creator's intentions. What I tell you now is all that I know and believe."

"So if all this is true, then you guys really have been watching me since birth," Michael said, feeling a cold chill run up his back.

"I've never personally watched you but there are records of all the children given up for adoption then those records are crossed with hospital records. Every child has some kind of minor injury or sickness that requires some form of medical treatment. But not you, Michael. Of course, the other hopefuls didn't either, but again their presence didn't ignite the blood in the lamps."

"Okay, but I still don't understand how you'd know the Prophesized One would be an adopted child. I mean, if all this is true and I'm so important, then why would my mother give me up?"

"She didn't," Lori said in a very somber voice.

She didn't even have to say what happened; Michael could see it in her face.

"Childbearing is dangerous for any woman," she continued. "But giving birth to a child with spiritual blood is said to take every ounce of strength that a mortal can muster. In those critical moments, only one can survive. The mother decides if she'll give up or give her absolute all. That is the sacrifice necessary for yielding such a powerful being. For the mother to survive would literally take a miracle. I'm sorry."

"And all this time I've resented my biological mother. I've grown up believing she just didn't want me for some reason. I'd always thought she left because there was something wrong with me. And this may sound funny, but I even thought I must've been an ugly baby. And now to know that she had to die for me to be born is ..." Michael sighed and looked out the glassless window. "She sacrificed herself for me while this whole time I've held deep resentment for her. But why would my adoptive parents lie to me? Maybe I'm not this Prophesized One. I don't have any powers, and I don't believe Debra and Drake would lie to me about my biological mother."

"Maybe they didn't lie to you. Maybe they were just telling you what they'd been told. The Elders haven't only watched over you, they've also protected you. Michael, there are rogue pure humans that have gone off on missions and never returned. Then we learn of tragic reports that could only be the work of these rogue pure humans. Their goals are unknown, but their focus has been to foil any of the Elder's plans. There are even some pure human agents who've been specially trained and commissioned to apprehend rogue agents."

"Wait. So they fight?" he asked in astonishment.

"Yes, and with them both having powerful abilities, it can get ugly."

"What happens to rogues after they're apprehended?"

"They're given a trial before the Elders. The charge is treason, so if they're found guilty, the penalty is death."

"So if these rogues have turned against the Elders, then why don't they just expose the Village? Obviously the Elders consider their private seclusion extremely important. Wouldn't that seem to be a logical tactic for the rogues?"

"Yes, we've all had the same fears. Our only explanation is that they're waiting for the perfect time. We presume exposing our location may be a calculated phase in their master plan."

"So what do these rogues have to do with me?" he asked.

"All the rogues know we've awaited your coming. Capturing or even killing you would've been a major victory for them. So understand that the truth about you and your mother is valuable information. These details have been concealed from everyone to protect you. So I'm sure your adoptive parents haven't lied to you about her. They probably just didn't know."

"What about my mother's family? Was there no one from my family willing to take me in? No grandmother, uncle, or aunt?"

"I'm sorry. I can't speak on your mother's family. There's nothing I've heard in the prophecy about them."

"I understand, but I still don't have any abilities. This Prophesized One is supposed to be so powerful, but I can't do anything special."

"The prophecy says that his might will be shown upon his arrival. So we will soon see if all this has been in vain," she said.

"You really believe it's me? Even after I froze up like that in the forest?"

"If I was to go down a checklist, you'd have every item checked off. And if that alone wasn't enough, then I'd still know I've never felt this way about anyone. And it's not just because you're cute. You have the purest heart I've ever sensed from any another human, pure or impure. That has sealed the deal for me."

"I see, " Michael said, shaking his head. "My kisses have totally made your judgment too biased," he said, finishing with a smile. "So what's next?"

"Well, we meet with the Elders tomorrow morning, so we have tonight to entertain ourselves. I think we deserve a little time off to enjoy ourselves. When I was in training here, I'd sneak out the Palace and join in the festivities of the people down in the Village. Are you game?"

"Sure, but what if we're caught? I'm not as fast as you or anyone else here for that matter."

"Don't worry. I'm your guide, remember. It's really just an extension of your tour. There's no rule or law we'd be in violation of. We can just walk out the front door. With the exception of field training in the forest, it's the trainees who aren't allowed outside the Palace after dark."

"Were you ever caught?" he asked.

"Many times."

"What happened?"

"Imagine a football player who gets disciplined with a double morning practice. Then a double primary practice after school. And then after studying, another double night practice."

"What's a double practice?"

"It's just what it sounds like. You do everything you normally do twice. And our training makes football practice look like golf. It's excruciating."

"So you were a bad girl?" Michael asked with a smirk.

"I wasn't considered a problem. It was just the curiosity of what I was missing. When it was quiet, I could hear all the fun they were having outside the Palace. The sounds pulled me to my window, where I could see their faint lights in the distant night."

"Why weren't you allowed to wander outside the Palace?"

"The Elders said there was no need to make friends outside. We were told it was pointless, since we'd soon be leaving on missions anyway. Nevertheless, I indeed made good friends although I haven't seen them in years. I miss them," she said, in reflection.

"Sure I'll go. Check out the Village nightlife, yeah," Michael said, trying to hold back his slowly-returning feelings for her. He believed she'd finally been honest with him, but he wasn't sure if that was enough to open his heart again so soon. "Just let me wash up and change clothes."

"Okay, I'll be back in about thirty minutes," Lori said, and smiled.

As the door closed behind her, Michael thought he saw someone eavesdropping from the hall. Did she allow someone to hear our full conversation, he thought, as he rushed to the door. He swung it open to see two very muscular men. One stood on the left and the other on the right of the entrance to his quarters. They turned towards him simultaneously. Both men were well over six feet, towering above Michael.

"How may we assist you, sir?" the man on Michael's left asked.

"What's wrong, Michael?" Lori, who was only about ten feet down the corridor, asked.

Michael now understood these were his own personal guards. He still couldn't help but wonder if they'd overheard any of their conversation. "I'd like to ask you a question in private, please," he said, looking back to Lori.

The guards resumed their poses and Lori returned to his room. He closed the door behind them and walked her over to the other side of the room at the window. "Have they heard our entire conversation?" he whispered. "I thought you could sense a person's presence through their emotions."

"Michael, you'll have to trust me. They've been there the whole time. I've constantly felt their minds focused on nothing but keeping you safe this entire time. If one of their intentions would've shifted from protecting to inquiring, even for a moment, I would've detected it. Besides, I outrank those two by so much that I could have them collecting animal poop from the forest. I have friends in the Village who need fertilizer," she said, giggling. "They wouldn't dare pry into my affairs, not to mention those of the Prophesized One. So just relax and get ready."

"Okay, I'll see you in a few," Michael said.

As the door closed behind her again, he began to wonder if he was being too paranoid. After all, he was really at the mercy of their society anyway. What could he possibly do if they were manipulating him? he thought. Who could he call? There were no phones. Once again, he was forced to tell himself to just play it cool. He figured if all else failed, he still had his charm.

Michael couldn't help but to laugh a little to himself. The thought of angels having babies was a little farfetched; especially when he was supposed to be the baby. But with what his own eyes had already seen, he couldn't totally dismiss the thought either.

He felt a little insecure about bathing with two men right outside his door and no shower curtain. There was no lock that he could see from the inside. So since a relaxing bath was out of the question, Michael undressed and squatted in the basin. His hands moved in flurries as he spread soap over himself while keeping a steady eye on the door.

After finishing, he had one foot out of the basin when he thought he still felt some soap on his thigh. Michael looked down to see an insect the size of a small bird on his leg. He frantically jerked and swung at it, missed, and smacked his own leg violently. He instantly lost his balance. Michael's other leg was still inside the soapy basin and couldn't help him. His naked body fell hard onto the unforgiving marble floor. "Owww," he cried, rubbing his knee and hip in a puddle of water.

Michael looked up to see the large insect fly out the window just as the two guards rushed in. The two giants looked as if they were ready to battle whatever adversary they'd face in Michael's room. Then their expression quickly changed from excitement to confusion.

Michael looked up at the two soldiers and lost all his dignity. "You missed it. I had a little scuffle with a giant mosquito or something, but it retreated. So I guess I won," he said, trying to ease his embarrassment.

The two guards didn't take to the humor. He saw a sincere disappointment in both their faces. Their stares penetrated Michael's comedic shell and made him deeply ashamed. The soldiers turned back to each other with defeated faces and left the room. Michael didn't know what to think. He'd begun to feel an entire civilization of people was depending on him for something he couldn't deliver. Part of him kind of wished he did have powers and could help everybody; another part of him was still suspicious of their actions and motives. And the rest of him was just still trying to get a grip.

The last thing Michael needed was for Lori to walk in and see him lying naked on the wet floor. That would just be a perfect addition to this day, he thought. He got up, cleaned, rinsed off, and got dressed. Shortly after, he heard a knock on the door.

"Come in."

Lori entered, comfortably wearing her customary white robe. Michael thought if New Yorkers could see her, they'd beg her to model for a new and more attractive Statue of Liberty.

"You ready?" she asked.

"Sure, let's do this."

"I know there should be some type of celebration tonight for your arrival, although they won't be expecting you to show up. They'll be so surprised. You're really like a celebrity here," Lori said, smiling.

"Yeah, I just hope I don't let everybody down."

"Don't worry," she said, rubbing his shoulder. "You were born with a destiny. A destiny you control, Michael. You are who you choose to be. Remember that…no matter what happens."

"Thanks, that's pretty good advice." Michael was ready to get his mind off all this and just have a good time.

As they started past the two guards, the entire incident replayed in Michael's head. He walked past them as if nothing had happened. Neither of them said a word either. Lori and Michael continued back through the remarkable palace to the entrance.

"So what happened between you and the guards?" Lori asked, grabbing a torch from the wall.

"What?" Michael asked, startled. He quickly figured the guards told her what happened before she knocked on the door.

"Come on," Lori said nonchalantly as she lit the torch and handed it to Michael. "It's customary for a man to hold the torch. Kind of like an umbrella," she said, smiling. "Now why were you and the guards so embarrassed to see each other?"

Lori's ability had totally slipped Michael's mind. "Well, I tripped over and fell. They heard the noise, came rushing in, and saw me on the floor. That's why we were all embarrassed. They're expecting me to be this powerful leader and I'm tripping over furniture," Michael reluctantly admitted as they started down the long palace staircase.

"All right. But for the kind of embarrassment I felt coming from you guys, it's like they saw you naked or something," she said, smiling.

Michael looked over at Lori to see if she was joking. Then she suddenly looked up at him and started laughing. "I'm sorry," she said, laughing even harder. "I had no idea." She paused to laugh some more. "Until I mentioned naked and you got even more embarrassed."

"You see. Now right there, I wish I had powers to level the playing field. That wasn't fair. If you were an ordinary woman, you would never've found that out."

"Forget about it. Laughing is just one more thing I enjoy when I'm around you," she said, still giggling.

The night air was perfectly cool and, ironically enough, the moon was so full and bright, the torch wasn't really needed. The twilight atmosphere was dreamlike. The stars looked like giant sparkling diamonds that could fall at any moment.

"Has your journey been everything you'd thought it'd be so far?" Lori asked.

"It's actually been much more than I thought it'd be. The palace, as well as this village, is just so beautiful. And everyone has been so nice to me that I can't help but to feel welcome here."

"That's good, because you haven't seen anything yet," she said with a smile.

Michael could see the glow of lights ahead. He wondered how they could have a celebration without electricity.

"When we arrive, I'll tell everyone you're relaxing tonight. I'll ask them to keep their distance so you're not overcome in a sea of people. Kind of like a V.I.P. area. I should also inform you that only those pure humans who were trained in the Palace can speak and understand English. Those out here in the Village only speak our native tongue. Although, as the Prophesized One, they'd probably expect you to already know our language. It's been forbidden for impure humans to even hear us speak it."

"Well, if I'm not an impure or a pure human, then what am I?"

"Something else. Something special," Lori answered.

"Oh yeah, I get it now. That really explains it all. Thanks for the detailed explanation."

"Maybe sarcasm is your power," she said, smiling.

"You realize you've just used sarcasm to make fun of my sarcasm, right?" Michael said, grinning.

"You see, this is what I mean," Lori said, with a newfound enthusiasm. "I can't just talk with anyone else like this. Of course we talk about important issues, but I like how we can also have silly little conversations like this. Can you feel what I'm saying or is it just me?" she asked.

"Yeah I understand, but you kind of ruin it when you call it out like that," Michael said with a chuckle. "I mean, we both know it's there, but you almost take the mystique from it when you bring it up like that." He looked over at her with a smile to check her reaction.

"Why do you sound as if you're joking, but I sense you're neither joking nor fully serious?"

"It's because I'm joking about the truth. This concept may be a bit complex for you, even with your fully-operational super brain."

"Okay bright boy," she said, smirking. "Would you mind waiting right here while I let everyone know you're coming?"

"It's cool, I'll be here."

"I'll be right back after I find a place for us."

"All right," Michael said, giving her the torch.

Lori smiled and walked off, leaving Michael alone in the pale moonlight. He walked over and took a seat under a large tree just off the grassy path. He looked up at the sky and tried to take Lori's advice and just have a good relaxing time tonight. He couldn't help but notice the strange fruit dangling from the tree branch. It was almost pear shaped, but what caught Michael's eye was the texture. The fruit seem to have small spikes growing out all around it and as if that wasn't enough, he looked closer to see it was almost a florescent-blue color. If it weren't for the spikes, the fruit seemed edible. This reminded Michael he hadn't eaten since he'd arrived.

At that moment his imagination began to run wild. He remembered how Lori said this was the geographical place of the Garden of Eden. Could this be the fruit that…no it couldn't be, he thought. He struggled to see if he could spot a serpent slithering around the tree's branches in the twilight.

"Michael," a voice whispered.

Michael's heart dropped as he considered the impossible.

"Michael," the voice repeated. "Are you alright?"

He turned around to see Lori, standing on the path. "Yeah, I'm fine. You came back awfully fast," he said, laughing at himself.

"What were you doing?" she asked.

"You wouldn't believe me if I told you."

"Try me."

"Sorry, this one is really embarrassing. I'll tell you what. After all this is over, ask me again."

"I hope you don't think I'll forget. I can't imagine what in that tree was causing the bewilderment I felt from you."

"Why were you whispering?" he asked.

"You looked like you were concentrating. I thought maybe something was wrong. I just didn't want to startle you."

"Anyway, are we ready?" Michael said, trying to quickly move on.

"Yeah, come this way," Lori said with a suspicious smile.

Michael followed her past a couple of huts to where he could see a meadow ahead. There was plenty of light coming from the area but the voices he heard earlier had all been replaced with silence.

Just as they came over a slight incline on the path, Michael could see numerous white robes lined on both sides once again. Another burst of cheers and screams erupted from all around them. Michael couldn't even hear himself think. He walked in a combination of excitement and anxiety. Up ahead, he could see of a pile of mid-sized boulders. Michael and Lori made their way through the sea of white robes and took a seat amongst the surprisingly comfortable rocks. Michael just continued to smile and nod, occasionally waving and feeling a little presidential. It took about two or three minutes before the crowd settled down. The cheerful multitude seemed to be dispersing into assigned areas.

Now that words could be heard again, Michael leaned over to Lori. "So what's all this?"

"Our version of a party. Just a little song and dance. Except the song and dance is actually about you."

"What do you mean?" he asked.

"Since it won't be in English, you should know the song is about how long we've all waited for the day of the new beginning. It's about patience and faith during the hard times. The dance symbolizes the transition from our past way of life to our rebirth and inheritance of the earth."

"Not to belittle that or anything, but will there be any food? I'm starving."

"Yes, there will be bread served shortly. I'm sorry; I ate while you were asleep. I came by to see if you wanted to join me but you were in a mouth-wide-open sleep. I tried to wait but when I came back, you were still comatose."

"I'll be fine. So where does the music come from with no electricity?" he asked.

"Just watch, they're about to start now. It would be considered very impolite for you to speak during the celebration."

Michael looked up to see a portion of the mass had assembled a small distance from them across the meadow. The crescendo of sound that Michael heard was mind-boggling. He knew the extraordinary harmony was coming from the collection of white robes about one hundred and forty yards away, but the melody seemed to be in stereo. Being outside, he knew there were no acoustics so he was baffled at how a sound coming from one direction could totally surround him. Soon he was so hypnotized by the beautiful voices that how he was hearing it became irrelevant. It made no difference to him that he didn't know the words. Each voice was like an instrument. Since instruments don't use words, Michael felt as if he was attending a symphony. Which was strange, Michael thought, since he figured he'd never enjoy a symphony.

Just as he was really becoming consumed in sound, the dancing began. The combination was breathtaking. The movements were beyond graceful; the fluidity of their turns and sways were unimaginable. There were so many of them yet they were perfectly synchronized with each other, as well as the choir.

Michael began trying to coordinate their movements with the story Lori told him earlier. Until now, their movements had seemed very soft and refined. Now he noticed a stronger and more emotional style of dance. Then his skin suddenly erupted in goose bumps. Both men and women began jumping high into the air, reaching almost ten or fifteen feet. They were so high it almost seemed as if they were flying. He was even further impressed with how effortlessly they were springing and landing from such heights. Just at the peak of their implausible leaps, their refinement appeared to be suspended in slow motion.

Michael's eye caught an attractive woman soaring through the air with hair and features similar to Lori's. He tried to look closer but lost her in the beautiful sea of swaying white robes. He turned his head to see if the real Lori was enjoying the celebration, but she was gone. In her place was a plate full of sweet-smelling bread. Ignoring his hunger, he looked around for a moment before he finally realized the woman he saw dancing was actually Lori. He'd been so mesmerized by the performance that he hadn't even noticed when she'd slipped away and joined in the festivities.

The tone of the choir changed simultaneously with the style and mood of the dancers' movements. Michael had to look close and hard, twice, to fully understand exactly what was happening before him. At first glance it seemed as if everyone was disappearing, then reappearing again in slow motion. Telling himself this was impossible, he looked a second time. This time he could see how they'd move blindingly fast, then come to a seductive slow twisting of bodies. He marveled at the extent of self-control needed to appear so sensual, yet avoid any collisions. Michael was visually astounded. He couldn't find Lori amongst the others but it didn't matter. He was truly being entertained.

Soon the choir began to fade their singing and joined in the hypnotic dance. The scene was even more intriguing to Michael in silence. The celebration appeared to have peaked.

There were a few unidentifiable words everyone harmonized before they all began cheering again. This time Michael stood and joined in the applause.

He finally recognized Lori again. She'd separated from the crowd and started towards him. "There are no words for that," Michael shouted over the cheers, still in disbelief of the exhibition.

"I told you that you hadn't seen anything yet," she said in delight. "You didn't even eat any bread. You didn't like it?"

"No it's not that. I just got so caught up that I wasn't even worried about food anymore."

"I'm happy you liked it. This is a perfect time to get back to the Palace," Lori shouted back. "Like I said, you're a celebrity. If we stay any longer, people will start trying to meet you. Once you meet one person, then you have to meet everybody. And I do mean everybody."

"Alright, but I really enjoyed the performance. You guys do that all the time?"

"Often enough. Do you maybe want to eat on the way home?" Lori said, picking up the tray of bread that hadn't been touched.

"Sure. With all the excitement my stomach forgot, but it remembers now," Michael said, grabbing a roll of bread. It was still soft after sitting out for so long. He took a bite and was surprised at the sweet taste. "It's almost like cake," he said with crumbs falling from the corners of his mouth.

"I knew you'd like it," Lori said, leading him behind the boulders. "There's a way through back here. That way we won't have to pass by everyone again."

"We won't need a torch?" Michael asked, still eating.

"The torch was really for you. I can make it back with my eyes closed and I doubt we'd lose each other in this moonlight."

With the exception of Michael chomping away, there was silence for a moment. He finished his piece and looked over to Lori. "I wish I had your ability right now. I'd love to know what you're feeling."

"Why don't you just ask?"

"I guess that kind of was my way of asking."

"Well, I know we agreed to just have an evening free of all the emotional weight this entire circumstance involves but tomorrow you're meeting with the Elders and I don't know how much time we'll have to talk alone after that," she said.

"So this is our only time alone before it all goes down and you want to give me some last-minute pointers? That's cool, but can I get something off my chest first, please?"

"Sure, go ahead," she said, looking over at him.

"The way these people live out here isn't right."

"What do you mean? They love it out here. I even wish sometimes that I had grown up out here under the stars," she said, looking up.

"Lori, if Max can arrange to have that extravagant palace up there, with piece by piece being flown in, then he can also have materials flown in to make real homes for these people."

"All right, but like I said, they're happy with the way they live."

"Have you ever asked them? I mean, really sat down and talked to them about their living conditions? If they had a choice, I'm sure they'd choose to have better materials to build with. Okay, I understand I have an outside looking in perspective, but this is a clear case of separation by class. Since these guys' abilities aren't special enough, they have to live outside in huts while those whose abilities are deemed worthy are allowed to live in the luxurious palace. We're talking about how they were born. People can't help that."

"Michael, you're not seeing the full picture. Max cares for the people of the Village. Whenever they have any problems, Max helps them in any way he can. I've seen it with my own eyes."

"I'm not saying he doesn't keep them alive, I just…" Michael stopped to take a deep breath and regain his composure. "I'm not saying this isn't a beautiful place. I wouldn't even mind spending a relaxing weekend in a hut just to get away from all the technology and smog. But that wouldn't be acceptable as a way of life. Maybe this is just why some foreigners don't like Americans. Maybe Americans are just always trying to push their values on other cultures. It's just that so many people have fought and died for equality in my country. Maybe that's why, when I see segregation here, it disturbs me so much. In America anyone born in the poorest home in the poorest neighborhood of the poorest city can work hard and become successful. They can literally go from a shack to a palace. These people don't have that chance. No matter how hard they work, Max has already chosen a destiny for them. You guys are collected and analyzed then separated and used for the will of the Elders."

"Michael, I can sense your apprehension towards the Elders and even a little towards me. Just let me say that I know this has been overwhelming for you. But please understand as I told you before, the Elders are the closest to the Creator. They explain His will to us."

"And you follow them as if they were the Creator Himself. You didn't feel anything at all on this mission? There wasn't anything tugging at your heart, telling you something wasn't right? Listen, Lori, the Elders are human. Pure or not, they're still human. And just like you, they may have been made from the hands of the Creator, but there's danger in blindly following anyone who encourages lies, concealment, or murder."

"Murder! The Elders are not responsible for any murders," she said in a louder voice.

"Maybe not, but you're familiar with the terrorist attacks in America, right? Particularly the tragic destruction of the World Trade Center in New York, on September 11th?"

"Yes, of course," Lori answered.

"Okay. Well, these suicide murders have caused so much death and pain that no one would believe these terrorists were righteous men. I know I don't. But the terrorists themselves did. These men were convinced the will of Allah was to murder innocent civilian men, women, and children. Now all I'm saying is there had to be something tugging at their hearts. Something had to be telling them killing innocent people was wrong. You yourself told me the Supreme Being is pure love in its simplest and greatest form. I believe, deep in our hearts, we all know that. So since when is murder part of love? When did concealment and lies become attributes of love? And just as those terrorist probably did, you felt in your heart that this wasn't right yet you chose to carry out your mission anyway. You chose to follow man, who dwells on earth instead of following the Creator, who lives within you." Michael looked over at Lori to see her looking away from him, into the night.

"I don't believe you're evil. I'd never believe you could murder anyone. But look at the situation from my point of view. In order for the terrorist to even get on board those planes, there had to be lies and concealment. And that's what the Elders did to get me here. Now, what would be so different if the Elders decided to wage war on impure humans because they believed the Creator wanted them to? Or, even worse, if they've grown impatient and taken it upon themselves to decide the time has come for their inheritance of the earth. I don't know, but this is a very delicate and dangerous situation. This is why you sense that I'm apprehensive."

Lori finally turned towards Michael to reveal a face full of tears. "Michael, there's never any need to explain your intent to me. I've always felt nothing but the best intentions in every word you've spoken to me. And as ironic as it seems, that's what hurts. It'd be easy to dismiss your words if I could sense even a hint of resentment behind them. But as you speak now, your heart is as pure as it's always been. That forces me to consider your words as truth. And when I do so, my reality begins to crumble. Michael, this is everything I've ever known. The Elders are like parents to us all. If I choose to believe you then my entire world changes and everything I've ever done is in question. Or I just disregard the obvious truths you've mentioned and risk living in ignorance."

"I'm sorry," Michael said, with his head down. "I guess I hadn't really thought of any of that. And even though I shouldn't, I feel guilty for putting you in such a position."

"Michael, you should never feel guilty for exposing the truth. What if that's the real reason you're here? If you can make me have second thoughts, then maybe you really can convince the Elders to reconsider their motives. I still believe they fear the Creator."

"I remember when you said something similar to this back in America on campus. I said something about not have any powers, and you said maybe I'm just supposed to convince them not to wage war on impure humans. Do you remember?" he asked.

"Yes."

"Thinking about it, I just have to know. Did you believe it at all back then or were you just saying what it took to get me here?"

"As bad as it sounds, it was both," she said humbly.

"How could it be both?"

"Well, she prophesized that you'd come to usher pure humans into a new way of life although the prophecy never gave details on how you'd do it. We've trained all our lives for overtaking the earth so I guess I made it right in my mind by telling myself that if you convinced the Elders not to attack pure humans then that would indeed be a new way of life for us. Even though, at the time, I thought it impossible to change what we've believed for centuries. And Michael, please understand this is all in hindsight. At the time I was on my mission, these weren't my conscious thoughts."

"So basically this was one of those things you felt tugging at your heart but you unconsciously tried to make it right within yourself."

"I believe so. And I have to say that looking deep within yourself and analyzing what you find is not pretty," she said.

"Don't be too hard on yourself. You were being misled. Most people are deceitful without being misled especially since I can see how you look at the Elders as parents. They took you in and cared for you, just as my parents adopted, loved, and nurtured me. I can relate to feeling grateful and even in debt to those who take on the responsibility of raising you from birth. "

"Yeah, but you were right. I still should've listened to that voice inside tugging at my heart. I felt it just like you said, but I chose to let my fear of disappointing the Elders drown out that voice. Since birth we've been told the Elder's actions represent the Creator's intent. It's hard for any of us to imagine otherwise, even when I've been given immoral orders."

"Part of learning from the past is leaving it there. You take what you need to grow from past mistakes and leave all the feelings of guilt and shame behind."

"I don't believe I'm learning from someone who is a hundred years younger than me." Lori sighed, with a smile.

"Well, if words are my ability, as you say, then I'm not responsible. I'm just a tool for the Supreme Being. There's no way I'm smarter than you, so my words must come from Him."

"When you say it like that then I have no choice but to agree with you. At least about being a tool."

"You know if you were anyone else that would be a pretty sly joke, but I know you didn't mean it like that," Michael said with a confident chuckle.

"Like what?" Lori asked.

"Like nothing. Really, I shouldn't even have said anything. It's not worth the time to explain."

"Okay…"

Michael was happy they had this talk. He felt closer to Lori after understanding her point of view. He wished the Palace was much further away so they could have more time to talk. He could just barely see the top of the shiny fortress above the trees. "Let's just say we do make it through all of this. Do you know how strong the bond of our friendship will be?"

"So that's it? Our bond is just friends from now on?" Lori asked in a disappointed tone.

Michael stopped and grabbed Lori's hand. He grabbed her by the waist with his other hand and kissed Lori without warning under the pale moonlight. Startled at first, Michael felt her submit and they continued passionately. He didn't want to be the first to pull away, and she showed no signs of stopping. Suddenly an unnaturally strong gust of wind blew past, reeling them back into reality. "I trust you," Michael whispered.

"I feel tingly all over," Lori said, trying to regain her poise.

"Yeah, if we were in a movie that would definitely win best kiss at the Academy Awards."

"We should get going," Lori said with that iconic smile Michael hadn't seen in a long while.

Still holding hands, their walk became a romantic stroll back to the Palace. They took their time getting back to Michael's quarters. He wasn't surprised to see the guards still posted at his door but he couldn't help feeling their eyes on him as they entered his room. After closing the door, they indulged in another fiery kiss.

"Speak from your heart and don't be intimidated by their might," Lori said, looking into Michael's eyes. "I believe in the power of your words. Use them as if the Supreme Being Himself has given them to you as a sword and shield."

"If I do pull this off, it'll be because of you." Michael kissed her goodnight one more time. "I'll see you in the morning."

She smiled and walked off into the torch-lit corridor. Now with Lori in his corner, Michael felt much more confident about whatever he'd be facing in the coming day. After talking to her, he at least felt as if he had a game plan.

CHAPTER 13
INEVITABLE CONFRONTATION

The next morning he woke up to the sound of a sparrow perched on the edge of his window. He opened his eyes to the bright ray of sunshine that flooded the room. Michael remembered thinking he'd have trouble falling asleep but he actually felt great. He wondered if Lori would come and escort him to breakfast. He bathed and dressed in anticipation of seeing her comforting face. Michael went to the window and looked out across the Village once more before he heard a knock on the door.

"Come in," Michael said.

"The Elders are ready for you, sir," a voice answered.

Michael assumed he had a new guide because Lori had other duties to tend to. He opened the door to see a totally different guard. His garment was the same style as the other guards, except the color was a deep luxurious maroon. Michael followed him around a few corners and down another corridor into a massive hall. There were large paintings on the walls, sculptures, and a massive table in the center.

The five Elders Michael had met the day before were spread around the rectangular table. There were seven chairs. One seat was set at the head and another at the foot of the giant table, then three on one side, and two on the other. Max sat at the head of the table while the other four sat on the sides. Michael reflected on the conversation from yesterday, when he was told of two Elders out on missions. He wondered which of them sat at the foot of the table. Probably the woman who prophesizes, he thought.

Michael continued to follow the guard until he was led to the foot of the table. "Good morning, everyone. Thank you for such an honorable seat," Michael said as he sat down.

"It is a very good morning," Max said with a vibrant smile. "In fact it is the best morning of any of our lives thus far. We missed you at supper."

"Ah, yes. I'd like to apologize to everyone. Apparently I was a lot more tired than I thought."

"Did you sleep well, Michael?"

"Like a baby."

"Sorry to hear that," Max replied.

"Sorry to hear what?"

"I'm sorry you slept like a baby. Most babies wake up every few hours throughout the night, crying. I'm sorry you've had such a restless night."

"No, actually I slept fine. That's just an American expression for good sleep."

"I know, Michael, I was just making fun of it," Max said with a smile. "That's just one of the many things I don't understand about your culture."

"Well, if it makes you feel any better, now that you've brought it up, I don't understand it either," Michael said, smiling back.

"Yet you said it anyway," Max quickly replied.

Michael wondered if this was some kind of intellectual test. He'd barely sat down and he was already being drilled about the validity of his small talk. All the other Elders were watching closely and analyzing his every response. I'd better stay on my toes, he thought. "Yeah, that's probably why they're called expressions. I don't have any children yet but I imagine when a baby does finally sleep, there is a peace that finally falls on the entire home. Not to mention how beautifully serene an infant looks asleep. They're called expressions because they simply express how we feel. They're not to be taken literally."

"I understand. Well said. Shall we begin? First, do you fully understand why you're here?" Max asked.

Michael didn't want to expose Lori for anything she may have told him against their wishes. He decided to play dumb. "Well, first there was an earthquake back on campus in Arizona. Then I saw on the news how strange things were happening all over the world. That's when my friend, Lori, told me this could be the end of the world as we know it. Then she suggested that maybe I could help in some kind of way. She said she didn't know how, but you guys would. Now, I admit her story was a little hard to believe but I figured if she was crazy then so what. But if she was right, well I'm here to do whatever I can. I also have to admit that my love of travel influenced me, as well as Lori's charm." Michael ended with a smile.

"That's a good enough start," Max answered. "But first let me tell you I have my doubts. Even though you set the blood aflame, I pictured the Prophesized One to be a bit older, somewhat more experienced in life. Maybe even a little bigger in stature. I only see a child sitting before us. The Prophesized One has a role of major leadership. I don't understand how you're supposed to lead anyone."

Michael wondered what happened to the polite and seemingly humble Max that he'd met yesterday. "Well I never expected to be leading anyone either. Is there a problem with the leadership now?" Hearing his own voice, Michael knew these were bold words. But since Max started the game of hardball, Michael wasn't going to back down.

"No, there's nothing wrong with the leadership now but the prophecy holds a much higher precedence than my pride as leader."

"So if I may ask, what exactly is this prophecy?" Michael probed.

"Well, as you may or may not know, all pure humans in the Palace have abilities. One Elder, who is missing here this morning, has the ability to see what is to come. She has compiled her visions into different prophecies. And there's one that's very important to the future of our people. This same prophecy is, strangely, related to your life so far. You have never had a broken bone or been sick. You were born of a mother who died during labor. You'd be surprised at the number of people who match this exact same criteria but you've been the first to ignite the blood of murderers. That's the only reason we're sharing this privileged information with you."

"So you've watched me since my birth?" Michael asked as if he didn't already know, being careful to protect Lori's disclosures.

"Yes, we have, Michael. You, along with others. The prophecy says that an outsider will usher pure humans into a new way of life. Michael, the Creator has promised us the inheritance of the earth. The time of impure humans is over. We believe the Prophesized One will lead us in attaining this inheritance. Of course, you can see why knowledge of this information can be undesirable for impures so you're the first being from outside the Village to learn of this."

"So what you're saying is that my role in all of this is to lead your army of pure humans into battle against the rest of the earth?" Michael asked calmly with a disturbed look on his face.

"Not exactly, we already have a general to lead our army. As a matter of fact, you're sitting in his seat as we speak. Your role is a little different. Our agents have already infiltrated many major governments across the world. Our influence is already felt throughout several political arenas. But you…Michael. You are the one. You're the one who is said to perform great works and gain the favor of man. You're the one who shall have them all at the mercy of your words. You will persuade men to follow you. It has been your destiny to come here. It is your destiny for us to collaborate."

"I'm confused," Michael said, scratching his head. "I don't even like politics. I've learned in my short time here on earth that you can never make everybody happy. But that's exactly a politician's job. No politician can stand firmly on his or her views. If they want to be re-elected or move up the political ladder, then they have to compromise. They have to get votes or contributions from people they may not agree with, or even like. I'm sorry but I don't see myself in politics."

"That's exactly why you may be the one. People can see through the same old political game nowadays. They thirst for someone fresh and new. Someone just like them. A person who says something and sticks to it, no matter what. Even if it means their downfall. It's called principles, Michael. You will bring principles to the political arena. You will find most people will rally behind you just for that alone. The world thirsts for such refreshing beliefs as yours. And when you face a controversial issue they may disagree with you on, they'll re-evaluate their own values to support you. You will lead as we see fit, for the glory of the Creator. And don't worry about the credentials, son. We have more than enough power to put you in the top seat."

"Okay, now let's just say I did rise up in power. Exactly what would you have me do? If you really want me to be a part of this, then I need to know what the plan is."

"All right, fine. I won't sugarcoat it anymore. The future of impure humans has already been decided. It was not my decision, but that of the Supreme Being Himself. No matter what religion or race, they all believe the same outcome. That's the simplicity of it. They already know they're doomed. They expect it. We're merely the tools of execution. And Michael, you have one of the most vital roles in this preordained re-habitation of the earth. You will give them their last days of happiness. You see, the Creator is not without mercy. With our help, you will end world hunger. You will balance major budgets of countries in massive debt, such as yours. And after saving the people from their economic crisis, you will then use the money to cure terminal diseases that have plagued impure humans for centuries."

"I don't get it. I mean I know I don't have the pure human intellectual abilities of you guys, but how would helping impure humans advance your goals?"

"Simple, Michael. After everything you'll have done for impure humans, they'll trust you. Even more than that, they'll love you. And when the moment is right, Michael, they'll even worship you. When that time comes, then you will unify the world to your order. From that point on, you will enjoy power and wealth as you have never dreamed."

"And what of the people who refuse to serve me under my new world order?" Michael asked.

"Michael, this is a war ordained by the Creator. There are casualties in every war."

"And the impure humans who decide to worship me?"

"No harm will come to them. They'll become servants of pure humans. This is their destiny. We're to be the inhabitants of the earth. Impures have had their time. And look what they've done with it. There's been war across all continents, war between nations, and, my personal favorites, civil wars and genocide. Impures are killing each other, killing the animals, even killing the plants which give off the oxygen they breathe. Now tell me, Michael, is it a crime to kill a murderer? Osama Bin Laden, who killed thousands of men, women, and children, was killed by your American soldiers. Was that a crime? I'd personally consider those brave individuals heroes. Would we not be the same? Would we not only be taking what's rightfully ours anyway? You seem like a logical man, Michael. Where is the flaw in the logic of our inheritance?"

"Well, first of all, Max, you don't inherit anything until someone dies. And killing or enslaving a person, or better yet a species, to inherit anything is criminal. The flaw in your logic is using logic. You don't know the Creator, Max. If you did, then you'd know that He is love. Pure and simple. And anyone who has loved knows that logic does not apply. Logic and love are like oil and water. After someone you love does something terrible to you, it's illogical to forgive them. Logic says to disassociate yourself from them to avoid further pain and disappointment. But love is forgiveness. Love is faith. Love is hope and encouragement. And most of all, love is patience. Not a single word that has fallen from your lips this entire conversation has displayed any of these qualities."

"Such a strong tongue," Max said to the other Elders with a smile. He stood from the table and began pacing. "I'm beginning to believe in you more and more, Michael. Let me shed some light on a few things you may not realize. Every day we allow impure humans to hold dominion over the earth is a show of patience for us. Do you not realize our power?" Max said, raising his right arm into the air. With his hand in a tight fist, the wrinkles in his forehead pushed his eyebrows down into a distraught expression.

Michael saw the rest of the Elders rising from their seats as well. They took steps back towards the walls of the great room, leaving him alone at the enormous table. Michael heard Lori's words in his head. "Don't be intimidated by their might."

Max smirked and opened his hand to reveal a flickering flame in his palm. The flame quickly matured into a basketball-size fireball. The deadly sphere shot from his hand into the air towards the ceiling. Max raised his left arm half way up on his side and the fireball sailed down around the room before returning to his left hand.

He then raised both his hands, and the entire room was covered in flames.

Michael was petrified yet he stood his ground. He just kept his eyes fixed on Max and refused to move a muscle. He needs me alive, Michael told himself.

After about two or three seconds, Max dropped his arms and the flames immediately dissolved. "Creation and total manipulation of fire," Max said, while the entire room cooled in light smoke. "Do you not understand we can devastate entire civilizations at will? As I told you, we have agents in place around the world. At my command, they have the power to overthrow governments as we speak. Yet we have not. Why? Because, Michael, we have exercised patience," Max said in a very stern voice. "For centuries we have exercised this same patience you say we lack. Do you even understand the amount of humility needed to take the time to explain our centuries of patience to someone who has barely existed two decades?"

Although Michael was doing an excellent job of concealing his emotions, he was truly intimidated. Not only could Max conjure fire with his bare hands but his control over the flames kept himself and everyone else from being harmed in the blazing room. He just kept telling himself that he was too important to them to be killed. It was taking about seventy percent of all Michael's energy to simply keep his composure leaving the other thirty percent to concentrate on countering Max's snake-like notions of ethics.

He took a deep breath and rested in the faith that he was the good guy. "Actually, I can understand how humbling it must be to listen to someone of my age disagree with you. I'm sure it matches my frustration that someone of your age and wisdom cannot comprehend the simplicity of right and wrong. Of course, you understand what's right for you. But what happens when what is right for you is wrong for a multitude of others? One perspective verses that of millions. Such actions are no different than that of a tyrant. I'm sure you don't believe the Creator created you with his own hands for this."

As Michael finished, his heart dropped when he saw Max's jawbones clench. Michael's intent was to try and win him over, not to upset him. He was attempting to show Max that he just needed to look within himself and recognize his own decadence. It discouraged Michael to see he was pushing Max further away.

"A tyrant you say?" Max smiled. "A tyrant acts on his own, without any regard to the thoughts of his peers. I have established this Council of Elders, myself, just to prevent such unenlightened claims. These you see before you are the most powerful beings alive," Max said, turning to acknowledge his fellow Elders, who stood back in silence during this war of words. "We make coherent decisions with precious information gathered from agents in the field, as well as our prophecies."

"Why don't they speak for themselves?" Michael asked.

"I'm the voice of the council. If everyone spoke at the same time, we'd be as confused as your congress," Max said, smiling. "I convey our collective position."

"Well, in that case, I do apologize, Max. I should be addressing this entire council instead of just you. Maybe someone else may understand what is just and what's not."

Michael saw a few of the Elders behind Max exchange glances. But before any of them had a chance to speak, he heard Max's voice again. "You know, Michael, all this back and forth is beginning to get a little old. You think one of us will eventually crack?" Max asked with a smirk.

"I wouldn't consider it cracking if you were to re-evaluate killing and enslaving the world," Michael said, smiling back.

"I do like you, Michael, but the time is getting closer to either, how do you say, put up or shut up? Yes, I believe that's the phase I was looking for."

"So we're reaching the end of diplomacy?" Michael asked.

"Regardless of what you may think of me, Michael, I'm not like the short-tempered impure humans you've lived amongst. This isn't anything I haven't anticipated. We're simply reaching the end of this phase of diplomacy although I doubt you'll find the next phase as comfortable."

"Just for the record, I'd gladly perish if it meant saving the world," Michael said without even thinking. It just sounded like the right thing to say. But even as his own voice echoed in his head, he wondered if those were the best choice of words.

"Really!" Max said with raised eyebrows. "You're determined to make us look like villains while you stand here in a heroic fashion. Your religions have recorded how the earth has been cleansed before. And from that cleansing, came a new beginning, which has brought us here. Here, where it also is recorded in your religions that the end of this time will come. We're not villains, Michael. We're simply the tools and benefactors of His will. But if it has been your childhood wish to be a hero, well, I just may give you a chance to show just how heroic you are." Max looked past Michael and called out. "Lori. Please enter if you will."

Michael's heart began to pound on the inside of his chest so hard that he just knew Max could hear it. He turned to see Lori enter from a side room in her glowing white robe. Her gaze never left the floor as she came and stood beside Max.

"Lori is prepared to except her destiny, Michael. Are you?"

"What do you mean? What's Lori's destiny?" Michael asked desperately.

"She has fulfilled her mission, and for that we're grateful. But she has also committed the unforgiveable crime of treason."

"Treason? Lori has been loyal to your Council of Elders the entire time I've known her."

"It's alright, Michael," Lori said.

"You see, Michael, there have been preparations made that Lori wasn't even made aware of. First of all, her ability is like mine. It only triggers when she concentrates. So if Lori is preoccupied, she won't detect someone's emotions or motives. With that being said, one of our Elders has the ability to control the wind. You probably just felt a couple of cool breezes last night when, in reality, my fellow Elder was hovering above you. Listening closely to Lori's betrayal."

"I still don't understand how she committed treason," Michael said firmly, looking over to Lori.

"There are oaths that agents, such as Lori, take before they leave the Village for their first mission. Included is an oath of confidentiality. Now it seems that you insisted she explain everything to you that she knows. And it seems as though she did. The moment she decided to tell you anything of her mission or our intentions, she knew she was putting her life on the line. So now it seems she has disregarded her oath. Siding with someone from outside the Village against her own pure human family. At first I didn't want to believe it but after being questioned, Lori admirably admitted to her crime."

"And what have you decided for her punishment?"

"Well, the punishment for treason is death," Max replied in a grim voice.

"Death?" Michael shouted in disbelief. "Seriously?"

"I mentioned earlier that she put her life on the line for you. I don't like it either, Michael, but she made her decision. Now I do have some good news in the midst of such a disappointing morning for you. Do you still have those heroic intentions from a moment ago?" Max asked with another confident smile.

"You will spare Lori's life if I play this role you want," Michael said somberly.

"I know this may seem like some movie where a bad guy kidnaps the good guy's girlfriend and uses her as leverage. But the truth is Lori has admitted her guilt and is here without shackles or force. The truth is that her betrayal is really your fault. You just had to know what was going on. The truth is this could be a win-win situation for us both. I don't want to see Lori executed either. And you two could live happily ever after with the fame and fortune of a king and queen. Michael, can't you see this is all part of the Supreme Being's plan? It is an obvious choice for someone who speaks of love the way you have. This is your destiny, Michael. Embrace it."

Michael stood in total anguish. He didn't know what to do. Allowing Lori to die because of him was not an option y et he couldn't agree to be sent out as a puppet for Max either. He stood there in the middle of the most important moment of his life without a clue of what to do next. He tried to regain his wits and conceive a quick plan. He considered agreeing to Max's proposal but then going on the run after they left the Village but that would mean looking over their shoulders for the rest of their lives. Michael imagined never being able to lay their heads down to sleep in peace again. Who am I kidding? Michael said to himself. These guys could make the CIA look like unarmed rookie security guards. The might and political power of these being were too much for them to hide from.

"I understand this may be hard for you, Michael, but you can't just stand there looking like the confused child that you are forever. Come. Let us stop this foolishness and begin this journey together. Remember, everything has a beginning and an end. The Creator has condemned the earth. You and I are simply his servants that have been designated to carry out His will."

"DON'T DO IT, MICHAEL!" Lori screamed.

"All right, if that's what you both want then I'll show you the consequences of your decisions," Max said as he grabbed Lori by her robe and threw her to the floor. "The time for talking is almost over, Michael. I warned you this next phase of diplomacy wouldn't be as comfortable for you. Now you have your final chance to fulfill your destiny." Max raised his left hand and stood over Lori. His hand ignited into a flame so intense that Michael could feel the heat from where he stood ten feet back.

Seeing Lori thrown to the floor about to be executed enraged Michael. He began to sense the familiar sensation building in him. He felt warm deep within himself. The warmth quickly became a hot pulse, which made Michael feel as if he'd pass out. This was the worst he'd ever remembered feeling the intensity of heat inside him although at this point Michael was too infuriated to even consider losing consciousness. He kept his focus on Max and Lori, but he felt his body's vitals going haywire. He tried to figure his next move. What could he do? This was the very moment of helplessness that he'd feared. Here was another moment like in the forest. Once again he stood frozen, watching Lori in the same danger he promised he'd protect her from.

"No change of heart. What a shame," Max said, and drove his flame-engulfed fist into Lori's abdomen.

"Ahhhhh!" Lori screamed in agony, grabbing Max's arm as he pulled his glowing fist from her torso. She curled up and turned on her side, still shrieking in pain.

Before Michael could even fully process what was happening, he felt something snap inside him. As he heard Lori's cries of torment, the burning sensation within him suddenly stopped. It felt as if someone had lifted a thousand pounds from his shoulders. After a moment passed, Michael consciously realized the events that had just transpired. He looked down at Lori once more then looked up at Max. Before Michael could even take his next breath, he found his left hand around Max's face. For a split second, he looked into one of Max's surprised eyes through spread fingers. In a flash, Michael found his hand crushing Max's head into the wall of the great hall. Michael removed his hand to see Max's eyes half closed. Michael clenched his fist and prepared to pound it through Max's face.

"Noooo!" Lori screamed looking up at Michael, coughing up blood onto the floor.

Michael turned back to Max and released him. Max's head remained in the wall, holding the weight of his body. His feet dangled five inches from the floor. Michael turned and was instantly at Lori's side, leaving Max hanging in the wall.

"Don't let them leave," Max whimpered from inside the wall.

Michael saw one of the Elders point both his open palms towards them. Holding Lori in both his arms, he turned his back and bent over to shield her. Michael felt as if someone had thrown a blanket over them both. He looked up to see black feathers surrounding him. Was this some kind of trapping ability, Michael asked himself. He felt a little chill. He decided to try and shake loose of this trap. He stood up and stretched out, feeling as if he'd extended his arms, yet he was still holding Lori. He heard a cracking sound and saw what looked like ice shards falling all around him.

Michael noticed the black feathers were still there. Not only were they still there, but they were outstretched, just as he was.

He felt everything was different. He saw everything different. The walls didn't look like ivory or solid porcelain anymore. Michael felt as if he was surrounded by cardboard. He looked at the wall again and before he knew it, he was looking over the Village. He was in the air. He felt dust from the Palace wall clearing his hair in the wind. Michael was reacting so instinctively that he hadn't even stopped to think what was happening to him. He was much more concerned with Lori's wounds.

Michael decided to land deep in the thick forest that surrounded the Village. He felt his powerful wings knocking down branches as he slowed to a soft landing with Lori in his arms. He quickly pulled one of his massive wings around and laid Lori's head down on his comfortable feathers. He looked down at her wound again. Surprisingly, she wasn't losing as much blood as Michael thought, although, without a hospital, he didn't expect her to survive. Michael felt a tear roll off his face and saw it fall onto her cheek. She opened her eyes.

"Michael," she said.

"I'm sorry," he said, holding her close, another tear escaping his eye. "I shouldn't have insisted on you telling me everything. I didn't know."

"Don't worry, Michael," she whispered.

"What do you mean don't worry? Max put his fist into your stomach. If I'm not supposed to worry now, then when do I start?" Michael asked, wiping the dried blood around her mouth.

"I'm going to be alright," Lori said in a weak voice. "Pure humans are very hard to kill. Our bodies can heal at a much faster rate than impure humans."

"Yeah, but you still need a hospital," Michael said, insisting.

"There's no hospital for pure humans. A wound either heals or we die. I can feel this wound healing from the inside already. I just need a little time."

"Are you sure?"

"If I was dying, then my body wouldn't have the strength to heal itself. I'll be fine in a day or two." Lori looked up at Michael and rubbed the side of his face. "Look at you. I knew you were the Prophesied One. More powerful than any of us."

"What am I?" he asked.

"One of the Supreme Being's most precious creations."

"Lori, I'm so sorry."

"No, Michael, I'm sorry. I purposely kept things from you. You had no clue of my oath. There's no way you could've known this would happen." Lori closed her eyes. "I can feel myself healing, but I need to rest."

"Don't worry. I'll be right here. Rest as long as you need to," he whispered.

Lori fell sound asleep in his arms and wings leaving Michael to try and figure out what metamorphosis he'd just experienced. He looked down at his Ed Hardy t-shirt, which was barely hanging on to his new muscular frame. In fact, he noticed the outstretched neck of his shirt was the only piece intact. The entire back of the garment had been obliterated by his overpowering wings.

Now what do I do? he asked himself. His mind began filling with more questions and concerns. How could he ever return to America looking like this? He'd be considered a freak. Would the government run a million tests and try to use him as a military weapon? How could he ever make any more friends? Could he ever have children? He was too afraid to even check his underwear, especially while holding Lori. And why were his wings black? Was he some kind of demon? Michael had begun to overwhelm himself with all of these questions. He tried to just relax. One thing at a time, he told himself.

CHAPTER 14
ANSWER MY QUESTIONS

Michael woke suddenly, still holding Lori in the middle of the forest. It was now early in the evening and the sun was just barely lighting the woods. He hadn't even realized he'd fallen asleep. He wished he'd woken up in his dorm and all this had been a weird dream. But since it wasn't, he had to quickly gather his wits.

Michael knew he heard something that woke him. He looked down at Lori to see she was still in a deep sleep. He also noticed he had the body of an athletic nineteen-year- old once again. There was a brief sense of relief before he heard the sound that woke him once again. He was unprepared. Now that he needed it again, he had no clue how to become his stronger self. His eyes cut from left to right, surveying the area, but he saw nothing. He looked up, figuring maybe it was another training session for those pure human kids. But he saw nothing in the trees.

"Relax," a familiar voice whispered.

Michael gently placed Lori's head on the soft grass and dried leaves of the forest ground. He then stood to find the owner of the voice he knew so well. He didn't want to leave Lori's side so he walked a ten-foot perimeter around her. Once again, he saw nothing. Then, just as he turned to rejoin Lori, Michael couldn't believe his eyes.

After everything he'd experienced in the last forty-eight hours, Michael didn't believe anything could really surprise him anymore but his brain couldn't even begin to figure the whys and hows of Eric standing before him.

"I know. It's crazy, huh?" Eric said, smiling.

Michael continued to stand there, dumfounded, in shredded clothes.

"You look like a low-budget You Tube video of *The Incredible Hulk*," Eric said, looking Michael up and down, laughing.

"It really is you?" Michael asked in total disbelief. "Man, this is just too much. I don't understand anything anymore. I don't know who I am, what I am, or even where I am. And now I don't even know who you are. This is just way too much. I don't even care anymore," Michael said, falling to his knees in defeat. He was so mentally exhausted, he didn't even want to try and understand anymore.

"So that's your solution?" Eric asked. "You're going to have a nervous breakdown? Sure, all right. Be like everyone else. I mean, who could blame you. The average person would've had a mental meltdown well before now anyway. Of course you're supposed to be the only one who can take it."

"Everyone has expected me to do this or say that, but no one has told me anything. No one but Lori, and look at what that got her. This just isn't fair," Michael said, still slumped to his knees, looking at the ground.

"I have your answers, Michael. I'll tell you everything you need to know."

"How did you even get here, Eric? None of this even makes any sense. How do you even know about this place?" Michael asked in pure frustration.

"You're understandably confused. It's all right. Just take a deep breath and relax."

"Eric, with everything going on with me and the possibility of Max coming around the corner at any minute, this is about as relaxed as I'm going to get. Now please, what in God's name are you doing here?" Michael demanded.

"Ironic word choice," Eric said with a smile.

Michael fixed his lips in frustration to respond to Eric but was instantly blinded by a white light. He shielded his face with his hands, and peeked through. As his eyes adjusted, he saw that the light seemed to be coming from Eric. Michael looked closer and saw magnificent white wings spread from Eric's shoulders. He could now see the full picture. He was looking at a real life angel.

"Don't be afraid," Eric said in the most subtle, yet most powerful voice Michael had ever heard. Then, just as quickly as Eric's true form appeared, he instantly diminished back to his human form.

"You're an *angel*?" Michael asked in total disbelief. "But-"

"I know. We have much to discuss," Eric said, taking a seat beside Michael. "I thought that little demonstration would eliminate a lot of explaining and doubt. You must listen very closely to me now. We don't have much time. Like Lori, I was once a pure human," he said, pointing over to Lori's unconscious body, which had now curled into a fetal position. "Long ago I was raised and trained in the Palace, just as all the other agents. We looked at the Elders as if they were our parents. We never even thought to question the motives of the Council. I had completed many missions and was favored by the Elders. Max promised I'd have my pick of land to rule after we inherited the earth. And everything was going according to plan…until I fell in love."

"Lori said you guys weren't allowed to be involved in relationships. Were things different back then?" Michael asked.

"No, they were not. In fact, since my wife and I were the first to ever publicly announce our love, Max made an example of us. He accused us of adopting ideals from the outside world and trying to implement them in the Village. This way Max could twist the charge into treason."

"How could that be treason?"

"Pure humans believe that impures are very undisciplined. They believe impure humans do as they please when they please, without thought of consequence to future generations, their own offspring, or even themselves. Max sees both impures and their way of life as enemies. So, falling in love before the time of inheritance had shown that we were also undisciplined. According to Max, we were trying to bring impure ways into the Village. Max believed these so-called, 'impure values' would spread like a disease, until the Village was just as condemned as the outside world."

"I can see the connection but that's still a pretty far stretch to treason," Michael said.

"Max is the oldest of us all. And, besides the general, he's the most powerful. My love and I were the first and the last pure humans to defy him for a reason."

"So Max hates impure humans so much that he was willing to execute you both. He has that much fear of the Village embracing anything from the outside world? Even love?"

"It wasn't always like this. Imagine you'll soon inherit a car from an older sibling, but you see them crashing the car every weekend without any regard to even their own safety."

"That's how you see impures treating the world?" Michael asked.

"That's how Max groomed us to feel. At first pure humans felt pity for impures. We'd go on missions where we gave very influential men the information they needed in medicine, engineering, and political peacekeeping. We wanted impures to succeed while they could. We knew the Father would eventually take everything from them and give it to us in the end but even pure humans are still human. The sympathy we felt for their future slowly became an awkward impatience as the centuries passed. Senseless wars of pride just kept escalating. Along with starvation, genocide, prejudiced hearts with smiling faces, I could go on and on.

"But time passed and there came a day when the Council began to change our missions. We were no longer helping scientists, doctors, and engineers anymore. Instead we were assigned more and more political positions of influence. We infiltrated corporate boardrooms, where there was even more political puppetry. Even worse, we knew we were no longer helping impure humans, yet we never said a word. Most of us were beginning to wonder if it was pointless to help anyway. It was obvious that impures were on a path of self-destruction. The more the outside world fell apart, the more we felt that all our efforts were in vain. But when Max actually began to speak about impure humans as pests in the way of our inheritance, everything changed. He strangely made us feel better about their downfall. He told us this was all part of the Father's plan and we shouldn't be discouraged. He explained that without the destruction of impure humans, we'd have no inheritance. He urged us to look forward to their end. Eventually we became impure human's unknown enemy, consciously pressing the accelerator on the road to their end. Max was intimidating back then and I see he has not changed. And today Max has agents in positions of power around the world."

"So what became of you and the woman you loved? Weren't you scheduled to be executed?" Michael asked.

"Yes, but we escaped."

"Escaped? How?"

"With the help of others who also believed Max's intentions were beginning to stray from the Father's plans for us. There was an organization of pure humans that planned our escape as well as their own. I was totally unaware of the extraction plan. There were guards, agents, and even an Elder involved in our rescue. By the time Max realized we were gone, there were thirty-eight of us crammed on a private plane over the ocean."

"The rogues," Michael said in reflection. "Lori told me that rogues were agents who never returned from their missions. She said their only known goals were random acts of terrorism and opposing any plans of the Council of Elders."

"Yes, we were called rogues from that day forward. Max was infuriated. He immediately sent out his most powerful agents to begin hunting us. I'm sure he told all the pure humans the same story Lori told you. Max wanted everyone who participated in our escape executed for treason. We fought them off several times, with many close calls. But we made the tragic mistake of letting our guard down one day. We accepted a new rogue into our circle that no one knew of. We didn't have the heart to turn away a pure human and leave him to stand alone against Max and his agents. Besides, we needed as many pures as we could get in the fight to one day overthrow Max and return to the Village. Well, of course, this new rogue agent was planted by Max to infiltrate us and learn our plans and locations. It wasn't long before Max himself blew down the walls of our compound. Within minutes, Max and his powerful agents had brutally slain one-fifth of our unsuspecting resistance, and the momentum wasn't shifting. I gave the order for my wife and the others to retreat but I stayed with two other rogues. It was the only way to ensure that my love would live. We fought courageously for as long as we could. My ability was that every time I was injured, I'd heal and become stronger. My two friends and I held them for at least forty-five minutes. There were too many of them to spend enough time to put even one down for good. As soon as we injured one of them, we went to the next. Our only goal was to keep them from following the rest of the rogues. Inevitably, we became fatigued. In the end, Max had his agents hold us down as he came down the line, one by one, killing the three of us. He made me watch as he plunged his flaming hand into their torsos. Hearing their cries was worse than my own death."

"So you actually died? I thought the more you were injured, you healed and became stronger."

"My gift became my curse. Being held down by countless agents and unable to fight back from exhaustion, my ability made my death excruciatingly long. Since my wounds were simultaneously healing, Max had to burn my organs from the inside to ensure my death."

"And now you're an angel? Do all pure humans who die become angels?"

"No. I'm the product of a murdered pure human the Father was pleased with and merciful. The murder of a wicked pure human would produce a demon."

"Hold on a second," Michael said, scratching his head with a confused look in his face. "If you're an angel, then how is it you can be in a physical form as you're in now? And what about all those girls you slept with in college?"

"Well, Michael, you know how people say you can rest when you're dead?"

"Yeah."

"Not true. As an angel, the Father sends us on assignments. But don't misunderstand me, I'm not complaining at all. There's nothing I'd rather be doing. All the assignments I've had as an angel have been directly from the desires of my heart. The Father somehow custom fits all my assignments to me. It's a million times better than any dream vacation I could imagine. It's truly euphoric. "

"So you get to sleep with multiple women? I guess that would be euphoric," Michael said chuckling.

"No," Eric said with a short laugh himself. "Actually my desires are a bit different," he said, looking at Michael with a more serious expression. "Most men want a son so they can make what they consider a good man; someone to pass on the family name. They want to pass on the life lessons of women, successes, and even the failures they've learned from. They want to steer their son from the mistakes they've made, and be there for them when they make their own. Most men want to grow old and sit back to see a strong, successful, and smart version of themselves, marveling at their work as if they'd built a supercar from scratch. Not me though. I've always wanted a daughter. I'd always dreamed of holding my little princess. She would've been the daddy's little girl that every other girl wanted to be. And she would never have had any boyfriend problems. I would've taught her every trick men have in the book. There wouldn't have been a guy alive that could put one over on my daughter. She would never have settled for anyone but the best. And even then, she would've brought him to me for approval. But then again we don't always get what we want," Eric said, looking into the distance of the forest.

"You never had a daughter?" Michael asked.

"No, I had a son," he said, laughing again. "But this specific assignment has satisfied every one of those duties I was yearning for with a daughter. Every girl you saw me with in school had a father or an older brother in their home. They were as naïve as a fly landing on a spider web to look for food. There were no better pleasures than showing them how a man can and should be their friend. Sure I slept with all of them but sleeping was all we did. We talked throughout the night about past relationships and held each other. I assured them that my feelings were still very much alive for my girl. Sure they were attractive, but they were like daughters to me. I showed them how a man should be attracted to more than just their bodies. My assignment was essentially to break the cycle of single-parenthood in the lives of these girls. And as beautiful as Monica is, she would never have found a life-long mate. She was pretty much a sweet prude," Eric said with a short chuckle. "But she's also a believer. And we were the unknown answers to her whispered prayers. She always wanted to be more social, but she associated fun with drugs and sex and since she doesn't do drugs and isn't ready to have sex, she never wanted to have any fun. She just needed to see that people can laugh and just have a good time without drugs and sex. We showed her that. Now she still has her values, but she's able to open up and enjoy life."

"So what happens to her? Her heart just gets broken when you leave for the next assignment? That doesn't seem fair," Michael said.

"Where's your faith, son? How many times must I tell you? My assignments come from the Father. His knowledge is infinite. She came to tell me how she'd begun to have feelings for someone else when I told her I had to leave school for personal reasons. She was relieved that her honesty wouldn't have to break my heart. Without our intervention, she would never have met her future husband."

"Okay, but you even encouraged me to sleep with girls too. In fact you even criticized me for not doing it."

"And what did you do?" Eric argued. "You stood your ground. No matter how much sense my arguments may have made, you stayed the person you are. But most importantly, you experienced leadership. You even had a little taste of my assignment yourself. Do you remember how you changed Katie? She never knew if a guy wanted her or just wanted sex so she would sleep with men first, to see if they would leave her or not. Even if she did come across a good man, her tactics would make a guy lose respect for her anyway. You helped her. You showed her there were still decent men out there who weren't just looking for sex. You surely saved her from a disease or unplanned pregnancy. Do you remember how that felt?"

"Yeah, that did feel good."

"Better than good, son; that experience planted the seed of persuasion that leaders need. That small success you experienced showed how you actually could make a difference in a person's life."

"I would never have thought of how all that affected me. Or that you were so caring," Michael said in pure amazement.

"Well, that was the idea," Eric said with a smirk.

"What do you mean by that?"

"If you recall, I told you how you'd be surprised if you really knew what I was doing with all those girls," Eric said, chuckling.

"I do remember that," Michael said, smiling.

"Well, all the conversations we had were also ways for me to see what kind of man you'd become."

"What? You mean you had to make sure I was the Prophesied One too? You had to test me, like Lori, to see if I had a pure heart? Why does everyone around me have some kind of hidden agenda? It feels as if no one has been around me lately because they just wanted to. Like there's always a reason behind anyone befriending me."

"I'm guilty. I admit it was part of my assignment. But I also took pleasure in personally witnessing the man my son had become...as his friend," he said, looking at Michael.

Michael looked dead in Eric's eyes then quickly looked away and started laughing. "Man, you better stop playing," he said, still laughing. He looked over to see Eric hadn't even cracked a smile. Then Michael felt his heart, once again, take a nose dive to the bottom of his belly. He could hear Lori's words echoing in his head. She'd told him his father was an angel. Michael stood up and began pacing. "What's going on? I mean how much can a guy take in one day?" Michael asked, looking up into the sky.

Eric began laughing. "I'm sorry, but I was going for the whole sentimental mood and you just smashed it. And what's even funnier? Even though it was a legitimate outburst, we both know you're mentally strong enough to process everything you've been learning about yourself so come back over here and sit down next to your dad. There's more you need to know," Eric said, smiling.

"I'm sorry but this is just too weird. You look my age. How am I supposed to accept you as my father?" Michael asked.

"Michael, we don't have time for this. You saw how your eyes could barely stand the light my angelic form? Well, who you see me as now isn't the physical form I had as a as a pure human either. This appearance is what was appropriate for the assignment. A young college student. Looking your age is how we became friends. And after everything else you've been through today, this shouldn't be hard to believe."

Michael took a deep breath and sat down next to his father. "Okay. So let me see if I got this." He took another deep breath. "You were a pure human who fell in love with..."

"Your mother. Her name in English was Nicole," Eric quickly interjected.

"Nicole," Michael said, letting her name sink in. "The woman who died so I could live."

"I was there for your birth...and her death," Eric said in reflection.

"What! How?" Michael asked with the eyes full of wonder.

"As I told you earlier, each assignment is custom fitted to your heart's desires. One of my worst fears was that your biological mother, my love, would die alone. In fact, as a pure human, I'd shudder at the thought of anyone dying alone so one of my assignments involved holding the hands of people as their souls passed on. People who would've breathed their last breath alone had the Father not placed me in their hospital. They all departed with peace in their heart, and sometimes a smile."

"Didn't other doctors suspect you were responsible for the deaths if you were always present? Were you the angel of death on this assignment?" Michael asked.

"No I wasn't the angel of death," Eric said, laughing. "I was a doctor who became known for his compassion. When a patient passed on, I'd follow protocol and try to revive them; and that's what other doctors saw when they rushed in. I'd be in a crowded room amongst busy bodies, racing around trying to bring him or her back. And only I knew their soul had already peacefully vacated. See, I'd have already held their hand and talked them through their fears and regrets, just moments before the flatline."

"A doctor? How'd you pull that off? You went to med school?"

Eric giggled a little. "Med school? With the Father, nothing is impossible, Michael. How does a baby know to cry, blink, or even breathe? Although I wasn't doing any complex surgeries, I was performing all of my medical duties as if I had done them a hundred times before. It's just so natural, you don't even realize you didn't know it all before. This also happened to be the only assignment where the Creator placed me in my original pure human body. I didn't understand why until the day I was called into a room to deliver a baby. The woman was your mother, Nicole. She recognized me immediately. She called my name and I called hers. I hadn't seen her in weeks."

"Weeks?"

"See after my death as a pure human, my love for your mother still burned within me. And since the Father is love, how could He not acknowledge it? So I was allowed to visit her in between assignments."

"So you get a break in between assignments?" Michael asked.

"Something like that. My heart was full of so much love for your mother, that He allowed me to visit her in physical form. Otherwise I could've chosen to stay and enjoy paradise between assignments."

"And this is when she became pregnant with me. When you were visiting her between assignments?"

"Nicole will always be my wife," Eric said. "Not time nor death has ever changed my love for your mother."

"How often does this happen? Are there angels and human having sex all the time?"

"Michael, this is the one time you can be sure that it was making love," Eric said, looking Michael in his eyes. "And no, this never happens. Your mother and I were an exception. This exception is how the Father planned to deal with Max. This exception has brought us to this day. There was a purpose to His merciful consent of our love and conception. You were to be born of spiritual and human blood."

"So there has never been anyone like me?"

"Never. Your path is a tale that will be spoken of throughout eternity."

"I still wish I could at least meet her."

"On that miraculous yet tragic day, we were together for a single unforgettable moment. As a family," Eric said with pride. "I stood there coaching and looking in her eyes as she tried to talk between her short breaths."

Michael could see his father's eyes welling up.

"Her last words were that she loved me. And Nicole never even got a chance to hold you," Eric said as the tears quietly slid down his face. "I almost forgot how stimulating these emotions are that come along with physical vessels." Eric quickly cleaned his face and continued. "But I held you. I was allowed to watch over you until you were adopted. And when my assignment was over, I returned to paradise where your mother was waiting for me."

"She became an angel too?"

"No. Only pure humans who have been murdered can become angels or demons. Since she chose to die to ensure your life, she didn't become an angel but her soul will reside in paradise for eternity. There's no need to feel sympathy for her. We spend what feels like fifty years together between each assignment. When I return to this realm, I'm always amazed to see I've actually only been gone a few hours."

"So if a pure human dies but is not murdered, then their soul will reside in paradise or in torment, just as regular impure humans?"

"You're getting it."

"Can everybody up there see down here? What does she think of me?" Michael asked with wide eyes.

"I can't tell you too much more about what happens after this life but I can tell you she's watching us right now. Your mother and I have watched you grow and love the man you've become. When I return from an assignment, the first thing she does is fill me in on what I've missed. We've joked and laughed alongside you, Michael. We also have smiled at your tears because we know your pain is so brief in the span of eternity."

Michael looked over at his father and they hugged. Michael felt as if his body was being squeezed dry of tears. He didn't want to let go. They hugged and cried for a few moments before they released each other and put their man faces back on.

"Now what?" Michael asked, still sniffling.

"Well, first, thank you for giving me my sentimental moment back," Eric said, smiling. "But now we get down to business. There's still much you must learn in such a short time. Now stand up," he said and took a few steps back. "Do you remember what happened when you summoned your powers for the first time?"

"Yeah, well first I remember feeling tiny spikes of heat all over my body. Then after I saw Lori injured, I felt something just snap and the pricks of heat and nausea all stopped. I thought about smashing Max's head into the wall and as soon as I decided to move, I already felt his face in my palm,"

Michael said, looking down at his hands, still in awe at what he'd done.

"Okay, stop right there. Do you remember exactly how you felt before you felt the rush of heat through you?"

"Yeah, I was pissed! I mean I was angry," Michael said, looking over at Lori's curled- up body. "I had just seen Max pull his blazing hand from her stomach. If Lori hadn't stopped me, I probably would've killed him."

"Maybe, but it wouldn't have been because you're a killer. It would've been because you had no idea of how strong you really are in that form. Your power can't be summoned from anger or hatred. Every time you receive your strength, it comes from the Father. He wouldn't bless you with such power for any unworthy purpose. You may think it was revenge that drove your transformation, but it was actually protection. You wanted to protect Lori so deeply that your body responded, with the consent of the Father. Max and the rest of the pure humans' power have free will. Your power is from the Creator. You can only use it when your will is one with His. Then your power is almost limitless. This is the only way Max can be stopped. The Father has limited my role in this assignment therefore I can't physically interfere. But this is your dance anyway, Michael. You are His plan to confront this issue."

"I can understand that, but it just took me by surprise when he...I just never thought Max would really try to kill her."

"Well, he knows how durable pure humans are, especially Lori. He oversees the training of all the agents. He knew she wouldn't perish from just one of his blows. I believe he may have eventually killed her, but he needed her alive longer to see if you'd transform."

"You mean he was hurting her just to clear his doubts if I was the Prophesized One?"

"Exactly! And after you transformed, he would've kept her alive, only as leverage for you to participate in his plans. He would've threatened you with her life anytime you opposed him."

"And this is the leader of the guys who are supposed to inherit the world because we're so bad."

"Careful. Don't mock your own purpose, son."

"What do you mean?" Michael asked.

"This is the Father's plan. And Max is the leader because pure humans need to learn from this experience before they proceed. And you will teach them. But you first need to understand your power's purpose is protection. Try and summon your strength right now."

"What? Didn't you just say I could only do it if God allows it? Why would He permit it now?"

"So this is what it feels like to be a parent," Eric said, smiling. "Always having your kids question everything you tell them."

"Okay, that was kind of a good one," Michael said with a short grin. "Go ahead."

"Look, we have an inevitable showdown in a few hours and I'm sure the Father will understand if you need to test drive your abilities. Now, just concentrate on protection. And make it intense, like you were in the Palace."

Michael took a step back and tried to bring about his transformation, but he felt silly just standing there. "I can't do this. I'm not some super hero. I don't know what to do," Michael said, bowing his head in frustration and disappointment.

Eric walked over and lifted Michael's head with his index finger. "Do you remember all the times you woke up sweating on broken beds?"

"Of course, how could I not remember the one disorder that has plagued my life?"

"You weren't having dreams, you were having visions. Visions of the future, when you were desperately needed. You broke those beds because your body became so dense that the bed could no longer support your weight. Your brain couldn't tell the difference between your vision and reality and your body would come close to transforming in your sleep, but you weren't mature enough yet." Eric put his arm around Michael's shoulders. "Son, look over there," Eric said, pointing his finger to Lori's sleeping figure. "If you hadn't protected her when you did, there's no telling what would've happened next. Max wasn't expecting you to be as powerful or as fast as you are. But do not be mistaken, he will not underestimate you again. You have to stop him. Believe it or not, you're the only one who can. Michael, you've been preparing for this since birth, but today you have truly begun fulfilling your destiny. You have to finish this chapter before you can move to the next. Imagine Max standing over her right now. Imagine him raising his glowing hand to strike her again. Because he will."

Michael felt the flame ignite deep inside him again. It was starting.

"Imagine all the people who can't heal as Lori can. Millions will perish if you cannot master your strength. And if all else fails, think of me. Think of how he murdered me and kept your mother on the run. Do you want another child to suffer the same fate as you? Do you want another woman to grieve over the murder of her husband, or another man to look into the eyes of his wife as she dies? Don't you want to protect them?" Eric said as his voice grew louder and bolder. "Don't you want to protect Lori?" he said, even stronger.

Michael straightened his posture and turned away from Eric. "I won't allow Max to hurt Lori or anyone else. I accept my destiny." As the words fell from Michaels lips, he felt a momentary explosion of heat then his body felt cool again with a slight tingling sensation all over. He looked down at himself once again to see bulging muscles he'd only seen before on the covers of bodybuilding magazines. He clenched his fists and felt power in his grip. He hadn't noticed before that his hair had grown down just below his neck. The deep darkness of his hair matched his exquisite black wings. He looked over at Eric and was amazed. Even though his father wasn't in his angelic form, Michael could see a light glowing all around Eric's body that he hadn't seen before. Then, before he could even comment on Eric, he looked over at Lori and lost his words. Michael could see her wound. She was lying on her side with her back to him, but he could see through her body to where she was injured.

"It's called spiritual sight," Eric said, breaking Michael out of his dazing exploration of himself. "If you live long enough, it'll become very useful to you during future escapades."

Michael looked down again to admire his arms and caught a flash of light in the corner of his eye. He looked over to see Eric in his true angel form once more but this time Michael could see him clearly. Now he saw that this was really his father. He could see traits of his own jawline and eyes in this radiant being before him.

"I've dreamed of this day for years," Eric said with a look of pride on his glowing face. "Okay now, move one of your wings."

Michael looked over to one of his wings and instinctively moved them both, propelling himself into the air. Eric chuckled as Michael spread his mighty wings to land.

"Angels aren't supposed to laugh at people," Michael said, marveling at the sound of his new deep voice.

"You'd be surprised at the Father's sense of humor. And don't feel ashamed; all you've done with your wings is fly, though they're far more than just instruments of flight. They're also your defense. Nothing can penetrate your wings. They're indestructible."

"I remember back at the Palace, I think they tried to freeze us. My wings covered us without me even trying."

"Just as when you penetrated the wall of the Palace and fled to this forest. Your wings shielded Lori when you broke through."

"You saw that?" Michael asked in amazement.

"Yes. I've been watching over you since you left Arizona, I've just not been permitted to interact with you until now. It's good to see your body's reflexes have already synchronized with your powers. This tutorial should be easier than I originally anticipated. Okay, now really concentrate on moving just one wing at a time. Try and imagine one of your arms were tied, and think of your wings as another set of arms."

Michael looked over at his left wing again and, after a moment of concentration, the massive extension of black feathers folded across the front of his body like a thick cloak. "I got it," Michael said with confidence.

"Perfect, now your wings can act as a shield for your front as well as your back. This way you can completely shield yourself without kneeling into a helpless ball."

"This may be a little off the subject, but why are my wings so dark? I almost feel like a demon or a giant crow compared to your gleaming white wings," Michael said.

"Don't let the world's perception of the color black influence you. You've been exposed to a society which portrays black cats as bad luck, depicts villains in the color black, and even the term 'black sheep' is used to describe family members in a negative manner so it's only natural for you to see your black wings and associate them with wickedness. But the truth is your dark features actually represent your distinction from the Father's original design of His angels. You were born from a pure human and an angel. This biological miracle has given you the strength of an angel but with a human soul. This is because the Father has restricted any of His original angels from engaging in physical confrontation with humans."

"But wasn't there a recorded account where an angel actually wrestled a human? Lori and I just spoke about that yesterday."

"Yes of course, but the angel was not wrestling with a wicked man. In fact, the man was blessed by the angel after they wrestled. Your encounter will be an incomparable situation. You must give Max a chance to repent from his centuries of immorality. If he chooses not to take advantage of the opportunity given to him, then the Creator has given you the power to end his reign over pure humans."

"I understand," Michael replied in a solemn voice.

"In this realm, our battles are only against powers and principalities. You aren't bound by this restriction. You're a hybrid, Michael. Your battle is also against flesh and blood. This is the reason you were born, the reason your mother sacrificed herself, so don't be discouraged or ashamed of your beautiful black wings. Instead, let the wicked tremble at their strength. You have a pure heart, Michael, never forget that."

"Thanks. What's next? I'm ready to learn whatever I need to fulfill my destiny. And I won't let you, Mom, or Lori down," Michael declared.

"Bold words from my bold son. I expected nothing less from my blood. Now, let's continue."

Michael resumed his training, learning how to use his extraordinary new abilities for the next three and a half hours. Eric showed him how strong and fast he really was. Michael began to feel more and more confident. He was even surprised at how easily he was acquiring every small trick and big power move that Eric demonstrated.

The final phase of the tutorial was sparring. Initially, Michael was afraid to strike his newfound father. But after taking a few of hard hits, he began to come around.

"Now that's what I'm talking about!" Eric shouted. "Show me something."

"I can't believe you can talk like that when you're an angel," Michael said, finally beginning to breathe a little heavier.

"There's nothing foul or vulgar in my words. They're spoken from a spirit of love and jubilation. And most importantly, they're words you can fully relate to. Now, let's go," Eric said before moving so fast it seemed as if he almost disappeared into thin air.

Michael's eyes adjusted to the high speed sparring until he could plainly see Eric's lightning fast movements coming. Eric's next attack ended with a spin, which he used to sweep his intimidatingly majestic wings at Michael's feet. Michael quickly launched himself into the air and struck Eric from above, driving him deep into the earth. There was a ten foot wide, three foot deep crater, with Michael and his fist in the center. Michael slowly lifted his fist in concern but before he could even inspect any damage he'd done, he felt a slight breeze and turned to catch Eric's fist in his hand. "I think I'm ready," Michael said, looking in Eric's eyes, still holding his angelic fist.

Eric lowered his fist and they both stood at ease. "Magnificent. It really helps that your brain functions are elevated to that of a pure human when learning."

"You mean I'm using one hundred percent of my brain right now?" Michael asked in delight.

"That's right. I was counting on that fact to help with your training at this time, but you've almost mastered everything I've introduced to you."

"All this just feels so natural, almost like I've done these things before."

"No doubt that feeling is from all the visions in your sleep over the years."

"The ones I can't remember?"

"Exactly. Your muscle memories have lain dormant in your subconscious until now. You're definitely physically ready, but there's one more thing we need to discuss before you proceed."

"What is it? I'm ready," Michael asked with the eagerness of a child.

"Listen close and keep an open heart, son. The Father has loved you and will continue to love you. Your pure heart has found favor with Him but you lack a major method that's necessary for complete victory. You have never called on Him."

Michael lowered his head, reflecting on Eric's words.

"Even when you saw Lori being crucially injured and even facing death yourself, you still didn't call on Him. I know you believe in the Father, but how often do you speak to him?"

Michael stood in silence as Eric's words continued to soak in. After another moment of digestion, he finally broke his silence. "I feel both ashamed and confused. I guess I've always thought God knew my every thought, so why even bother. I know it doesn't sound right, but when I did pray, I felt as if He already knew what I was going to say anyway. I almost felt silly. Like I was boring Him by listing my wants and needs when He was already aware of them. So I guess I just took it for granted that He could hear my heart. But I'm not saying this as an excuse," Michael confessed in complete sincerity.

"I understand more than you know, son. And He does know the wants and needs of our hearts. But children cannot be fed unless they open their mouths. And we are the Father's children. Tell me, why do you think the Father allows us to experience the hardships of life?"

"It makes us stronger to go through struggles," Michael said with confidence.

"That's part of it, but the primary reason is to show us that we can't make it through life without Him. Think about it. If everyone was completely content, then why would anyone need to call upon the Father? It's all part of the perfect test. As you've seen earlier today, a person's true self emerges under pressure. Some people call upon the Father just to thank Him. The same people will call upon Him again when their back is against the wall, and they shall be recipients of His mercy. Others don't even consider the Father when their life is good so giving Him thanks doesn't even cross their minds. But when the chips are down, they become that person who only calls when they need something. The reason we are all standing here today is because His mercy is so passionate. The Father will never turn His back on you, but you must develop your own relationship. He should be your best friend. Then you can walk in the faith that no one can stop you. After you add this to your arsenal, you will truly be unparalleled."

Michael looked up into Eric's eyes. "I understand."

"I believe you do."

"What kind of response can I expect from Him?" Michael asked.

"Just listen to your heart. That's how He speaks to us. Some people hear His voice, but they don't recognize it. Sometimes they listen and sometimes they don't. Others hear His voice and recognize it, but they still choose to take their own path. And most people just aren't listening or don't pay attention. You have to be one of the few that listens, recognizes, and understands that you're choosing His path. Remember this, most of the time, the hardest thing to do is the right thing to do."

"That makes sense, even though I don't like the way it sounds. Do you really think I'm ready?"

"You have to be. You have no choice. Always be careful, precise, and stay on guard. If you do these things, there's no need to doubt yourself, my son."

"I understand."

"But you must not approach in that form. Diplomacy is always the first option. To return at full strength and ready for battle wouldn't imply peacekeeping."

"Isn't it obvious that Max is far past negotiating with?" Michael argued.

"Max isn't your only audience. There are many others who need to see Max's true iniquities. Remember, Michael, if others are to look to you for leadership, they must see your struggle for peace or else they may come to fear your power as they do Max. You must have an influence of love, not fear."

"Okay, I get it. But how do I change back?"

"Close your eyes and simply thank Him. Thank the Father for granting you His strength. And with your thankful heart, humbly return the power."

"Okay, but it seems like one of those things easier said than done." Michael closed his eyes and meditated as Eric instructed. When he opened his them again, he was back to his original self once more. When he looked up Eric was gone. "How could you just leave like that?" Michael yelled into the open evening air. "No goodbye or anything? When will I see you again?"

"As soon as you turn around," Eric said chuckling, back in his human form as well. "I'm sorry for laughing, but that was a little funny. I was just over here checking on Lori. She's already healed some but she still needs a lot of rest. There's no doubt Max will be fully healed of his mild injuries. And if he doesn't repent...well, you'll need to apply everything you've learned today if a battle begins."

"You've taught me well, I'll be fine. But really, when will I see you again?" Michael asked.

"Soon I hope. I don't make the assignments. But when I do see you again, I trust it'll be at the right time. You should prepare to leave before she wakes and tries to follow."

"Wait. When I pray or call upon God, what do I call Him? Lori and the rest of the pure humans call Him the Creator or the Supreme Being. You call Him Father, but I'm guessing that's because you're an angel now. What is appropriate for me?"

"I may call you son or Michael, your children may call you father or dad. Your friends and your wife may also have different nicknames for you. But none of those names change who you are. The Father is called many names by many different tongues. He is still the Alpha and the Omega. What He's called does not define Him. The heart is what He sees, not the names He's called."

"So it doesn't matter?"

"Precisely. It's all about love. But I do like to end my prayers or talks with, 'It's just me and you.' I feel like that just makes it a little more personal. It reminds me in my darkest moments that He is still right there. So I'm never alone."

"I'm going to miss you," Michael said as he hugged his father. "Thank you for everything. I wouldn't stand a chance if it weren't for you."

"Thank the Father. Like I said, I don't make the assignments. And Michael, beware. Max may still have some tricks left. Stay focused. I'll see you soon. I love you, son."

Within the blink of an eye, Eric was gone, as if he had never been. "I love you too," Michael said, standing alone, looking into the darkening sky. There was no more time to ask why me. He now knew all the hows and whys. He now understood he was the only one who could stop Max.

He looked over at Lori once more and started off towards the Palace. He felt bad leaving her there but he had no choice. Michael knew she was much safer here in the falling darkness of the forest than where he was headed. He thought of how much easier it would be to just fly to the Palace, but he believed what his father told him. He decided to take this time to talk to God.

"Well, I thank you for bringing me this far," Michael said aloud. "I know I would've perished earlier today had it not been for you. I thank you for allowing me to meet my biological father. Knowing and understanding the history behind where I come from has made me stronger and more secure. And thank you for not taking Lori. I appreciate that. She's very special to me. Of course you probably already know all of this, but I've always felt awkward talking to you. I mean, what could I say to you that you don't already know? But then Eric told me how you should be my best friend and that's made it easier. When you're talking to your best friend, it's a lot less stressful than talking to the Creator of the universe. After talking to Eric, I feel as if I don't have to use all the most appropriate words when we speak, because you can see my heart's intentions. That's made this a lot easier for me too. And thank you for the power you've given me. At first I was reluctant to except the responsibilities of this mission but now I can see how much of an honor it is for you to entrust such tasks to me. I will do my best to protect all those who cannot protect themselves. Please grant me the words that will bring peace. And if battle is inevitable, then give me the strength to crush my enemies. Thank you for listening to me."

CHAPTER 15
DIPLOMACY VS. BATTLE

Michael carefully entered the courtyard. He looked up to the hole on the side of the Palace wall where he'd made his earlier exit. The sun was giving its final farewell before sinking into the far horizon and there were torches lit around the entire courtyard, and up the stairs to the entrance of the Palace. There was no hiding. He was cautious but not afraid. His clothes still hung from him like rags. He briefly wondered how far he'd get before he was confronted. He immediately found out.

"That's far enough, Michael," Max said, stepping from the shadows atop the stairs. "It's good to see you again. That's quite an alter ego you have there. I was wondering if he could come out and play again."

Michael could see the other Elders stepping out from behind Max. "I'm fully aware of everything I do in my other form," Michael shouted from the courtyard of the Palace. "I'm in control, it's no alter ego. And I was hoping we could try to resolve this without anyone else being hurt."

"Oh yes, how is Lori?" Max asked. "You know if I really tried to kill her, she'd be dead. My intent was merely to show you how serious I was about you fulfilling your destiny."

"You know that's funny. Fulfilling my destiny is exactly what I came here to do although I don't believe we share the same vision of my destiny."

"That's too bad. And I was just beginning to really like you."

"So you still plan on challenging me? Even though it's been proven to you that I'm the Prophesized One. Can't you see your plans are not the Creator's will? Open your mind! Just maybe I was sent here by Him to stop you. Suppress your vanity and listen to reason. I'd much rather my words stop you."

"Of course you would. No matter how powerful you may be, you're outnumbered." Max turned his head towards the other four Elders. They immediately began to race down the steps and in seconds they'd surrounded him, standing strategically in the four corners of the courtyard.

"Can't you see this is not your purpose?" Michael said, looking around at the Elders. "Max is using all of you for the same old plans of world domination that all tyrants and oppressors have had. He's only human. And humans make bad judgment calls because we have emotions motivated by flesh. As long as impure and pure humans alike are walking in flesh, we're capable of being immoral. Do you all really believe killing me and conquering the world on your own is what the Creator wants? If you do this, there will be no difference between you and the impure humans you'd be eliminating. Search yourselves," Michael said, looking around at the Elders. "Something in your heart is telling you I speak the truth! Something in you is hesitating! Deep within yourselves, you all know that somewhere along the way, Max has lost his integrity." The last word fell from Michael's lips softer than the others, but just as strong. The word seemed to haunt those who heard it. It appeared the Elders surrounding the courtyard were actually listening to him.

"That's enough!" Max commanded. "Your attempts to poison our minds with this nonsense will cease. Michael, if you won't listen to me, then try listening to your loved ones."

Michael had taken his eyes off the Elders to look at Max. Two figures walked up beside him and Michael strained his eyes to see who they were. He felt a shot of pure terror shoot up his spine. His first thought was to deny what his eyes were showing him. The figure on his Max's left looked like a woman and on his right was a man. The man, the woman, and Max started down the multitude of steps towards Michael. The closer they came, the more Michael realized his fears were justified. "Let them go right now, Max," Michael snarled as he felt the flame deep within him begin to ignite.

"Aren't you even going to ask why they aren't shackled in any fashion?" Max asked with his snide smile. "Isn't there a bit of curiosity as to why they walk alongside me as if we've known each other for years?"

"Mom! Dad!" Michael roared. "No, this is some sort of trick. These aren't my adoptive parents. This has to be someone's ability or something."

"Remember I told you two of our Elders were away on missions." Max gestured to his guests. "Behold, Drake, the general of the Supreme Being's pure human army. And behold Debra, our very own window to the future. The woman who told us this day would come."

"So all of this is true?" Michael asked Drake. "You conveniently said you had a government job so you could be off doing your duties as the general of Max's army."

"My army!" Drake barked in a powerful voice.

The sound of his voice intimidated Michael. It was a tone that Michael hadn't heard his adoptive father use before. Even if all this was true, Michael had looked at Drake and Debra as any child looks up to their parents. He still saw them as authority figures. Until two minutes ago, he yearned for their approval. And as much as he tried to ignore it, the fact remained that he loved them.

"And you, Mom," Michael said in a broken, weak voice. "I guess all you had to do was just tell Drake here your visions, and he'd just get the word to everyone else on his next trip out while the whole time the Elders got to keep their eye on me. Well, I guess you two did a terrible job at grooming me for this moment, because I'm not buying."

"Michael, listen. Be upset but just look at your options here," Drake said. "Do you think because we raised you as part of a mission that we don't love you? Do you think we want to see you slaughtered here? What we're doing is best for everybody."

"Everybody?" Michael cried in disbelief. "How is it good for impure humans to either die or become servants for you guys?"

"They've had their chance. Michael, why do you think we raised you to be such a loner? Think about it. Is there really any impure human you care about enough to risk your life for? We've thought as you have for centuries. You'd understand had you stood beside us, watching for ages as impure humans just take for granted every year the Creator gives them to turn from their ways. We will vanquish them when the time is right. That's why the Creator gave us these abilities. They'll shudder with fear in service to us."

"Well then, why would I be standing here now? Wasn't I prophesized to usher in a new way of life for pure humans? Maybe my mission is to show that your perspective on impures as enemies is not His will. And the way pure humans with lesser abilities are disregarded and segregated is also not His will."

"What do you know of His will?" Max asked with a snide smile. "You are but a confused child to everyone here."

"Lori taught me something I'll never forget. The simplicity of the Supreme Being. He is love. Pure and simple. And your intentions are not His because there's simply no love in them."

"Do not let his words of confusion waver you, Drake," Max sneered. "In our span of time he was only born five minutes ago. What does he know?"

"A war is imminent! Choose your side here and now, Michael," Drake ordered.

Michael couldn't believe these words were coming from the man he'd looked up to as his father for all these years. He looked over at his adoptive mother to see her reactions, but she was looking away into the distance.

"I remember asking you a question, Michael," Drake repeated impatiently. "Would you be willing to risk your life, here and now for any of them?"

"Are you saying you'd try and kill me if I did...Dad?"

"Don't misunderstand me, Michael. The feelings that I have for you are conditional. If you prove yourself as an enemy to pure humans, then I'll see you as nothing more than a wasted babysitting mission."

"I see." Michael looked down, sighed, and continued. "That was hard to swallow, but I'm so much stronger now. I met my biological father today. His love for me has helped to soften this brutal blow of manipulation. He finally told me the truth behind my birth, my purpose, and his death."

"Enough of this talk!" Max thundered, taking a few steps back. "If he's not with us then he's against us. Bring him down, using whatever it takes. If you can apprehend him, fine. If you must destroy him, then that's his destiny."

Silence fell on everyone. Michael didn't know what would happen next but he hoped that Max hadn't just turned these conversations into the beginning of battle. He looked over at the Elders surrounding the courtyard. He saw them looking amongst themselves as if they were torn about what to do.

Finally, Michael saw movement on his left. He instantly thought of what would happen if they found Lori in the forest. I have to stay alive to protect her, he thought. He began to feel the heat of his new blood race throughout his body. Michael then saw movement on his right. He closed his eyes and pictured the millions of women and children butchered and enslaved at the mercy of Max's intentions.

Michael opened his eyes to find he had indeed summoned his powers, but he couldn't move. He felt his new body tingling a little differently than it normally did. His ribs felt as if someone were poking him with a hot pitchfork. Michael struggled to look over and see what was happening. He turned his head just a little to see there was an electric current coming from the extended hands of an Elder. He had come within ten feet of Michael and was attempting to electrocute him.

"Would you like to change your mind before you're roasted, Michael?" Max said to Michael's sparkling body.

Michael could see Debra was still looking away into the night. He then looked to see Drake standing with his arms folded, without any trace of concern.

Michael closed his eyes and concentrated. Seconds later, there was a bright flash of light. A potent burst of power followed that knocked everyone within one hundred yards of Michael a few steps back. When Michael opened his eyes, the Elder who had been shocking him was thrown to the ground from his blast.

Michael remembered there had been movement on his left side too but just as he turned, he felt as if someone had tossed a cup of water in his face. He wiped his eyes to clear his vision but then realized something was terribly wrong. He couldn't breathe. He felt as if he was drowning right there in the dry courtyard. Looking to his left, Michael saw another Elder with his left arm extended towards him. He couldn't help but notice the Elder glaring at him with a pale stare. Michael tried to cough up the liquid as the Elder approached him. With a lightning quick turn, Michael spun around and used his powerful wings to sweep the Elder off his feet although, when the indestructible feathers touched the Elder's legs, they went right through them. Michael was afraid his wings had cut through the flesh of the Elder, but he was wrong. There was no flesh. Not only did the Elder have the ability to somehow manipulate liquid, but he could also make his entire body as permeable as liquid.

Michael didn't panic but instead quickly devised a plan. The Elder who was shocking him was just getting back to his feet. Michael quickly used all his speed to dart over to him. He grabbed the Elder by his collar. The shook-up Elder instantly began shocking Michael. Michael grimaced and turned to the other Elder, who still had his hand extended, preventing

Michael from breathing. In one quick movement, Michael hurled the Elder he held by the collar into the other. Their collision caused a small detonation between them.

After the explosion Michael immediately began coughing up the liquid from his lungs into the air. The courtyard began to reek with the smell of an electrical fire.

"One of the first things you ever taught me," Michael said, looking at Drake with smoke still rising from his unyielding wings. "Liquid and electricity don't mix. You'd think pure humans, who use one hundred percent of their brain, would know better than to attack me with those two abilities at the same time."

"Quite impressive," Max said with a smile of delight. "Your tough body can take quite a deal of punishment."

"In case you missed it, I can dish some out too," Michael replied.

"Tell me, what was that first technique you used to break free of such a powerful electrical current?" Max asked.

"I just learned that a few hours ago. If I'm ever overwhelmed, I focus all my power into a single pulse, which temporarily overpowers anyone in my immediate vicinity. And as you saw, it also temporarily disrupts any ability. My father taught me that. My real biological father," Michael said, looking at Drake. "The one you killed, Max! But that's all right. He's more powerful now as an angel than he ever was before."

"Who exactly is this biological father of yours?" Drake asked.

"Why is there still dialogue?" Max yelled in frustration. "There should be no more talking. Didn't I say I wanted him dead or alive? Why are the rest of you just standing there? Take him down."

Michael immediately turned his attention to the two Elders who were still standing at the edge of the courtyard. For an awkward moment, they both took their eyes off Michael and looked at one another in hesitation.

"Now!" Max's voice bellowed.

One of the remaining Elders shook his head. The other looked at Michael and launched into the air. Michael began to feel the wind pick up around him. He looked up to the Elder, who had both of his hands to the heavens. The wind picked up even stronger but as Michael looked around, he realized the gusts of air were only affecting him.

"Tear him apart!" Max shouted.

Michael noticed small pieces of the earth beneath him had begun to crumble and rise up. He looked back up to see a very thin funnel cloud dropping towards him. The Elder was attacking Michael with his own personal tornado.

"Rip his limbs from his body," Michael heard Max's voice hollering out.

Michael felt the wind pick up even stronger and could no longer make out the figures behind the wall of wind and debris spinning around him. Then, without warning, Michael's dark wings stretched out. With a mighty leap, he shot up, spinning to the top of the funnel cloud. In a flash, Michael grabbed the Elder by his neck and drove him back down through the wind cloud of tree branches and leaves. Michael could feel him trying to resist but with one flail of his mighty wings, his dive picked up even more speed. Michael, the Elder in hand, bashed into the ground with tremendous force.

There was dust and debris scattered all over the devastated courtyard. As the haze began to clear, a crater could be seen, at least twenty feet wide. The pit was too cloudy and dark to tell the depth. Suddenly a dark figure sprung from the crater, followed by a trail of even more dust and dirt. Michael's breathtaking wings extended magnificently as he softly touched down.

"That was a little rough, Michael," Max complained. "Aren't you worried about killing any of these beings the Creator has made with his own hands?"

"They can take it. I just don't want them getting back up any time soon," Michael said, looking over the faces of those left standing in the courtyard. Debra was still unable to even look at him while Drake had a disturbing smirk of pride on his face.

Michael saw that Max had his eyes fixed on the last Elder, who remained in the far corner of the courtyard. Michael also turned to see what ability this Elder had for him.

"My brethren have foolishly fallen," the Elder said as he approached the rest of the group. "I'm just grateful Michael has used restraint in suppressing them. It seems he could've surely slain them if he wished. I speak for my defeated comrades when I say we've all had our doubts in Max but most of us have followed him for so long that considering the fact Max had become immoral was too difficult to accept. To accept his iniquities would mean we'd also have to face the fact that we'd become envious of impure humans. And that Max's envy and hunger for power had made us instruments for his wickedness. A few of us have also feared his power, but most of us just didn't want to face the shame of our transgressions under his leadership. So instead, we stood in our foolish pride. Conveniently persuaded by Max's words, we believed impure humans were beneath us. We proceeded with offenses we knew in our hearts were not honorable. We began to take advances to inherit the earth on our own terms each Elder justifying their actions in their own way to find a synthetic peace. I will stand with you, Michael. And if need be, I will fall with you."

"And we will stand with you too, Michael!" a voice screamed from the darkness of the forest.

Michael couldn't believe the crowd of pure humans from the Village that had gathered to watch the battle. He also couldn't believe Lori was leading them. Bandaged and limping, she still found a way to show the smile that always cut straight through to Michael's heart. He was happy to see she was doing fine but didn't want to see her in harm's way once again. "Stay back!" Michael shouted. "We're not done yet."

When he turned back to face Max, he also noticed that Harold, along with all the agents and pure humans that were training to be agents were in every window, doorway, and on the roof of the Palace.

"You're right. We're not done yet," Drake said, pulling Michael's attention back to him. "I don't know if you've noticed or not, but all the Elder's robes are ranked according to their power. The brighter the robe, the more powerful the Elder," Drake said as he removed his cloak to show his illustrious robe.

"Behold the brightest robe of the Elders. Max leads us because he's the oldest, not the strongest."

"Dad…" Michael hesitated, in a confused state. "I can't fight you."

"You've just defeated most of the officers in my army. That alone cannot be forgiven. As their wounds heal, they'll rest in the satisfaction of knowing their general has avenged them and defeated their foe," Drake said in a harsh voice.

"But Dad-" Michael spoke softly.

"That's enough!" Debra cried desperately. "I've seen all I need to see. That's enough. Max, this does not end well for you. Stand down. And Drake, how could you?"

"Look at him. He's the aggressor. He wants to end our way of life. Our way of thinking. Max even says Michael feels the Villagers, with their meager powers, should live amongst those who walk the halls of the Palace. Do you believe that? You live according to your worth," Drake said, looking back at Michael. "That's why we live in the Palace and they live in huts. Their powers are worth nothing, so they live like nothing. We were just babysitters for this…boy," he said, looking back to Debra. "We knew this day would come."

"No, I knew this day would come," Debra said in a formidable tone. "And I also knew he would defeat us."

Silence fell over everyone. Even the Villagers at the edge of the forest focused their attention on the woman who'd accurately predicted their futures throughout their lives.

"Yes, I knew he would come to overwhelm us with his might. That's why I raised him to be the man that he is, and that's why I stand silent now as he thrashes through Max's Council of Elders. Max has steered us wrong for centuries," Debra said, stepping forward to address the people of the Village. "My vision showed me this day. But this is not a day of defeat for pure humans. This is a defeat for Max. His reign of subtle tyranny is over. I couldn't speak of the true meaning of this day because Michael would've been killed as an infant." Debra turned to Michael. "Just as I couldn't tell you the truth about your family. If Drake had found out I was telling you such information, your entire childhood would've been compromised. Michael, I knew your biological, pure human mother. She was a good and strong woman. I raised you as my own son with her in my thoughts and memories. I almost told you many nights but then I was shown a vision of what would happen if you were told the truth too soon. That tragic outcome was nothing like what you see here. Please forgive me. I did what was necessary for you to become this strong, this humble, and this pure-hearted."

"You lying witch," Max shouted.

"I never lied," Debra replied quickly. "I told everyone the Prophesized One would come to usher in a new way of life for pure humans. And that's exactly what he's doing. You just assumed the prophecy meant you inheriting the earth."

"Well, I don't care what she says. I still can't let you just leave after all of this destruction," Drake said.

"Dad, I-" Michael started, but was cut short by the sight of Drake bolting towards him. Michael barely dodged his blow before resetting. He saw Drake's momentum had carried him a few yards behind him.

"You're pretty fast for such a big powerful guy. I must say I can't hold back a sense of pride just looking at you. Your long dark hair, sculpted body, and impressive wings…maybe that's why I feel I just have to challenge you," Drake said in excitement.

"What do you mean?" Michael asked.

"I mean the feeling a father has when he sees his son thinking he's hot stuff. You feel a sense of pride, as long as the son doesn't forget that he's the prince and you're the king. I'm the king, Michael. You will come to understand that," Drake said and came at Michael again.

This time, Michael had to use his wings for extra propulsion to dodge the attack. He couldn't believe the speed Drake possessed. He was definitely faster than any of the other Elders he'd faced so far. Michael could feel the forceful wind of his blows as they barely missed him. He wondered what damage he'd suffer if Drake connected with one of his powerful swings.

"That's it? Dodging me? You're not going on the offense at all?" Drake snarled.

"Dad, I don't want to fight you."

"Stop calling me dad. You said you met your father, so stop trying to bond with me. Okay, I know. I'll just hit you one good time and we'll see if that'll get you going." Drake started his move then completely disappeared.

Michael looked around, but didn't see him. Then, out of nowhere, Drake appeared on his left. Before Michael could even brace himself, he felt his body flying across the courtyard from the blow. He flailed his wings once to stop himself but it barely slowed him down. Again, he used his wings to catch the wind and dug his hand into the ground to finally stop himself. Michael couldn't believe it. One punch had knocked him halfway across the courtyard and almost into the forest. He quickly tried to shake off the dizziness from the solid strike. He couldn't understand it. Before he could fully get to his feet, he saw Drake coming again. This time Michael prepared himself. He swung his left wing around as Drake moved in.

Drake whacked onto Michael's indestructible wing and stepped back, shaking his hand. "Okay, your wings work as shields. I get it. That's pretty cool. So I guess that eliminates the sneak attack from the back," Drake said and charged Michael head on, disappearing once more.

Michael closed his eyes and concentrated. "I know I'm not strong enough on my own, Father. God, please help me. It's just me and you," Michael whispered. He then lifted his left hand just in time to catch Drake's fist. The force Drake put behind Michael's palm pushed him back in the dirt about a foot. Michael slowly opened his eyes to see Drake's surprised face. "Is this what you wanted?" Michael asked, and punched Drake so viciously that he could hear the spectators gasp in awe.

The impact from Michael striking Drake was so powerful that the vibration could be felt through the ground. Drake's burly frame was instantly airborne, flying thirty-five feet back before tumbling down onto the courtyard surface. His body finally came to a violent stop, crashing head first into the bottom steps of the Palace.

Michael instantly regretted not using more restraint. He slowly started walking towards Drake, but then instantly froze.

"That wasn't bad," Drake said, wiping blood from his mouth. He sat up and a chunk of the steps crumbled where his head had shattered the marble staircase. He rose to his feet and dusted himself off. "That wasn't bad at all. I can't remember the last time I saw my own blood. This may actually be fun," he said, smiling.

Michael couldn't believe it. For Drake to take that kind of hit and just shake it off showed Michael that he'd been in many battles with very powerful beings. At that moment, he made up his mind that Drake was just too strong to let him get away. Michael felt he'd regret it if he let this opportunity to stop Drake pass him by. He balled his fists and mustered the strength to attack.

"Wait!" Drake said. "What were you whispering back there?"

"Why does it matter to you?"

"Even warriors can talk as gentlemen amidst battle. Don't you agree?"

"What's all this conversation, Drake? End him." Max's voice sounded in the distance.

"No, I don't agree," Michael argued. "I believe you're stalling because you're hurt. And every second we speak, you regain a little more of your strength. But that's good. I want you at full strength when I defeat you," Michael said, slowly walking towards Drake. "And I want you to know it was my biological father who trained me for this moment. My true father mentored me and taught me to pray."

"It couldn't be. That fighting style, I should've…what was your father's prayer?" Drake asked.

"He didn't give me a prayer. He taught me to give thanks to the Creator, and call on Him when I need Him. But my father did give me his little tagline. It's-"

"Just me and you," Drake interrupted.

"How did you know that? You knew my father?" Michael asked in puzzlement.

235

"I knew a great man," Drake said humbly. "Eric was his American name. And he was my friend."

Michael's eyes widened. "That is my father."

"And you say he trained you?"

"He's an angel now. He told me if a pure human is murdered, then they either become angels or demons."

"And you said he was murdered by Max? Max told me that the other escaped rogues turned on him and killed him." Drake looked into Michael's eyes. "I can see him in you." Drake then turned from Michael and took a few steps before he disappeared.

Michael looked around, but couldn't find him.

Seconds later Michael heard Max scream in pain. He looked up to see Max flying into the edge of the forest and crashing against a tree. Michael darted to the center of the action.

"You killed Eric. You murderer," Drake said, approaching Max.

Debra rushed between them. "You know what'll happen if you kill him. He'll become a demon and possibly become even more powerful under the authority of the Beast. Don't do it, Drake," she pleaded.

"Listen to her. Don't do it, Drake," Max said as he made his way to his feet, leaning against the tree, his face bloodied.

Drake looked at Max. "You will be tried and executed for your crime."

"He was a traitor!" Max shouted as he lifted both his hands together and instantly ignited them into a giant blow torch.

Drake and Debra were both consumed in flames.

Michael quickly swung his mighty wings to his front and approached Max, blocking the flames. After a short moment of fending off the concentrated blaze, he no longer felt the heat outside his wings.

Michael pulled his shields back to see Max had once again found Lori. She stood helpless in his arms, still wounded from Max's earlier attack.

"Everyone stay back or I'll have a beautiful corpse at my feet," Max said to the restless pure humans of the Village.

"What do you plan on doing now? There's nowhere to go, Max. This makes no sense," Michael said.

"You'll understand in a moment, my young-"

"You will not use me again!" Lori interrupted, twisting herself away from Max. Her spin left her facing Max with her back to Michael.

Before Michael could react, he could see Lori's back begin to glow. An intense flame burst entirely through her and almost hit Michael. Lori fell to her knees.

"Nooooo," Michael cried. He was under her with his supporting arms before her back could fall to the ground. "Lori, you're going to be alright. Your pure human body will heal itself again," he said frantically with a tear in his eye. "AHHHHHHH!" Michael's roar to the sky echoed throughout the courtyard. He gently laid Lori on the thick grass. "I'll be right back. I promise."

"Don't kill him," Lori whispered.

"He's already dead," Michael said and stood up, looking Max straight into his eyes.

"You going to make me a demon, Michael?" Max asked. "Come on," he said, and began hurling massive fireballs at Michael.

Michael brought one wing forward and started walking towards Max; each blazing cluster of destruction dissipated as it crashed into the dark shield.

"Whoever heard of feathers that don't burn?" Max said in a frustrated voice of panic as he shot even more concentrated boulders of fire.

Michael drove forward without pause. Each step was a challenge from the thundering amount of pressure that bashed against his wing. Suddenly Michael felt a powerful blow from behind that knocked him to one knee. He felt pain from his lower back on down to the back of his legs.

Michael had forgotten that Max could also manipulate the direction and speed of his projectiles. Max was conjuring flames from both his hands. One fiery palm was attacking

Michael head on, while his hand was directing a second attack to any openings that Max could find on him. Michael considered using his powerful pulse again but he was fatigued and had no time to concentrate while blocking Max's simultaneous attacks.

"Look out, Michael," Debra cried.

Just as Michael heard her words, his eye caught the tail of another fireball on his left. In the split second he picked up on Max's attack, he also saw Lori's defeated face, looking on with worrying eyes. The moment seemed to have been cast into slow motion for Michael. Then, just as Eric taught him, Michael swung his other wing back on his side to deflect Max's second attack. He continued his advance towards Max without any concern for the painful burns he was acquiring.

Max had increased the volume of fireballs until he'd become exhausted. He'd thrown all the artillery he had at Michael. His last few bursts of flames were comparable to an overweight boxer swinging wildly in the last round of a fight. With desperation and defeat in his eyes, Max continued to taunt Michael. "Go ahead. I'd rather be a demon than wait another century for Him to eradicate those pathetic impure humans."

Michael brought his steaming wing back behind him. "You murdered my father. You've hurt the ones I love and the ones I've sworn to protect," Michael said as he marched closer to Max.

"You won't make me a demon. Deep in your heart, you believe there's hope for me. You believe I can change and become the person the Creator meant for me to be. You won't make me a demon," Max said with a smile.

"You're right. I won't make you a demon. I won't murder you as you deserve. As a matter of fact, I won't even touch you."

"I knew I liked you, Michael," Max said, falling to his knees in exhaustion. His smile grew wider and blood dribbled from his nose and mouth.

"What's that trickling off your face?" Michael asked, still stepping forward. "It looks like the blood of a murderer. Wasn't

I greeted with the blood of murderers in this very courtyard upon my arrival?"

Max's eyes bulged until they almost popped out of their sockets. "No. No. Stay back," he said, raising his hands that still glowed from his assault.

"I believe it was you who told me about how a murderer's blood had a special kind of reaction when I came in close vicinity with it. Of course oxygen is the catalyst, remember? And those look like open wounds," Michael said, taking his final steps towards Max.

"Michael..." Max started in a pathetic voice.

"You won't become a demon because you will not die by my hand. Lori told me the Creator made me like this for a reason. Now I understand. You will die because of your own murderous actions. Your soul will suffer an eternity of torment alongside the wicked impure humans you've hated so much." Michael spread his dark, intimidating wings and stepped up to Max. He could see small sparks begin to flicker on Max's wounds.

"I was-" Max's words were cut short by the ignition of his entire bloodstream.

Michael looked into Max's eyes as they filled with a bright blue light that began to split his face and burst his body from within. Michael's widespread wings kept Max's organs and other body parts from spreading onto the speechless spectators.

Michael looked behind him and immediately returned to Lori's side. "Okay, we're going to get you up to the Palace," Michael said as he kneeled down and held her in his arms, tears falling uncontrollably down his face. "There you can rest in a real bed. That'll probably help the healing huh," Michael said, trying to smile.

"You did it," Lori said, smiling and caressing the side of his face.

"No. We did it. I wouldn't even be here if it weren't for you," he said, smiling back, the tears rolling off his nose and onto her cheek.

"You're fulfilling your destiny," she said, her smile beginning to weaken.

"No, Lori, you're part of my destiny. Please don't leave me. Please, Lori."

"I'll never leave you, Michael. I promise."

"IS THERE NOTHING ANY OF YOU CAN DO?" Michael screamed at the crowd. "All the abilities all of you have and none of you can help her?" Michael continued to shout through his tears. "Don't worry. The Creator wouldn't do this to us. You're going to be fine," he said, purposely disregarding her lethal wound. He wanted to wipe his eyes so he could see clearly, but he wanted more to keep holding her with both his arms.

"Michael, I need you to promise me something," Lori said softly.

"Name it. Anything," he answered quickly.

"I want you to promise me that you will never lose your faith."

"Sure, sweetheart, you got it. I'll never lose my faith," Michael said quickly, forcing a smile across his wet face.

"No, Michael. Really promise me that no matter what happens, you will continue to believe that everything occurring is..." Lori stopped to cough up a significant amount of blood. "Promise me you will believe that everything occurring is in the Creator's plan. He does not make mistakes."

"I believe it."

"I need to hear you say it, Michael."

Michael looked up to the night sky and closed his eyes. "No, no, no," he said, shaking his head.

"Say it," Lori mumbled louder.

"I'll never lose my faith," Michael said looking back down to her. "I will continue to believe that everything that happens is in the Creator's plan. He does not make mistakes."

Lori presented her genuine smile that first captured him in their class that day. "Death is not strong enough to confine my love for you," she said, looking so deep into Michael's eyes that he felt she could read his thoughts.

"I love you," he whispered back to her.

Her eyes stayed fixed on Michael as her smile began to weaken.

"Lori," Michael whispered. He tried to adjust her head but her eyes did not follow him any longer. Michael brought his head up, his mouth wide open. He looked as if he were screaming, but there was no sound. "Ahhhhhh!" he finally cried, his wings so extended they looked as though they were screaming with him. His shriek was so intense the tree branches seemed to sway from its force.

Michael sunk down and hugged Lori tight. His long hair covered both their faces. After a moment of sobbing, he felt a gentle hand on his shoulder.

"Come and rest, Michael. Let the people of the Village handle it from here," a soft voice said.

Michael raised his head once more to see the multitude of pure humans weeping in chorus with him. He then looked up to see it was Debra's comforting words in his ear.

"You've done everything you could, and more, Michael. There's nothing else you could've done. Please, come and rest," she asked again.

Michael continued to hold Lori tight for a little longer then carefully placed her head onto the grass. A new wave of tears began when he realized there was no more reason to be careful with her anymore. He closed her eyes and pulled some strands of her hair from across her beautiful face. "I love you," he whispered.

Michael stood up slowly to find his sadness quickly becoming anger. He turned to Debra and looked past her to Drake; they both had minor burns from Max's brief previous attack on them. Michael's bloodshot eyes fixed on the man he had called dad his entire life. "Are you happy now?" he roared at Drake. "Is this what you and Max wanted? Is this what you fight for?"

"Michael, I'm sorry," Drake said with a sincerity Michael hadn't heard from him in years. "Lori was under my authority. I helped raise her and saw her become an agent, as well as a woman. I've suffered a loss, just as you. I've not fully

241

agreed with Max's methods for some time now. He earned the excruciating death he experienced."

"And what about you? Is there innocent blood on your hands?" Michael said, taking a step towards Drake.

"Michael, no! Has there not been enough bloodshed tonight?" Debra shouted.

"Listen to her, Michael. For the moment, I've lost the will to fight you. Max kept the fact that you were Eric's son a secret from me. Your father and I were like brothers. And now, after the death of Lori, I will take time to mourn. I have no desire to slay the son of my best friend this night," Drake said quietly and turned away.

"Who says that choice is yours?" Michael said as he raced towards Drake. Michael was upon him before he knew it. He was fast, but he amazed himself at how quickly he reached his hands around Drake's neck.

"Michael!" Drake gasped, trying to speak.

Michael tightened his grip. "If I let you live, then you'll just show up later with the same plans as Max."

Michael loosened his hands. Something isn't right, he thought. For some reason, when he looked into Drake's eyes, they didn't match. These eyes were from another familiar face. Michael finally realized that these eyes were from his adoptive mother. Michael let her go and stepped back. "What's happening to me?" he asked.

"It's Drake," Debra said, coughing and rubbing her throat. "That's his ability."

Michael turned around and saw Drake in the crowd, heading to the forest. Again, he was instantly upon him. Michael lifted Drake up with one arm and looked into his face. And again, he did not see Drake's eyes. He refocused to see he was holding a pure human bystander two feet in the air, by his robe. Michael put the civilian back down and apologized.

"Don't be in such a hurry to die. Enjoy this time I've given you. When we meet again, I may not extend such consideration." Drake's voice rang from all around him.

"Come on! Let's go right now, you coward!" Michael growled back.

Silence fell on the bloody courtyard. The mass of pure humans from the Village were tending to Lori's body.

Michael looked over at Debra. She tried to smile but a tear accompanied her attempt of consolation. Michael's tear fell in correspondence before his wings spread and launched him into the night air.

He could feel the chill of the wind against his tears as he soared away from the smell of blood and ash. The only sound was his mighty wings dominating the wind. He soon began to feel numb. A subtle state of shock set in as he refused to fully accept this brutal new reality. He flew with no destination and temporarily ignored all his thoughts.

Michael flew for what seemed like hours before he finally realized he simply didn't want to land. If he landed, then this horrible day would have to continue.

He eventually came across the distant lights from the torches of the Palace. He slowly approached and landed gently at the top of the staircase. Michael turned and looked back across the recent venue of combat. The crumbled stairs, the deep crater in the ground, the damaged trees, burnt grass, debris, and bloodstains, all told the story. "Please show me how this is part of your plan," he said, looking up into the sky.

Michael closed his eyes and attempted to return to his original form. He remembered Eric told him to thank the Creator and give Him back His power. Michael tried to have a thankful heart, but he could not. He found it difficult to thank God when he felt that Lori's death was of His will. He tried to concentrate harder, but just couldn't force himself to be genuine. He was beginning to feel trapped in his body of war. His frustration quickly became anger. "WHY!" Michael's potent voice resounded throughout the courtyard and entrance to the Palace.

He leaned against a pillar and dropped his head. "What do I do now?" Michael asked, his thick dark hair falling over his face.

"Now you rise and show your true strength." Debra's soft voice came from behind him.

"I have no strength left," Michael said, without even looking up. "No inspiration. No motivation. No family. No nothing," he said, sliding down the pillar onto the ground.

"Michael, you have all that and more. You just-"

"What if I did?" Michael interrupted her, finally looking up. "Say I did believe whatever little inspirational speech you're about to say. Why?"

"Why what?" Debra asked in confusion.

"Why do anything? I promised I'd protect Lori. What am I good for if I couldn't even protect the woman I love? Who can I help if I couldn't protect her? She was right there, and I couldn't…" Michael's tears took over and he lost his speech.

Debra sat down next to Michael. She remained quiet for a moment as he wept. "I don't know if I can make you feel better about any of this. I don't even know if I can restore our relationship. But I do know a few truths. I know there was never a destiny for you to follow. Michael, you make your own destiny. Each decision you've made has brought you to this point. And the truth is that you couldn't have done anything more honorably today. There's nothing you could've or should've done differently."

"That's exactly the problem. I've been sitting here trying to change back, and I haven't because I can't find it in my heart to thank Him for granting me with His strength. I'm trying to thank Him, but I just …if I did everything I was supposed to, then why did He take Lori? If I couldn't have done anything more right, then why must I suffer like this? Was that a win? Is this what victory tastes like? I mean, why even fight the good fight, if this is what happens when you win? I would've rather had lost the battle and still have Lori."

"Michael, there are truths you must hear and understand. Please listen to my words carefully. You mustn't allow your strength to falter now. First, you must build your foundation of faith once again. You don't have anything to stand on when your faith is shaken."

"My faith." Michael responded in reflection.

"Yes, you must not blame the Supreme Being for Lori's death. If He allowed her to be taken, then that was part of His plan."

Michael's eyes streamed with tears as he sat in perfect attention.

"And His plan is without a single flaw," Debra said with perfect confidence. "To disagree with Him is to say that you know better than Him. And it would be saying a lot to suggest the intellect which He gave you has surpassed His. So our job now is to show our true faith. For if your faith isn't tested, then who's to say that you truly have it? That's what I meant when I said it was time to rise and show your real strength. Sure you have brute physical strength but do you have the strength to put your own desires aside, and accept His will over yours? To truly believe if you're a faithful servant, then you'll find favor with Him. You're not alone, Michael. You'd grown close to Lori just within the past several months. I've known her for over a hundred years. Now I'm not saying you hurt any less than I do, but understand we all must apply this faith I speak of."

"I don't believe it," Michael said.

"What?"

He closed his eyes and sincerely thanked God. When he opened them, he looked down to see his original teenage hands.

"That was amazing! Truly indescribable! Looking at you now, I forgot you're experiencing all this at just nineteen years old," Debra said in awe.

"No. Hearing Lori's last words coming through your mouth was amazing," Michael cried.

"What?"

"Everything you just said about faith was almost exactly what Lori made me promise her. And I know you were too far away to hear her mumbling."

"Really?" Debra replied.

"I mean it was just about verbatim. I know this sounds crazy, but it was like she was reminding me of my promise through you. Whatever the reason, it's enough for me to build on. It won't be easy, but we'll find a way to push on. I just have to work on believing that we did the best we could, so in His perfect plan all this had to happen. After all, I will not break another promise to Lori."

"Now that kind of strength is just as powerful as the might it took to take on Drake, and defeat Max."

"So what do we do about Drake now?" Michael asked.

"Drake believes, as Max did, that impure humans are no longer worthy of their dominion over the earth. They are both certain the only way we'll inherit the earth is to seize it. The difference between them is that Max's plan was to simply overpower the impure humans. He eventually came to believe the Creator gave us abilities as weapons to conquer the world. On the other hand, Drake prefers to take over the earth's governments strategically. He'd rather have the impure humans live under the Council's rule. Instead of annihilation, his arrogance demands reverence from those he considers lesser beings. "

"What's his ability? Why did I think he was you? And is he really so fast that he just disappears?"

"No, his ability is far more powerful than just blinding speed. Drake can control the body's senses. He never disappeared the whole time you were fighting him. At least the rest of us saw him the whole time. He can decide what a person sees, hears, tastes, smells, and even touches. It's as close as you will probably get to having the power of hypnosis."

"So he was making my eyes see him disappear, and making me to see you as him. That truly is a powerful ability. His voice even came from all around me, so I didn't know in which direction to follow him."

"We believe that Drake's abilities are what have kept him in the field so long. It was obvious to many of us that Max was uneasy about Drake's superior power. Besides Eric, Drake was the only one to ever oppose Max's methods. Everyone else either sat in silence out of respect or fear. But since he'd been given the title of general, Max has kept Drake in the field most of the time."

Michael looked at his adoptive mother in disappointment. "I never saw this in him. I mean, we were never really that close but I loved him. I even think I still do. Was he always like this?"

"No he wasn't," Debra said eagerly. "He and your biological father, Eric, actually were really good friends. This was early in the sixteenth century. Everyone and everything was different back then. Max was actually sending Eric and Drake on missions of scientific advancements together. Our intent was to truly help the impure humans. There was a collective sympathy for their situation. Everyone felt that any day the Creator could take everything from the impures, and we would be the new kings and queens of the earth. We wanted to help them make the best of the precious time they had left. Drake and Eric made major strides in science and medicine throughout the years. Of course they've used many aliases and have kept their images out of any public records."

"So what happened to change everything?"

"All the benefits that impure humans had unknowingly received from us were only distributed or made available to the wealthy or powerful. And this was not under our influence, but strictly the will of impures themselves. Even if the resource was abundant, they made it too expensive to help the masses. All of the Elders were becoming more and more frustrated with impures but it seemed as though the sympathy Max initially had for them was now more like one has for a sick pet. Pretty soon Max was tired of tending to pets he was waiting on to die so he could live better. We all felt the change in Max, but he was the oldest of the Elders. And some, like Drake, seemed to follow his new mindset. Before all this, Max and the rest of the Elders lived in huts alongside everyone else but soon the Palace was erected for the most powerful of the pure humans. And after such an act of superiority over their fellow pure humans was demonstrated, well, you can imagine how they easily came to see impures as nothing."

"It's still hard to believe that my adoptive father and my biological father were best friends."

"They did have their disagreements when Drake began to lean towards Max's new outlook on impure humans, but everyone knows Drake was the one who helped Eric escape."

"What?" Michael said in bewilderment.

"When your biological father, Eric, announced his love to your mother, Nicole, they were both imprisoned and awaited execution for treason. Drake and Eric were rumored to have had a huge quarrel about Eric staying in his hut. Eric was the only agent who refused to move into the Palace. He, like you, didn't believe it was honorable for the others to remain in huts while he slept in luxury. He would speak of many others who'd worked just as hard as he had but weren't offered quarters in this new fortress. Drake had no problem moving into the Palace. In fact, Drake was rumored to have said that Eric was trying to make all the other agents look bad, as if Eric was insinuating Drake and the other agents were wrong for accepting the comforts of the Palace. They hadn't spoken for months at the time of Eric's and Nicole's imprisonment. Then, all of a sudden, they escaped and evaded death. Drake was one of the only agents with enough influence to pull off such a sophisticated escape although he's never mentioned it and no one has ever dared questioned Drake about his participation."

"So are you trying to make me believe he's a good guy or a bad guy?"

"There's a difference between doing wrong and being wrong. But when you have options and you choose to live wrong, are you still good?"

"Why are you playing with my head?" Michael said with a smile.

"It may seem like I am because I'm trying not to influence you. Your feelings for Drake should be your own. The next time you two meet, my feelings shouldn't have any impact on your interaction."

"You sound as if you've already had a vision of it all."

"You have always controlled your own destiny, Michael. My visions only show me what happens once you do."

Michael looked out into the courtyard. "Who will lead them now?" he asked. After a moment of silence, Michael turned around to see Debra staring at him with a sarcastic smile. "You've got to be kidding. You heard Max. Everyone here thinks I'm a child. And he's right; I'm only nineteen years old.

How am I supposed to lead a colony of super humans that are hundreds of years old?" Michael chuckled at the thought.

"It is written that a child shall lead them," Debra said.

"Yeah, that sounds real good, but how?"

"The same way you singlehandedly defeated almost all of the most powerful of pure humans. With courage, wit, and what Lori taught you…the simplicity of the Creator's love."

"And how can I expect those Elders to follow me after my battles with them?"

"I told you they only followed Max out of fear or respect. Even those who are powerful are sometimes weak-minded. And the weak-minded will follow a strong leader, whether he's completely just or not."

"I still don't know. It all sounds crazy to me."

"Crazy!" Debra said in disbelief. "After everything you've been through, *this* sounds crazy? What would be crazy is letting another leader step forward that doesn't possess the pure heart you have, Michael. And what happens when Drake comes back? We could possibly be in an even worse situation."

"Is my leadership of pure humans part of a vision of yours?" Michael asked.

"One of the rules of my ability is that you can't inquire about your future. What I tell you could alter your decisions and make you change your own destiny for the worse. I couldn't live with that. This is your life and your decisions. I'm just laying out the facts and options."

"As beautiful as this place is, I don't know if I'm ready to just give up the modern world and live here."

"What if you didn't have to live here?" she asked.

"How would that work?"

"If your president makes a decision about Americans in another country, does it not still stand? Does it matter where he is? You're still the Prophesized One. You're not held by any guidelines."

"I'll think about it. I've got a lot to process. I just need a little time."

"What if I told you the Council of Elders has access to a fortune?"

"You've never raised me to be materialistic. Why do you think I'd be interested in money?" Michael said then looked away.

Debra sat in silence.

Michael tried, but after another moment of silence, he just couldn't take it. "How much is a fortune?" he asked with a smirk.

Debra chuckled. "I don't know exactly, but it's in the billions," she said nonchalantly.

"Billions!" Michael said with bulging eyes.

"But you don't care about the money?" she said, smiling.

"Actually, I don't. It means nothing if you don't have anyone to share it with," he said, looking away again to hide his impatient tear.

"Sometimes it's painful to go to the doctor. But you have faith that your doctor knows what he's doing, or you won't get better, right?"

"Right." Michael looked back to her and smiled, wiping his tear.

"Well, if you can have faith in a human doctor, then it should be no problem putting your faith into the Creator," Debra said.

"I know you're right. I understand that now. I'm not upset with Him anymore; I just miss her so much." Michael felt his adoptive mother reach over to him. They hugged and cried for a short time.

"That's understandable, we all will miss her. But now you need to bathe. That hug was as sour as it was sweet for me," she said with a smile.

"I'm sure it was," Michael said, laughing. "I almost can't stand smelling myself right now." They stood up slowly. "Thank you for making me laugh."

"No. Thank you for laughing. It lets me know you're alright. Now I can sleep better. By the way, Justin is the name of the one Elder who didn't attack you. He's talking to the rest of the council as they heal. It seems you already have his vote as the new leader."

"That has to be awkward for them," he said.

CHAPTER 16
REASON TO LIVE

The next morning Michael woke up, refusing to open his eyes. He remembered last night, but couldn't recall going to sleep. Which meant everything could've been a terrible dream. Maybe he was safe and sound back in his dorm room. He was about to consider Lori could even still be alive, but decided not to ride that emotional rollercoaster. Instead, Michael opened his eyes to find the reason he didn't remember going to sleep. The dried bloodstains around the basin jogged the horrid memories of the night before. He recalled trying to bathe before going to bed, but began wondering how much of Lori's blood he was washing off. He remembered trying to regain his composure, but ended up crying himself to sleep.

Okay, I've got to man-up, he thought as he stood up and began to clean. He understood there was nothing wrong with a man crying, and mourning was healthy although he also realized moments like these are what define a man's character. Michael felt he had the choice of collapsing on the floor in tears, or redirecting his pain into motivation.

"Dear God!" Michael said aloud, suddenly falling to his knees and looking towards the ceiling. "Please hear me, Father. I can't do this alone. I'm not strong enough. Now I get it, I understand what Eric was telling me. I can't only call and ask for you to grant me physical strength. I also ask that you grant me the resolve to carry on. I could cry a million tears and it wouldn't be enough so I pray you give me the focus I need to move on. Please guide me. Father, I don't know what to do. I know you see my situation. I need you. Please speak to my heart." Michael continued to sit in silence for a moment.

"Michael!" A muffled voice spoke!

Michael's heart jumped for a split second before he heard a knock on the door. "Come in."

"Did I wake you?" Debra asked with a sympathetic smile.

"No, not at all. I was just ah…praying for some guidance."

"How are you?"

"Well I won't say it's a good morning to wake up to, but we have to push on, right?"

"That's exactly what I came to talk to you about. There's a celebration ceremony for Lori today."

"A celebration ceremony?"

"Yes. In our culture we celebrate the life of our loved ones. Pure humans of the Village as well as the Palace will all be assembled. The Council has requested for you to address everyone."

"Address them? I can't even speak your language. And even if I could, what would I say?"

Debra walked up to Michael and put her arm around his shoulder. "This is a perfect opportunity to see if you're capable of being a leader. If you find yourself uncomfortable, then decline. But please consider at least trying to give them some comfort and hope for the future. At the present, the pure humans are without direction. They need a vision for their future that I cannot give them. They've admired you and cherished your story for years, before you were even born. If you decide to address them, I'll stand by your side and translate for you."

"I just prayed for strength and now I'm being given an opportunity to show some. That can't be a coincidence. Tell them I'll do it."

"Great! I'll go let everyone know."

"Wait! When is it?"

"In about thirty minutes."

"I can't make up a speech in thirty minutes."

"Then don't. Just speak to them from your heart. If it's meant for you to lead, then it should show. I trust your words and you should too."

"I'll be ready," Michael said, figuring winging it would be better than reading through a last-minute, thrown-together speech.

"I'll be back in about twenty-five minutes," Debra said, turning for the door. She stopped and turned halfway around. "One more thing, Michael. This ceremony is very important to us. Pure humans do not perish very often. Especially women. In fact, Lori is only the second woman in our history to leave her earthly body. The first was your mother, Nicole," Debra said, then turned and finished her initial exit.

Michael sat in silence for a minute, then washed and dressed so he could form some kind of idea of what he was going to say. He was relieved that he'd brought two pairs of shoes, considering his other pair had been torn to shreds when his feet burst out of them yesterday. He checked himself in the mirror and hesitated a moment.

Michael saw something different about his reflection. He worried that his transformations may have distorted his face in some way. At first glance there was no significant difference, but then he looked closer to find the truth.

Michael no longer had the wide eyes of a naïve nineteen-year-old. The person that now gazed back at him possessed eyes which had seen more in these last few days than most people see in their lifetime. This gave Michael a confidence he wasn't sure he had before. His appearance wasn't necessarily sad, but his expression sketched new lines in his features that showed he'd experienced genuine hardships.

There was a knock on the door and Debra returned as promised. She paused for a second, looking at Michael. "I'm so proud of you," she said, accompanied with a tight hug. "I've seen this moment in a vision, but I didn't know I'd feel this way." She wiped her moist eyes and continued. "No matter what happens or what you say when you get out there, I want you to know that you've surpassed my hopes and dreams for you as a mother. And I'm sure your mother, Nicole, is in paradise with the same feelings."

"It means so much to hear that from you. Thanks," Michael said, proud of himself for keeping his composure. "Let's do this."

They walked through the Palace, holding hands until they reached the top of the staircase of the main entrance. Michael was surprised to see how much the courtyard had been restored and prepared since last night.

There were a multitude of gleaming white robes dancing around Lori's lovely body, which lay in a beautifully-woven basket of feathers and flowers. The intensely- decorated, massive basket was about ten feet long, and almost resembled the shape of a canoe.

Michael couldn't look at her too long. He was afraid he might lose his strength and break down. Instead, he focused on the crowd he'd be addressing. Michael sensed someone coming from behind him and turned to see a familiar face.

"Good morning, Justin." Debra greeted him as he joined them, looking down onto the beginning ceremony.

Michael turned to shake hands with the only Elder, besides Debra, who hadn't attacked him last night. "I'm happy you agreed to speak today, sir," Justin said in a sympathetic tone. "I understand that yesterday was probably the most challenging day of your existence thus far."

"There's no doubt about it," Michael said, looking directly into Justin's eyes. "But through the darkness, my only comfort has been the honor of participating in the Creator's will.

And please call me Michael, I consider you a friend," he said smiling, with hopes of Justin continuing to be a future loyal ally.

Michael saw the dancing had slowly come to a stop. Debra stepped ahead of him and walked down a few steps of the long staircase towards the courtyard. She then looked back and nodded for him to begin.

He took a step forward to speak but as he did, it felt as if he was stepping out of his prior life and into a new reality. "My friends," he began then paused. Debra translated in a language that Michael had never heard anything close to before. The assembly was standing in total attention. "I am Michael, son of Eric and Nicole. You know of my parents. You know their story. You have watched me battle Drake and Max, along with other Elders. You have watched…how Lori has been taken from us because she refused to be used as a pawn in Max's plans. And now, my friends, I ask you to take what you have seen and rejoice. We may not like what this day has brought us, but let His will be done, not ours. Lori didn't belong to us. She belonged to the Creator, to give and take her as He pleased. We must rejoice for, after last night, there will be no more pain for Lori. And yes, we may still shed tears. But that's because we'll selfishly miss her. But we also rejoice because she's in paradise. We rejoice because we know we'll see her again. And there will be laughter. I was told this was a celebration. Well, let us celebrate everything Lori has done. Starting right now with a standing ovation for her and all of her accomplishments."

After another second or two of Debra's interpretation, a deafening sound of cheering and applause erupted. The thunderous appreciation for Lori lasted a full ten minutes. Silence finally fell on the crowd again and Michael resumed.

"We rejoice because the Supreme Being gives victory through what our eyes see as tragedy. I was told the Creator sent me here to usher in a new way of life for pure humans. Well, that new way of life begins today. From this day forward, we'll receive materials for anyone who wants to build shelter that's as comfortable and stable as the quarters of the Palace. Or for those who want to move into the Palace from the Village, there will be notifications of available space. The quarters will be offered on a first-come, first-serve basis. There will be no more segregation. Quality of life will no longer be dependent on the quality of the abilities you were born with. The men and women with the nicest or largest homes will simply be those who work the hardest. We shall also return to the time of helping and working with impure humans instead of against them. We will include them in our prayers. And, most importantly, we will love. We will love as the Supreme Being intended us to love. When two people love each other and promise loyalty before the Creator, they shall be considered married. I did a bit of exploring last night and I saw plenty of space to expand. I've also heard rumors of those who want me to lead in Max's position. I propose we eliminate Max's position. I propose that the Council of Elders make decisions together, without a leader. This will prevent our human emotions of pride or envy from surfacing. A vote will be held for every major decision, where each Elder must provide reasoning for their vote. No decision will be finalized until every Elder is in agreement. And the people of the Village will decide who'll replace Max, as well as any future Elders."

As he paused to consider how he'd conclude, he heard Debra finish interpreting his words to an unexpected roar of cheering and applause that exploded throughout the courtyard. The ovation gave Michael the confidence he needed to figure his last proposal. "Although there will be no single leader for the Council, there will be a need of someone to speak for the Council. I will assume this position, but Justin will speak in my absence. Drake is still out there…and I will find him. He needs a new army. I believe his first move will be to recruit any rogue agents that he can. I'm aware that some rogues may have left because of Max, so I will not be on a search and destroy mission. My first option will always be to try and persuade any rogues to rejoin us under our new Council. Whether I find Drake first or find all the rogues, I have to stop him before he grows too powerful. I thank you all for your support, and I'll address you again when I've made any progress. Until then, may the Supreme Being bless you and keep you." Michael finished and turned back into the Palace.

THE END??

Made in the USA
San Bernardino, CA
14 March 2014